# RADIANCE

*A Novel*

Phil Kenney

We live in the night ocean wondering,
*What are these lights?*

Rumi

*For Lori, Joey and Georgio*

# ACKNOWLEDGMENTS

I am very grateful to so many good people who helped me complete this work. Some read the words while others comforted my psyche. Quite a few did both. A special thanks to my editor, Nancy Wolf, who uses a red pen with the utmost care. To Gary Smith, who read *Radiance* from the start and offered unwavering encouragement. To Larry Christensen, Jeff Whritenhour, Rob and Carol Bibler, and Lois Young, who let themselves be moved.

With deep appreciation to Howard Wascow, who even in the last days of his life gladly gave of himself and his incredible insight into the written word.

To Warren Allen Smith, my high school English teacher, who taught me how to read and the beauty of a sentence. And to Kate Lee, who helped quiet certain voices from that time.

A special thanks to Andy Robbins and his magic camera for the cover and author photos.

My heartfelt thanks goes out to my wife Lori whose radiance has always dazzled me. You let me know in so many ways that you are my biggest fan while not hesitating to comment when I've gone off the mark. And who would I be without my boys, Joey and Georgio. They bring more life to the table than this cup can sometimes hold.

# CONTENTS

PART I: The Dream of Remembering

Prologue:   The Compassion of the Dead                              1

    Chapter 1.  Waking                                         9

    Chapter 2.  Ruth                                         13

    Chapter 3.  The Mark                                     37

    Chapter 4.  A Birthday                                   57

    Chapter 5.  Matricide                                    67

    Chapter 6.  Brother                                      97


PART II: Radiance

    Chapter 7.  Daisy                                       125

    Chapter 8.  Hunger and Food                             153

    Chapter 9.  Forgetting: a History                       185

    Chapter 10. The Necklace                                213

    Chapter 11. The Last Breath                             247

Epilogue:   Walking                                                255

# PART I

# The Dream of Remembering

# PROLOGUE
# The Compassion of the Dead

∾

*I*t is now, in your time, twenty-six months since my passing. In those seven hundred and ninety days, while you circled the sun twice, I have been among the dead and my body has been with dust and ash. The atoms that congregated for a time, making and remaking the person I was, are now sprinkled throughout heaven and earth.

Nearly an entire year passed before death brought a kind end to my demise. Nearly three hundred days after that relentless disease crushed what few memories remained of my life. Moving like a glacier, grinding to nothing but pebbles and dust everything in its path, it destroyed the last remnants of the person known to my loved ones as Georgia Daisy.

Before that terrible disappearance there were three long years of erosion and decay. The present eaten by locusts. Those dreadful days followed the years when it was still possible to laugh and pretend that misplacing the keys, losing my glasses and notes to myself, were simply silly lapses in attention. These were easily forgotten in ways I had mastered much earlier in my life, managing the painful events of this world.

Eighty years of forgetting the painful. Eighty years of remembering all I could to prevent the memories of all I could not bear from breaking into pieces the glass figurine of happiness that was Daisy. The Daisy whose smile was sunshine on leafy trees. Whose smile made the sky blue and drove unhappiness away like a lioness chasing predators from her cubs. It was Daisy who hid from her friends, from her husband, and, with great success, from herself, the horrible reminder *living at the edge of her dreams, always threatening to wake her from forgetting this terrible truth: she lived divided. Cut in two like the pretty girl in a magician's performance, lying in the box that looks like a coffin, smiling and willingly sawed in half and still smiling and living as though magic will make everything right in a world gone wrong where the closest thing to magic is forgetfulness and the power of that smile.*

*Everyone dies. Every last bit of self returns in order to leave. The lost and unborn, the refugees who fled from armies of custom and conformity, the emaciated forms of personality that never found enough light to stretch and flower, all these and others never dreamed of return to enjoy a moment of life in the great expanse that exists between the final breaths.*

*By that time, Georgia was gone. Daisy's smile no longer warmed the night. By that time, the English teacher correcting the grammar of unrepentant students was gone, the mother of two boys was gone, as was the wife of their father. The charming little girl, the Southern lady, the story-teller, the pleaser - all of them, gone. What was left of me, what remained after the passing of every last character, every last impostor and ghostly spirit was what you would call a soul. No larger than my thumbnail. Weighing no more than a picture in your mind. It could be that light because it no longer carried what was so heavy: the burden of the forgotten.*

*It could be that light. That light. Enough so that following the final breath, which was more like a farewell kiss, a cottonwood blossom making its way on the wind, it grew smaller, smaller than the tip of a needle, smaller than a fraction of a strand of hair, and in that blessedness slipped from the body.*

*I didn't assume a voice to talk about death. What good is it? No one can tell you and you will know soon enough. That is not my purpose. But I know you have wondered and your mind is full of more wonder and dread. And if I tell you, perhaps you will settle and listen to what I'm going to say. Then, perhaps, you will be able to forgive. And that is my desire.*

*You will not forgive me, though I have committed many wrongs and you will hear of these. You will not forgive me because I am forgiven. That was immediate and complete. As was the expansion of my being into unfathomable dimensions, into a radiance that required no stars and galaxies, into an effortless delight that gathered my soul in its arms and brought me to the silence that is home. I will not tell you about that silence because I cannot. I cannot because in it I am not. But you will know it as do I.*

*Enough. It is time. There is no need for worry. What is needed now is listening and a readiness to enter into dreaming. Because many voices wish to speak and invite you into the dream that was their life, and if you are not prepared to understand and forgive, you will fall prey to anger and the judgment of the damned because no one can bear the murder of a mother without demanding such retribution.*

*I brought two babies into this world. Two sons. Each one dazzling to me as a glorious sunrise. Each one as different from the other as rain is to snow. I loved them more than the moon and the stars. I loved them more than my own self. A day did not go by that I did not cherish their presence and the gift of caring for them. And still they found it necessary to kill me. Each in his own way. You will be shocked, but I tell you, one must understand.*

*One has joined me in the radiance. He has suffered greatly, walking over hot coals, since leaving you. Understanding his motives will change the world. The other is among you and finds little peace in his heart. He stands condemned and you will do the same when you hear our story. You will feel condemnation, and you must resist, with all your might, the temptation to throw him to the ground and hurl stones at him, calling him a monster. "You monster! How could you do such an evil thing? How could you say those things about your mother?" And you would be wrong and doomed if you fail to see into the depths of his world and my life. And he will suffer an injustice for his efforts and die a slow death alone in the desert. Therefore I will help you. I will teach you the compassion of the dead, and then I will leave and you will be on your own to navigate your own tendencies, your own lust for blood.*

*It was a bewildering world. By the time my children were born, so much of the land lay in ruin. History was banished. Great gulfs existed among family members. Their father sat at the table and said nothing. He was missing his tongue. It was hiding under a rock like a lizard. Instead of speaking he shuffled his fork and knife over the napkin and made sounds that came from his aching stomach. Their mother sat at the table and talked without stopping. Her face was frozen, but so lovely was her smile that no one noticed. She told story after story that made the world out to be wrapped in gift paper and bows.*

*My first-born, Frank, sat at the table ready to pounce. Canines flashing. His words jabbed like a boxer's fists. It was a small table. We made no room for visitors. James, my youngest, sat and watched. Speechless. It frightened me the way he looked inside people. It frightened me the way it had when he was a baby slumped against the crib as though he were in shock. As though he sensed a great confusion in the air and could not move until it cleared. I propped him up urging him to crawl, but he did not. I urged him to smile and told him the world was a happy place. He looked at me with the strangest expression. Eventually he did crawl and walk and took to the world, but he did not explore it the way most children do. It was as though his interests were elsewhere, places we could not see.*

*James was the most unlikely of detectives. He showed little curiosity for the world. He seldom asked us questions. Certainly not like most young children who pepper their parents with "Why, Momma? Why?" This was so unlike his brother, who regularly disturbed the order of things by demanding answers to impossible questions. It was unnerving to watch James go inside, to watch his eyes go dull and vacant. We were intent on eliminating any sense of an interior life, but he seemed equally intent on occupying the very territory we deemed so dangerous. Treacherous.*

*Imagine my astonishment when I realized he was piecing together a puzzle. That one by one he was collecting clues. Bits of stories we had trivialized and stripped of meaning. Stories we laughed at over dinner. Expressions of the eyes and face that appeared like single-frame shots and revealed what I prayed would never be seen. Never be known. He was doing excavation on my psyche. He was a paleontologist, and the discarded scraps of our history were tiny bones he pieced together, becoming a skeleton in his little hands.*

*And James was right. He was right about the terror in my eyes. The terror I worked so hard to conceal. The terror that slipped into a scream when so much as a spoon dropped behind my back. The terror that revealed a crack in my story. And from that crack, a frightened bird flew shrieking and piercing the quiet, piercing the pretense. He seemed to have an instinct for the truth. For the forgotten and unwanted truth.*

*He was right about the dreams. It was a mistake to mention them. Quite reckless really. From time to time, as they occurred, Daisy recalled the dreams at the breakfast table. There was a need for the periodic repudiation of meaning, of inner life. A need to establish a family consensus. Weren't they silly? Wasn't she silly? The little man with the carrot-top hair, the strange little leprechaun. What a nut! She led the way with a good laugh, the half-drunken laugh that James took note of as over-ripe, that is, laced with anxiety. It took great effort to convince herself. To forget the experience of the night. Because the dreaming was not silly to the dreamer. It was a nightmare. A convict escaped from his cell menacing the innocent.*

*It was the same dream each night. The little man with the flaming red hair entered Daisy's room and sat by her bed. He sat beside her and stared down into her eyes. His lips opened slightly into a smile that made Daisy shiver. He said nothing but looked at her body until it filled with fear, until her muscles went limp and her throat closed the door to her voice. There were nights when she woke standing and facing the wall of her bedroom, moist with sweat and yelling into the plaster. Her fists were clenched. Her husband could not understand what she said and she could not remember once she came out of the spell. Most nights, however, she lay there quivering like a little girl, too frightened to move or speak, helpless under the gaze of the little man. When he left, she felt no relief. Only a sickening feeling in her stomach and the dread of his return.*

*James translated my dreams. For years he held them in storage. And as if they were his own, he dreamed the dream of remembering for me. All for the sake of a story never told. Many things floated through and settled onto the dream like lint on a sweater. There were certain facts: the angry grandmother who turned her back on Daisy in the last days, denouncing her daughter for failing to care for her properly; the brother who hid from Daisy and ate himself to death behind her back. And there were the subtle confessions; the throwing back of her shoulders in a studied posture of confidence, the arrangement of her dear face and smile, a portrait in oils, a total eclipse of the fear and bewilderment threatening to break through the well-rehearsed lines of her story. A story that barred trespassers. A story so tight it betrayed the censorship of chaos lurking beneath.*

*In the end, when forgetting failed, when the cumulative weight of memory tipped from the unknown to the known, when the dream could no longer be dreamed but stood before them like a lamppost, James knew that he was right about the secret. Daisy's secret. The secret I remembered by forgetting. The one I told him in my sleep.*

"Daisy."

"Daisy."
"I know you're awake Daisy."
"You'll like this. It will feel good."

"I won't hurt you Daisy. I promise I won't hurt you."
*"Please don't."*

"There, doesn't that feel good, Daisy?"
"Doesn't it?"

"I love you, Daisy."
"You're so pretty."
"You're so pretty and special."
*But it did not feel good. It felt like spiders crawling up my legs. And I felt ugly, not pretty. Ugly and foul. And the paralysis only made me blame myself more. Daisy hid behind the curtains. She hid from the hot anger burning in her throat. Hoping it would not find her. And she vowed to never allow silence to overtake her again.*
"Doesn't it feel good, Daisy?"
"Doesn't it?"
*The moment turned to days.*

"Goodbye, Daisy. Goodbye. Mother would be so mad at us, wouldn't she? She would be so upset. She would. We won't upset her, will we?"
*"No."*

*The house was large and made of stone. Large stones. The rooms were spacious and many. Or at least it seemed that way to Daisy. Bedrooms filled each corner on the second floor of the big stone house. Bathrooms and wide hallways separated the rooms. Daisy could not hear her father snore from her room, and he could not hear her door open, or the footsteps in the hallway leading to her room. No one heard her brother enter and sit down by her bedside. No one imagined him pulling back her sheets and touching her. Such a thing could not happen. And when it did, those many nights in the quiet, she learned to pretend it hadn't happened and she learned to forget the unforgettable.*

*Only many years later, when I wondered about the restlessness of my sleep, at the need I felt to sleep on my side with my knees tucked up, at the startled flinch of my body when the sounds of the dark intruded, at the ease with which I welcomed sleeping with a lamp left on; only those many years later while wondering these things did I come close to remembering what I knew I must not.*

*My boys were my life. Like any mother, I would have died for them. I was more than happy to have boys. Girls are such trouble. All the quarreling. And, truthfully, I was frightened of how I might react to a daughter. How could I manage watching her delicious body unfold into its beautiful fullness? The boys were so vital and they adored me. I easily ignored the problem of a penis. It caused me no revulsion. It simply did not exist but for a few stains on the toilet seat. I loved them in every way I could. But I could not let them touch my body. This was my crime.*

*And because I loved them but could not love with all of me, because my heart was divided and some of it wrapped in a hard shell, because I could not let them touch my body, I set about blindly to give them everything. I baked butter horns and made pancakes. I pushed them in the stroller and on the swing. I made their beds and ironed their shirts. I read them stories and tucked them into bed every night. I took nothing for myself.*

*But I could not let them touch my body. I could not let them take my milk or play with my face. I could not let them bury their little faces into my breast or take my nipple and flesh into their mouths and have me. I could not. I could not afford to remember what was hidden in every cell. And so they suffered. This was my crime. Remember this.*

*I could not let them touch my body and so they touched my shame. They drank it and their bellies ached and became swollen like those of starving children. They carried the mark of my shame and their father's loss like a long splinter from dry wood buried deep within the flesh. Therefore it was the within, the interior life, that was forsaken. Amputated. A frost-bitten finger thrown in the trash.*

*The oldest, Frank, developed a bite. Noticeable as a limp. What was a smile like any five-year-old became a display of fangs. A sabertooth tiger ready to sink its teeth into the hide of any beast in its way. He killed me and everything soft. Everything feminine. Every need and emotion. Every moment of silence, slaughtered. He killed me and went on killing me. And then he went in search of me. In search of my body. A touch. Something warm.*

*The youngest, James, developed a mask. Invisible to most. What was a delightful little boy became a shadow on the wall. A ghost in a body. Hiding from the nightmares of his ancestors. He delighted in my scream. He wept for my lost life. He adored me. He killed me. He fought me. He cut himself into pieces looking for me. He killed everything masculine. Every muscle of authority. He killed me and died by my side. In search of my soul. A glimpse.*

*You and I are nearly done. The moon is rising. The skeleton at James' fingertips is taking shape, piece by delicate piece. You have touched one of the fragile bones. The shame of Georgia Daisy. There are a thousand others. Many would turn to dust if you touched them. Some are fragments from a hundred years ago, too minute to identify. You can hear them murmuring in the wind. Stories lost to the world and yet echoing through the psyches of the bewildered children who followed.*

*Death is your friend. It returns to every person the greatest of what can be remembered and the most welcome forgetting of the small and insignificant. No story goes untold in the home of no stories. The final judgment is not judgment at all, but mercy. The unacceptable is accepted. The compassion of the dead is yours to hold and to cherish, to give away as water. It is the greeting of the fresh, the body of love. Touch it. Feel it.*

*Daisy is not in need of compassion. She is the new moon overhead. She is the morning dream passed into the empty sea. She is memory and dust. She died on the flameless fire, and the light of her eyes found its way through the maze of Daisy and Milwaukee and the graffiti of the little man with red hair and the marriage of Georgia to the man who would not talk. That light became her passport in the country of the radiant. As it will for you. As it will for the little man and every story and crime.*

*You will know the compassion of the dead when you remember the stories within your stories. When you awaken to the rise and fall of memory's magic and peer into the groundless depth of your being, that nothing, not the little man, not the blood on your hands, not all the sorrows in the world, can tarnish. Then you will not simply forgive Frank and James, but you will welcome them to sit at your table and add your own tales to the collection of bones.*

# CHAPTER 1
# Waking

∾

Deep sleep. Bottomless, dreamless. No beginnings: wordless and breathless. No endings: formless and timeless. Boundless as a sky without stars. No mind, no shapes, no dreamer making magic on the walls. Not a trace of the man lying at the foot of his mother's bed. Not a trace of the past and its gallery of relics nor the future in a motherless world. A geography of nothing. Limitless. Only the one with no arms holding the many. Quiet as death though not death. Still as death though not death. The great silence at the heart of all. That silence the wind searches for. That stillness known in the depth of oceans and lakes. The unborn, faceless and unfathomable, where the many come to rest, dissolving into the reservoir of forms. Where even the mind settles and finds in that baffling merger the most effortless sanctuary. Where even the most restless of boys looking for his mother is taken in.

Deep sleep. Selfless. No one moves. No one dreams. No one shudders. Not empty, not full. Unpeopled: a biography of zero. Featureless: an epic with no tales. Prior to worry, prior to want. Undisturbed.

But then, a stirring. Faint; too faint to recognize. A ripple. Far away. So far away. And again, a quiet, lasting centuries.

Deep sleep. The mind lying in shadows. Shadows lying in the mind. The first stirring passes. It is like that for another hundred years. Falling, settling: snow lighting on a leaf. Silent.

It is like that before the first sound laps upon the shore. Before the first sound makes a crease in the night sky. The first sound, which is more of a movement. More of a bend in the space that is not there. The first sound; the breath of breath, the bringer of worlds upon worlds, dream upon dream: image and light.

He is lost. Lost and bewildered. Memory tries to stand and falls. Where? Remembering is birth. It could be a womb: that sound. What is it? The distant hum of waterfalls. Confusion. That sound. Floating, floating to the sound. No body, no mass. Toward. Floating toward the sound. It is dreaming; the sound dreams a world. Sound and movement. A floating dream. A cell dividing in slow time. In slow time, in slow space, shadows grow forms and the outline of a mind opens and closes.

The sound is breathing, is breath, is calling. Calling a shape into being. Calling the forgotten forth. A confusion is lifting. Awakening is calling, breath is calling, death is calling, daybreak is calling. She is calling. The breathing belongs. It belongs to her. Mother. And more. The dreamer is born to waking. The breath belongs. Remembering breaks the seed open. Out comes a fragile stem moving toward. Breathing is calling; it is a flute and dancing and it calls across a valley. And a rustling amoeba self reaches out into the dark.

And in a moment with more space than not, figures come forth. One remembers and one breathes. One remembers the cot under his side. The night that began on the other side of sleep. The room that held the cot and the other bed and the breath swimming from the bed to the sea. And one by one the images line up. The son, the mother, the room. July warmly waiting in its own breath. Her breath settling over the room. The room breathing in the light of a new day. The son remembering, the sun rising, the room filling with the sound of the mother breathing long, long and slowing. His mind filling with the memory of his mother lying there breathing. Her breath calling him, drifting to him lying on the cot at her feet.

He can no longer forget that he is listening to her die. That he has been in this room for three days listening to her breath enter and leave her body. He cannot forget the sound of her efforts; the will of her lungs to pull in another measure of air. Without trying, he remembers that sound throughout his own body. Despite the fatigue and the aching, he remembers the first sound, the first impression upon the great silence surrounding his becoming. That sound, echoing through the room, through his cells, through the womb, through his psyche and the deposits of memory: known and unknown. And he cannot help but feel, despite the hour, despite the faltering arc, despite the tension, an annoyance beginning to crawl up his spine. Annoyance and the familiar wish to go away. And even as he lies there on the cot, wanting to fall back into the deep, wanting to forget her name and the place and that sound, he feels the spell of her breath and the calm it casts and the desire, as old as his own breath, to be near her.

And in that moment he is ashamed to be himself. Especially in that moment that he recognizes the change in the sound. In the same moment he comes more fully into himself, into the presence that is not a dream, into the yearning to be close to her, into the anger beginning to build and the impulse, the damned impulse, to turn away from her and leave her to herself. This causes the most dread, especially now, noticing the sound has changed and is no longer the crusty, protracted breathing of the past days but rather a simpler, far softer sound, more like a moth landing on his arm. And in that moment he notices the space between each breath has grown into what seems like an endless pause and that a new tension has arrived. Will she draw another?

It was within that dreadful, wonderful sound, within that gap between breaths that everything in the known world seemed to converge and all the emotion of a lifetime, and perhaps the lifetime and emotion of countless others, flooded his own permeable psyche. And within that blessed and cursed moment, bathed by the sound of his mother's last breath, the final song of her life, he wrestled with a pull strong as the undertow of the Pacific, a pull to stay in the comfort of his cot. To stay at her feet and pretend she would be there when he woke. Hadn't he done enough? Hadn't he made all the visits even when she was forgetting her name and his? He begged to return. Return to the deep. Deep sleep. Boundless. No constrictions. Perhaps he would dream a beautiful dream and find another world in which to be someone quite different. Without shame, without anxiety, and without dread.

In the same mysterious instant, as the sun began its silent ascent, as his wish to sleep pulled on his mind, he felt an urging, as if from a guardian of his soul, a compelling urge to go to her. To go to her side, to breathe her last breath with her, to touch the last warmth of her body, to gaze at her face, to ensure that she was not alone, not lonely again, not in that gap that might last an eternity. He felt the urge to preserve her breath in its softness, in the beauty of its rhythm. To hear in those remaining tones an invitation to something beautiful, a call of the wild.

And with the pounding of that urge and the pull of the deep crashing against each other, caught in this perilous crevice, this gaping seizure, feeling too weak to move, too strong to stop, too alone to know, in the hollow of his being he listened to silence, to the battle for his heart, to her breath and to his own. And then he closed his eyes.

# CHAPTER 2

# Ruth

∽

My name is Ruth. Ruth Brennan. The day is August 1, 1936. The morning of my funeral. My life ended quickly. It just withered away to nothing like a cornfield in severe drought. Five months and five days into the fifty-second year on this earth, the light went out and I made my way to the house of God, leaving behind my poor husband, Warren, and the three precious sons born from our union: Edgar, Earl, and Gerald. They are gathered in the kitchen of my mother's house. It is 6:00 AM on the Saturday they will place me in the ground. Already the air is terribly hot and humid as it has been the past five days. Sweat is beading from their necks and shoulders. Their shirts are wet and sticking to skin.

"We have a ton to do before the ceremony." Warren is standing near the sink drinking from a cup. "Edgar, you and Earl have to get to Grant Bros. and pick up the shirts for the funeral. They should be in from Chicago. Edward Grant promised. Then get back in time to help Grandma Turner with arrangements. Gerald, you get to polishing the shoes."

Edgar is at the table smoking and leaning back in the chair. "What are we supposed to use for money?"

Earl leans against the wall and looks for his father's reaction.

"Credit."

"Not again." Edgar twists in his chair.

"What the hell are you saying?" Warren's voice is hard and sharp.

"Just that it's getting embarrassing to go in there with no money all the time. What do they think of us?"

"The Grants will get their money. Nearly every man in Lake County is in the same boat. Now get on it."

"Then why don't you go in there?" Gerald's voice was audible but just barely. His eyes were red and sore, and he stared at the table like he was trying to read something in its lines.

"What's that, boy?" Warren looked at Gerald with contempt. The room got smaller.

Gerald didn't look up. He shuffled a salt shaker between his fingers. His tongue had yet to leave his mouth, and he was quite sure he had nothing left to lose in this world, so in a voice quivering with resentment, he muttered, "Cheap bastard."

"Gerald, don't." Edgar tried to head Gerald off.

"You shut up, boy. You shut your damn mouth."

"I won't shut my damn mouth and I won't polish your goddamn shoes."

"Gerald, not today." Earl was pleading but it was too late. Each was locked into the other's sights.

"You put her in a pine box. A stupid, damn ugly box. Our mother in a lousy colored person's crate." Gerald looked at him now and his eyes were bulging with hate.

"There ain't no money, boy. When are you going to get it? There ain't no money."

"Why don't you go out and make some instead of sitting around here feeling sorry for yourself, pissing and moaning?"

"Gerald, stop!" Edgar was agitated. He glared at Gerald and nearly shouted, "Stop! You don't know what you're talking about."

But Gerald wasn't stopping. "Damn kid." Warren started to turn but Gerald caught him with a right hook.

"And why'd you take her to that damn chiropractor besides? Cheap bastard! Mother'd still be alive if you'd taken her to a real doctor."

Warren turned and charged. Gerald was up in a flash and threw his chair at his father's feet, causing him to stumble and nearly fall, which left just enough time for Edgar to grab Warren and hold him back. Over his shoulder, he yelled, "Jesus, Gerald, enough. You'll make Grandma Chester a wreck. Get out of here."

But Gerald wouldn't leave. It took his big brother Earl to restrain him. He was screaming now, "Bastard, you cheap bastard." Tears were streaming down his cheeks and choking his throat.

"Goddamn little shit! You think you're the goddamn only one she loved. You momma's boy piss-ant, you think you're so goddamn special, I could spit."

He nearly did but by then Earl had pushed Gerald out of the kitchen and closed the door with his foot. Gerald was still yelling but allowed himself to be removed. The cursing continued but it was trailing off into his lungs. He slammed his fist into the hallway wall and ran to his room. In the kitchen Edgar kept his father from pursuing his little brother.

"Let him cool off, Dad. He's young."

"Damn brat, I should kick his butt out of this house." His face was red as a bad sunburn and he stomped around the front room another five minutes before cooling down enough to go on. By then only two hours remained until the funeral and there was plenty to do.

"I'll take care of Gerald, Dad. You go into town and get those shirts. Earl and I will see to Grandma and getting things straight."

"Okay, but don't forget those damn shoes."

⁓

And he was off. Off by himself. One of the broken men of Northern Indiana. Broken and bitter. He walked into town alone, angry at the boy, angry at the Depression and angry that he would have to ask for another loan he could not repay. The farm was gone. Brennan's corner: the store, post office, all gone. Everything his grandfather and father built. Even the family house was gone, and he'd been forced to move his family into the Chester house near the cemetery. And now his wife. The one bit of good in this desolate place. And because of the boy he could not send the others into town for the shirts and he would have to face another humiliation. On the day of his wife's funeral. He could feel their eyes staring at him. He could read their thoughts. Shame held him prisoner in a cell without a window.

He averted his eyes from the people he'd known all his life. Never noticing the sympathy on their faces. Never hearing the kindness in their greeting. Never feeling the generosity in their giving. Warren was blinded by shame. His face was like plaster. He cared for nothing. He was one of the defeated, the defeated men whose dignity lay trampled in a ditch. All the king's horses and all the king's men couldn't put these men back together. Nor could God or a good woman or three fine sons. He cracked and broke into pieces never to rise again. Bitterness owned him.

Warren walked into town. He made his way to the general store, bought the white shirts on credit, and left without looking at a soul. Even when Edward Grant expressed his condolences, Warren merely nodded and turned for the door. He walked home through the gathering heat oblivious to the odor coming from his skin. When he arrived home, one and a half hours before the funeral, he said nothing. He looked at no one. He placed the shirts on the table and went to his room.

The funeral was no different. A respectable crowd filled the church. He saw no one. Reverend Milnes conducted the service and Reverend Brown assisted but he refused to look up at them. Nor did he look at the guests as they shook hands and filed past him and the boys following the ceremony. His eyes were dead.

So it was not a surprise that, as the family stood by the grave site and the Reverend Milnes made his final plea to the Lord above for the salvation of Ruth Ann Brennan, Warren would not see a four-year-old boy crawl from the chest of his son Gerald and fling himself into the wooden casket bearing his mother. In fact, not one of those present saw that inconsolable child lie down with his mother in her grave. Not one saw the bag in his hand, containing his every hope and dream, collapse alongside his frail body. Likewise, they failed to see a ten-year-old version of Gerald sneak from his back and hide in the crowd. All were blind. Unnoticed, the boy dove into the hole and took dirt in his hand and ate it. He ate mouthful after mouthful. When he had enough, he climbed from the deep cavity and walked to the Reverend's side. There he took the Bible from the man's hands and made a pact with the devil. He vomited the dirt and from the clay of the land fashioned his mother's body anew. That piece of his soul wrapped the body in cloth and placed her in a sarcophagus made of walnut. He adorned it with jewels the way he had seen the Egyptians do in his school books. With that he left the graveyard, his family, and the townspeople. He strapped the sarcophagus to his back, headed for the Great Lakes to the North and never returned.

Gerald watched himself break into pieces. He made no attempt to stop the fractures. He thought he heard a limb break from the wind. He thought he heard thunder rolling in from the west. The last of his tears dried on his cheek from the heat. Without thinking he turned away from the grave and closed his eyes to all of it. In a short time he would forget much of this. And thus would he go about finding what he had lost.

∾

I was born on the 21st of February, 1884, in the house I came home to die in. It was named the Bradshaw house, after the man who built it forty years earlier. I was the second of eight children delivered to my dear parents, Elizabeth and Alexander Chester, good, hard-working people who helped others and always paid their debts. Mother says it was a difficult labor. She tells me it was hours before I moved into position for her to push, and by then she was so exhausted, the midwife feared for both our lives. Somehow she managed to bring me into this world around 9 o'clock the evening of the 21st. And she wasn't done. In the following years, she brought five brothers and another sister into our family. Each was a treasure to her.

It might have been the ordeal of birth that predisposed me to ill health. I'll never know. But I don't recall a time in my life when I felt secure in the health of my body. As a child I was not well. I suffered from fevers and strange bouts of fatigue. My lungs were always a problem. It seemed they were collapsed and breathing was difficult. Perhaps because of my fragility, from an early age, I sensed the presence of the Lord. During one of the fevers, I woke to the most glorious light shimmering over my bed. Without my asking, the light entered this body and filled it with a feeling I shall never forget. At that moment I knew that God was real and death should not be feared. I decided then to do everything possible to help others less fortunate than myself. Later in life I would find the Pythian Sisters, who would guide me toward realizing my goal of service to my neighbors. We believed in friendliness and charity. And while we read the Bible together, it was our belief in a benevolent Supreme Being that moved us in our work. Therefore we welcomed people of all faiths. And those with little or none.

Sometimes I wonder if it was my sympathy for the poor and unfortunate that led me to Warren. He came from a good family. Jeremiah, his grandfather, was one of the important early citizens of Wheeler, Indiana. People say he was a good man, a kind-hearted person. He was the first postmaster of our post office out at Brennan's Corner, where the general store bordered the family farm. That piece of prime farmland covered over 500 acres. It was well managed while Grandpa Brennan lived, but Warren's father Edwin wasn't the businessman Jeremiah was. Under his watch the farm began to deteriorate. As times grew worse, during the first World War and after, nothing seemed to come together for the Brennans. It hurt Warren deeply to see his father failing and his own prospects dwindle. I could see the hurt on his face and a darkening of his spirit well before we married in 1906. I guess I just assumed things would get better and starting our family together would bring happiness back to his life. But that is not what happened. Neither the birth of Edgar, nor that of Earl, brought any joy to his world. He grew more resentful by the day. More withdrawn. Prickly thistles grew from the pores of his skin. He closed his eyes to the world so as not to see the decline of all he had known. And bitterness oozed from his tongue like an infected sore.

As he grew more depressed, my health began to deteriorate as though the state of his mind and the state of my body were somehow linked. It is true that I loved him but by the year of Gerald's conception in 1919, there was little of Warren remaining to love. I tried to make him smile but I failed. And slowly but surely my body failed too. The doctor warned us that my kidneys were not strong and the difficulties I'd had with high blood pressure had worsened. He ordered me to bed rest in September and his cautions were such that I feared for the baby. It seemed unlikely I could carry a baby to term. And I did not.

Gerald was born eight weeks before his due date. It was an emergency situation. My water broke at midnight, shortly after the first signs of blood appeared. Warren woke Edgar and he ran to fetch Dr. Jeffries just six blocks away. Earl ran two houses down to wake Sara, my best friend and midwife. They were so frightened. Each showed their emotions in such different ways. Little Earl, only seven at the time, wore his feelings right on his sleeve. In fact his face, when he wasn't smiling, often appeared worried and fretful. Edgar was harder to read but if you looked closely you could see the strain around his eyes and his lips pressed tight together. Bless their hearts, they ran as fast as their young feet could carry them out into the chill of November in only tee shirts and trousers. Warren stayed and prepared hot towels. The house was cold and I was shivering badly, well before anyone arrived.

Sara was the first to get to me. The bleeding had worsened and the contractions were fast and like knives. The room began to swirl and before the good doctor was heard running up the stairs, I lost touch with my surroundings and the voices of concern at my side.

Instantly my spirit was with the golden glowing light that had come into my being those many years ago and had been my friend through much pain and illness. I thought certainly my time had come and the life of this body had been spent. Little of me fought. A swift shaft of sorrow swept through my heart for the life of the little one about to be born. But in truth, God forgive me, it was fleeting. For the most part I experienced a profound comforting. Everything seemed to be just fine. The time in the glow seemed endless. And then it was gone.

I must have passed into a deep unconsciousness and had no awareness of the flurry of activity around me. Of the hemorrhaging that turned the sheets on our bed the color of beets, of the frantic efforts to keep me warm, of Dr. Jeffries shouting instructions to Sara and Warren, of Edgar and Earl huddled together in the corner by the doorway, confused and shaken by the blood.

I was dying. Our little baby was going with me. Apparently there had not been enough suffering in this household. Never mind the grim pall that settled over the four of us. Never mind the disappearance of laughter from our table. Life took no notice of such things, took no pity on our lot, and, in fact, was gathering its forces and pointing us toward unspeakable tragedies. Why cry for one who would be spared these trials and hardships? Why mourn the life that would end before it began when living brought more sorrow than one could bear? But life is deaf and dumb. It insists on itself. And without my knowledge, blessing or help, our little baby, our dear Gerald, was born that morning in the hour before dawn. Born to a dying mother, he took his first breath as I took what others believed to be my last.

၏

And no sooner had he taken the first breath of air into his own pink virgin lungs, no sooner had he cried out loud, wailed the first announcement of his own grand and remarkable incarnation, than it happened: they took him from Ruth. In order to save his mother, they took him away. And placed him alone on a towel in a separate room. All three pounds of blood-covered flesh twisting and writhing in that motherless world. Taken. Screaming to no avail. Kicking to no avail. Taken from Ruth, his mother, at the moment of his coming into the world. Taken and not returned. And in that one act, in that single event, lost to all but those present in that room, lost in a blizzard of other events stretching over light years, like so many particles of cosmic dust, the curve and angle of a life took leave of possibilities and became, sure as a planet in orbit, a direction. That is, a destiny.

༄

My name is Ruth. I survived the morning of November 21, 1919. And I survived the following day as well. Another sixteen years of life waited for me to wake up. It was two days before I did so. During those days, which were not days, I died a hundred times and returned one hundred and one. The darkest night is pale in comparison to that place without light. Sleep, even the deepest sleep, is something in contrast to the nothing of that place. Dreams are cheap paintings next to the figures I met, thin imitations, like shadow puppets, compared to the magnificent world upon world of the other side. And much of those days I spent in the arms of the glow. I was never cold.

My name is Ruth Brennan although when I woke in the middle of the night forty-eight hours later, I could not remember my name. I remembered nothing of this life. Returning was impossible. What force carried me back I could not tell you. It felt like tumbling endlessly through thick cotton, like drowning and being washed up onto shore. There was the vague sense of something we would call being, shrinking, becoming smaller and smaller until it nearly disappeared. Until it stopped. Until there was pain and a heaviness that could not be lifted. Until the up and down of the breath of life began to say my name. Softly, so softly at first. Gradually, the calling was something I could hear. The name was something I could remember. Though the initial recollection was of Ruth Ann Chester, it was not long before I recalled my married name and recognized the surroundings of my home. I was grateful for the dark and the quiet. For the chance to get my bearings. I was awake long enough to realize exhaustion was my ruler. And then I slept.

That sleep ended as abruptly as a chicken's life. Terror as hot as the stove top ripped through the body into sleep and dragged me back screaming and dripping wet. I barely heard Warren running the stairs and then he stood over me like a giant. "Ruth!" He just looked at me and I could tell some feeling in him was trying to scale a twelve-foot fence to get to me. "Ruth, you're all right!"

He said my name a half dozen times. But I couldn't speak because the screaming had frozen up and sunk to the bottom. Edgar and Earl were there now and grabbing for my hand. "Mom! Mom!" They cried and put their heads on my arm. Their tears were warm and strangely calming. Though I couldn't yet talk, it was possible to turn my head and look at each of them though each movement was hard as trying to load a bale of wet hay onto the flatbed. The yearning in their eyes was heartbreaking and lovely. I struggled to say a word, but my mouth was numb and felt stuffed with clay. It was the mother who found the strength to break through the barriers and muttered in a voice that no one recognized as my own, a voice from the dead, a voice barely audible to the ears of my dear ones straining to receive something of me, the words I dared not say,

"The baby?" The words fell trembling from my mouth.

"The baby is fine. Fine. Dr. Jeffries took him to the hospital after caring for you. He's doing just fine, Ruth." Warren's voice carried a kindness I hadn't heard for years.

"Dr. Jeffries." My voice trailed off into the relief only a mother can know. A relief so thorough it lifted some of the weight from my muscles and I sank into a reverie that went uninterrupted for what seemed like hours until my eyes suddenly popped open and I heard myself exclaim, "He?"

"Yes dear, he." Warren's voice cracked ever so slightly. I might have been the only one to hear it.

"Another Brennan boy, Mom. Aren't you the lucky one?" Edgar was beaming.

"Yep, the nurses say he's a strong one, remarkable, they say. Strong and stubborn like a Brennan man should be." Warren was boasting of course, and the hint of an apology hid behind the wink of his eye that was for me alone.

We all had a good laugh. A big sad beautiful laugh.

"Shall we tell the boys their brother's name, Warren?"

"Sure. Sure we should." And he spoke slowly so any spirits visiting that remarkable morning, just days before the Thanksgiving holiday, would also hear and know his name.

"Gerald Warren Brennan." He said it with great pride, happy to be remembered in the naming. "That's one stubborn kid all right," Warren proclaimed out loud.

We laughed again. I laughed out loud: the first in a lifetime.

∞

Laughter echoed throughout the house and woke up the wallpaper in the parlor. They laughed and cried as they once remembered doing. Had they been made of the sky and sunlight and rain, they would have made rainbows. As it was, a light resembling sunbeams dancing on ice waltzed about her room. She saw it wipe the strain from their faces and lift up their hearts from her grave. Each privately wondered what the day was, in fact, heralding. Were better days ahead? Was laughter here to stay?

Ruth lay there dreaming of good will in the house. She dreamed with each breath that they might find it in their hearts to love this small, perishable life, that they might rejoice in the miracle of being here. That they might listen for and hear the song of life moving through and around the tree tops of the little town of Wheeler. All four held their breath and dared to believe in something other than hopelessness. And as they did, they were unaware of a light snow beginning to fall outside. An early snowfall that would bathe the land in white and dazzle children and grownups alike. Large flakes fell on the rooftop of the old house. Sunlight found its way through clouds and merged with the snow and made each crystal sparkle and sing. They were happy together. Ruth felt her blood quicken and stream through her flesh. She was alive. And as she felt life return to her body, the baby, only just named, some thirty miles away in a hospital tray, turned his head in the direction of the family. He wiggled and cooed. And his little hands and mouth, so tiny and pink, so moist and hungry, reached for them, reached into the spacious distance for his mother. And his blanket fell to the side.

◌◌

Gerald was a joy. From the time he came home to us, six weeks after his birth, he made our lives hum. He was such a happy baby, not fussy, easily soothed. Edgar and Earl liked holding him and making him laugh. Even Warren took his turn rocking and feeding his little boy. He was only three pounds at birth and the nurses called him their miracle baby.

Once home, little Gerald ate eagerly and put on weight. He grew like crazy and was of good disposition. I knew he was my last baby and so treasured every minute of being his mother. Every one. Not much upset him. The usual things, of course, from time to time got his lungs bellowing. But generally he was a content and jolly little fellow. That is, as long as he was near me. We were inseparable as spring from summer. Our bond grew and grew. We spent hours together playing and reading and now and then baking cookies. I pushed him in the stroller and pushed him in the little swing Warren had attached to our cherry tree out front. He loved that swing. Oh how he giggled and glowed moving through the warm summer air, back and forth, higher and higher.

"Higher, Momma, higher!"

"All right dear, but not too high."

"Higher, higher!"

It was a delightful demand. We both laughed fully and light-heartedly. He didn't tire of the motion. I didn't tire of the effort. Somehow I seemed to feel Gerald's exhilaration as my own.

"Momma, we are going so high."

"Yes dear, very high!"

"Momma, this is fun!"

And it was. And the days were wonderful for us. As the years passed we walked together into town, to the library and the park. We took the boys their lunch at school. He loved seeing Edgar and Earl at school, but on the walk home he would grow serious and ask, "Momma, will I go to school?" His little hand tightened around mine.

"Of course, Gerald, everyone needs to go to school."

"But I don't want to."

"Why not dear?"

"I don't want to be away from you and home. Can I stay home, Momma?"

My heart dropped into my stomach and the memory of his beginning tapped at my window. I didn't want to let it in. But it was impossible to forget what he went through to enter this world. I prayed it would not shadow him in his life but these questions reminded me of my foolishness and a grim worry intruded upon our reverie. This made me think of how everything came early for Gerald. Born fifty-six days before expected, he also walked early on, talked early and in full sentences, rose early in the morning to play and even learned to read by the age of three. Everything came early to Gerald as if he knew, in that mysterious way of knowing, that our time together would be short. My heart cringed for him. I rubbed his finger with mine, and said, "Oh Gerald, I love you so much. That will be hard for us both.  But I will bring you your lunch at school so we can see each other.  And you are such a smart boy, you will be a great student and make me so proud."  Something softened in him and we went on our way.  But both of us felt the shadow of uncertainty following behind.

Our walks were otherwise adventures in looking and questioning.  "Momma, why do birds sing?  Why is one cloud different from another?"  I embarrassed myself with my ignorance of God's world.  But Gerald didn't seem to mind; he just chattered along.  His four-year-old brain was quite happy with the asking and interacting with this big, big place, all its creatures and strange figures in the sky.  Who could have guessed that one day his tongue would sever and leap to the ground, scrambling like a startled snake for the cover of a rock?  Who could have guessed the terrible events waiting in the future to overwhelm the world?  Who could have foreseen the suffering?  And who can dare to imagine the next dream or the dream that will become history for the living?

Occasionally Gerald asked more startling questions.  Questions that asked for answers even as he feared what they might be.  "Why is Daddy unhappy, Momma?"

"Why do you think Daddy is unhappy, Gerald?"

"Because he sits in his chair all the time and doesn't talk to anyone.  I can't see his face, because the newspaper hides it, but I don't think he smiles."

"You are perceptive, Gerald."

"What is 'perceptive'?"

"You see things."

"Like clouds?"

"Yes, like clouds."

"Daddy has a cloud."

"Yes, he does."

"He doesn't talk to you."

"No, he doesn't."

"Why doesn't he?"

"Daddy's worried, sweetheart."

"Daddy doesn't like me."

"Oh Gerald, don't think that way. Daddy loves you. We all love you. Daddy has a lot on his mind. He worries about us. I know he loves you very much."

"No, I don't think so. Daddy went away, into the cloud; he doesn't love me."

I interrupted him, something I was loathe to do, but I had to, I couldn't bear it. What could I say that would make him feel better? What could I say that wasn't a lie?

He was right. Warren was far away and would go further in the coming years of pain. What did he love?

"Gerald, you must not think like that. You are a wonderful boy. Your brothers are crazy about you and you know Grandma and Grandpa Chester are too. Daddy has problems he can't work out and he feels bad that he can't give us what he wants. We can pray he'll come out of it, but in the meantime please, please don't ever think he doesn't love you. Some people can't seem to show their love very well."

He looked at me for a long time. I held my breath and tried to look into his heart. When he turned and skipped away without another word, I couldn't say what, if any, good my words had done. I would have marched right home and talked to Warren, but Gerald was right, he was hiding in bad news. It became nearly impossible to reach him.

As the losses mounted, Warren retreated further. About the time Gerald was to enter the first grade my health began to fade. We were all excited to see what Gerald would accomplish in school because it was plain as day how smart he was. It was equally apparent that he had the will to go far. The same will and resiliency that got him through the night of his birth and the next six weeks in the hospital were sure to help him do great things. And yet, what his father once with pride called "stubborn," he now said with derision in his voice. He could see through the cloud well enough to know Gerald would outshine him and he was jealous, plain and simple. To my great sorrow, he did what he could to tear him down. But

Gerald was his match and then some. His stubborn ways would become legend to his own children many years later. They would shake their heads and wonder how anyone could be so, well, pig-headed.

Gerald came by it honestly. He would need every ounce of it to escape what he saw as a nightmare. And so we should not have been surprised when shortly into his first year in school, our Gerald, who would one day become an accountant and steadfastly hold to his ideas of right and wrong, who never missed a day of work and was absolute in his sense of responsibility, who would come to berate his son Jimmy for threatening to leave college early, that same Gerald could not be kept in school.

Repeatedly, sometimes early in the day, other times later, after lunch, his teacher turned and found him missing. This caused great alarm in the beginning. But it soon became obvious to all concerned that Gerald had run away from school to find me. Many were the days I didn't feel well. Some of those days I was too weak to get out of bed. The kidneys that had failed during his delivery were beginning to show signs of degeneration. On those days, and others, when I felt strong enough to move about, Gerald would appear at the door looking for me. The expression on his face was enough to bring me to my knees.

"Gerald, what are you doing here? You belong in school." I tried to be firm.

"I don't like school."

"Gerald, you musn't do this."

"I want to be with you, Momma. Please, can I be with you?"

God in heaven, help me. "No, sweetheart. Momma's fine and you need to be doing your schoolwork." His face dropped. Followed by his shoulders. Then his eyes filled with tears and he stepped forward and wrapped his arms around me and pressed up close.

"Come on, I'll walk you to school."

There were unfortunate days when Warren came home and found him. "What the hell are you doing here? You get your butt back to school before I take my belt to it."

But all the shaming in the world did not persuade Gerald. It was a good six months before he stopped leaving school. There were intervals when we thought he had changed his ways only to find him sitting on the front steps waiting for me on a Monday morning. Why he finally gave it up, I do not know. But he did and he became a stellar student. His teachers said Gerald was the smartest child to come through their school in a long time. He liked doing well and being admired for his successes. The other children liked Gerald, though in some ways he was a bit removed from his classmates. He seemed older than most of the others, as though something in him knew how tough life could be and held him back so as to be ready when the going got rough.

My health was up and down for several years. By the time Gerald was nine, Dr. Jeffries said my kidneys were compromised and there was little he could do to help. At the same time the world was heating up. By the time he was eleven all the lies and greed had crashed. By thirteen the entire house of cards had fallen. Little food was available and less work. Warren's depression deepened when the misfortune everyone was suffering turned to a personal round of bad luck with the theft of his truck. That truck was his livelihood and to have it taken from him and sold for scrap left an already exhausted and fallen man with a bitterness that was unnerving.

Like most folks, we managed, but just barely, to get by. Edgar got a job with the city and that helped. And like most we lied to our young ones when we thought it necessary to protect them. It was a lie because times were so bad, for so long, we were not sure when, and if, things would get better. When the only thing on the plate for month after month is potatoes and beans, the children know things are not improving. Edgar and Earl were on their way but I worried so much about poor Gerald. To be so young and forced to grow up amidst such hard times. What would become of him? But of course I was really fearing the inevitable: what would he do without me?

☙

Darkness has covered the earth. A worse darkness is still to come. Humanity has gone mad. Ruth can see it and is filled with a despair she cannot fight off. Where has the light gone? What has blinded us? Were it a plague the people suffered, it would not be such a gross tragedy. She will not live to see the carnage. Her heart could not withstand the loss of 20 million boys, the murder of six million Jews, and the utter extinction of the hearts and minds of the multitudes surviving such chaos. The poverty of the past decade had weakened them all. Fear and hatred took advantage and moved in, disguised as strength. It would be several generations, during the time of the grandchildren she would never know, before the people would see a great light. Despite her love for the family, Ruth began to fail. New pains arrived on the shores of her body like immigrants from Europe. A strange cough took up residence in her lungs. But no pain was as great as that which accompanied the knowledge that by day grew clearer and by night haunted her sleep; the knowledge that no amount of pleading, no amount of prayer and bargaining, nor a mother's love, could protect her loved ones from what was to come. It was this realization that brought with it the terrible helplessness those standing in the way of fate must endure. Ruth knew her time was coming. The past sixteen years had been borrowed from an unknown treasury. She knew and she did not fight.

❧

My name is Ruth Ann Brennan. I was born the 21st of February, 1884, in Wheeler, Indiana. I died alone in the house I was born in on the 30th of July, 1936, leaving behind my husband Warren and my three boys: Edgar, Earl, and Gerald. My mother survived me as well, along with five brothers and a dear sister. I have grown tired from speaking, but I see that I am nearly done. After one hundred and twenty-five years, the time for complete rest is near. You see, on the day of the funeral when Gerald split himself into many, he took with each fragment a portion of my soul, each of which, in the course of his life, was handed down to his own children, Frank and James, in that most mysterious of all inheritances. I have existed over these past seventy-three years like the moons of Saturn, circling Gerald's bewildered psyche, on the rocky outposts of his divided self. For this reason I can speak to you. And now I am whole again and can find peace because at last it is reconciled. I know this sounds fantastic, but I can assure you there is no stranger story than that of this world and the creations of the mind.

And before the final story I shall leave you with, I pray to whatever God there may be to find the right words. May that God forgive me if I speak with pride. It may be obvious but let me say it out loud: I am the mystery. I am the absence at the center of everything that was made to happen from that day on. If you imagine a phantom limb, but instead of an arm or a leg, substitute his mother, you may have it.

To say I was a ghost is not adequate, although the notion of ghosts came from what I am describing. No, this is not original to our life and time. More ghosts exist than people on earth, believe me. Spirit is infinitely divisible. Therefore, by forgetting everything, by leaving Wheeler and the pain and all memory far, far behind, Gerald was able to remember fully what was his. By never once mentioning me, by eliminating anything resembling a story or a history or a fond remembrance, he was able to preserve me. I was a fly in amber. Not so much a fossil as a presence. A living presence uncannily cultivated and sustained by rituals of his design. Gerald lived his life in separate worlds. By day he worked hard, like any man, but not so much to amass status and wealth but to have the means to construct his refuge. He found his dear wife, Georgia Daisy, and she was the perfect replica needed to complete the arrangement. There he could dwell in his perfect reverie undisturbed by memory or emotion. Daisy sat in one chair and Gerald in another and I permeated the entire atmosphere. He was content to sit in his dream and not leave the house. World without end. Life without loss.

There you have it. In the last weeks of my short life on Earth, I had so little energy. The pain was terrible, but tolerable whenever I was visited by the glow of golden light, which was often enough to make everything bearable. I was leaving a world on the brink of disasters too grave to imagine. My own little community would be spared the bloodshed, although several sons of neighbors, boys I saw Gerald laugh and play with, would leave and not return. Their ghosts hovered near the lost and wandering mothers who saw no light again. We would go hungry for years, a hunger that made the soul flat and the stomach shrink. The townspeople grew thin and frail. Men kept to their homes, ashamed to walk the streets. Darkness never lifted.

On the days when I could, I reached for the Bible, not in the hope of finding solace but because I loved reading the stories. One of my last mornings with any strength, I opened by chance the Book of Isaiah. I could barely read a few lines. My eyes fell upon these:

**For behold...darkness shall cover the earth,
and gross darkness, the people**

My eyes shut and the Good Book fell from my hands. I cannot say how much time passed before I picked the book up again. When I did, it was to the following passage:

**The people that walked in darkness
have seen a great light
and they that dwell in the land of the shadow of death,
upon them hath the light shined**

Could it be? I tried to read it again but could not. Sleep was upon me. But I remember thinking well of Isaiah before falling into the empty place. Not because he gave me hope and not because of a sense of faith, far from it, but simply because it spoke to me of possibilities yet to be foreclosed. With that I dreamed my final dream. It was short and sweet. I am walking down the sidewalk

Gerald and I walked so many times. The sky is black and starless. I realize the town is asleep and I am walking in my nightgown and slippers. A single star appears in the East. It is blue and smaller than a pin prick. Light the color of a blue opal pours from the the star and fills the sky. The night is radiant.

When I wake up, Gerald is sitting next to the bed. Dark circles underline his eyes. I said to him so softly I feared he might not hear me, "Gerald, my dear boy."

He is struggling to look at me. It is too difficult to see me wasted away to nothing. I can see he has joined forces with Saturn, the planet of melancholia. The rings, consisting of all the unwanted memories and emotions of his life, are in place. Once he breaks into pieces at the funeral, the fragments will form satellites around the great planet. There they will orbit for millennia.

"Gerald, it's all right."

"Momma, don't go."

"I must, my dear. I must."

"What will we do? What will I do without you?"

"You will live a good life. You will find a wonderful wife to take care of you and love you like I do."

"Momma, don't." His legendary stubbornness failed and tears fell from swollen eyes one by one by one.

"Go to bed, sweetheart. You need sleep. Your father will need you."

"I don't want to sleep."

"Go, I'm tired. I'll see you in the morning."

ᘒ

It reached 102 degrees the day of the funeral. The humidity made it seem twice that. They stood under the clouds Gerald had once adored and watched her be lowered into the earth. Each was dizzy from the heat and escaped to thoughts of thunderstorms and a cool summer rain. All except Gerald, who was busy making vows to himself, only a few of which he recognized.

When it was over, each of the Brennan men packaged up his broken self and walked the short distance from the cemetery to the Bradshaw house in silence. Grandma Chester had gone on before them with her boys. They walked slowly. There was no need to hurry since the lack of money had prohibited them from inviting guests to the house for sandwiches and cold drinks. They walked slowly. The new white shirts were soaked in sweat. Their hearts were soaked in disbelief.

Warren cursed his fate. Edgar yearned to be with his new bride. Earl worried another fight would break out. Gerald cursed his father's stinginess. They walked slowly. Each step was heavier than the last. The neighbors who saw the sad procession coming hurried inside to avoid an uncomfortable encounter with misery.

Such terrible sorrow prevented them from noticing an intermittent breeze stirring from the east. The trees heard, as did the birds. Even the brown summer grass heard and leaned into the song of the wind: **Comfort ye, Comfort ye, my people** but not even those less grief-stricken than they could hear what was coming. Another thirty years would be needed to open their hearts to the sound **Speak ye tenderly to Jerusalem, speak ye tenderly to Jerusalem** They could not dare to believe what their ears told them so tattered were their hearts **and cry unto her that her iniquity is pardoned** So many days had passed since music touched their faces that not one of them recognized the caress of its hand. Not one of them perceived the body of light by his side.

Surrounding each of the Brennan men on that longest of walks was a line of ancestors, those who came before and those yet to come, all the spirits, young and old, who ever roamed the earth and ever would, accompanied them home. All the events of the past and the unfathomable future, everything that ever was or would be, untouched by the thick moisture in the air, accompanied them on that mournful day. But so heavy was each heart, so blinded were the bleeding eyes to anything but misfortune, none could partake of the grace that walked with grief. It was present, all of it, there in the midst of unbearable sorrow; in the most unlikely of places and among the most undeserving of common people, the light shone upon them.

But the four men, walking single file back to a motherless house, walking into a future without Ruth, into a world without a source of goodness, did not see a great light. They saw none of it, heard none of it, and turned their attentions to forgetting and the building of whatever fortress was within their means against the enemy they feared most: the mother of despair, longing.

# CHAPTER 3

# The Mark

&

Jimmy Brennan's family belonged to the band of rural Americans fleeing the quagmire of poverty that lay over the fields of the Great Lakes region. It was an exodus of people ravaged by war and depression seeking a clean house that would be a sanctuary from the past. The ugly past that pursued those lost souls through the solid walls of the new ranch house well into the defenseless rooms of sleep. They were a new class of people seeking refuge from the years of loss and the stench of shame left in the wake.

There were signs of that mark of inferiority. Sure signs. Signs that, for those with eyes to see, were large as billboards in South Dakota. Signs paraded every day. Not mysteries really, or hidden, like some things were, but telltale signs that were repeated so often they became familiar as neighbors walking past the front porch. Except by then, in the great Midwest states of Ohio and Indiana, the front porch had been eliminated, nearly outlawed, run out of town by vigilante groups protecting the interests of privacy. Garages multiplied and people disappeared into them. What was regarded as a success, a landmark of triumph over poverty and loss, was for most a place to hide. A place to hide from the stirrings of memory. To hide like a refugee from the authorities.

The signs were numerous: the friends who did not call, the brothers who did not visit, the disgust that grew on the tip of his father's tongue like mold, the painted face of his mother. And most of all the stories that were not told, that did not bear offspring, that were not repeated again and again but, rather, slumped in corners like moth-eaten blankets.

All the stories, real and rumored, cast aside as though a great flood had swept through the psyche of this family and washed away an entire history, the body of generations living here on this green earth, breathing this fresh air. All of it lost. Swallowed up like fishing boats in a storm.

What was left were scraps. Bits of living stories scattered here and there like discarded trash. A few photos of stern bearded men and women in dresses that squeezed the torso and touched the ground. People who never smiled, who spoke an Irish brogue, who drank homemade whiskey. Nameless people. People of the same blood who walked over the same ground, sat under the shade of the same trees, gave birth in the same houses. People who lost everything. Everything but grief. So much grief you could fill a silo.

What remained of that life was unwanted. Despised. Memory became the new enemy of the people and they adopted a commandment to protect against its return: do not remember. It was as though lifetimes had been consumed by a fire so broad and ferocious not even seedlings survived the purge. Why went up in smoke. How burned to ashes. When and where perished without a struggle. Incinerated. What was left for the children to breathe and dread was a haunted void. A world without causes. Without truth and light. They lived in an abandoned world of invisible shadows and strange echoes darting about like bats at dusk.

The exception was Gerald's mother, who was not despised, but cherished, yet was never mentioned and lived like an Egyptian queen buried beneath the sand in a gilded tomb. And Georgia, whose life was the stuff of illusion, a polished mirror. Her stories and laughter wrapped them all in a trance. They were hypnotic and convinced her children that life was a collection of happy endings.

And so a narrative took shape, shaped by exclusions. The past was bound and gagged. It disappeared and was believed to be extinct. This narration was tight as the doctrine of a cult. And it was deceptive. Bewildering. Theirs was a story without meaning told by a people without history. The unspoken concealed fear like a London fog and trampled grief, turning it to dust. Questions were not permitted even when the truth began to emerge like rust showing through paint. Tyranny ruled. The tyranny of forgetting.

Questions were exiled and inquiry forbidden. One question never led to another, never inspired tales of ancestors, adventures, or an understanding of the past. And yet there was a question turning at the center of their lives. A leading question with a prescribed answer, a question methodically repeated like a Latin chant. For Jimmy's mother, the question was, "How do I look?" And for his father the question was, "How am I doing?" These became the DNA of the family body.

With these questions asked, and the required answers given, they could believe the mark of shame that pursued each of them with the persistence of a stalker had been eluded. Their marriage was a pact, and each seized upon a symbol to place on the altar of salvation. For Gerald, it was the lock on the door that kept the past from intruding and his wife from leaving. It was the moat to his castle and the only insurance he could believe in, that she would stay and not disturb his reverie of an unbroken bond with his mother. For Georgia Daisy, it was the mirror; the mirror on the wall and the mirror of her inner eye, the scale of worth. It was the only protection she could count on to keep secret the shame and fear, so unsuitable to a queen, hidden in her body.

&

It was within such a mirror that Jimmy became lost. The mirror swallowed him like desire swallows judgment. He was a fly caught in an invisible web of shame. The mirror was not satisfied with his reflection but took his soul and kept him prisoner.

The mirror lived in Woolworth's. Woolworth's was the father of Sears and the grandfather of Walmart. It was the beginning of the era of the department store that would, over the next decades, gobble up city blocks and small businesses like a snake eating mice. Along with the television and the fluorescent light fixture, these mansions of waste and consumption cast a spell on those who came through the doors. They were body snatchers. More about forgetting than purchase.

Of course Jimmy went there with his mother shopping for dungarees and a shirt. Gerald was working and didn't have a clue what size Jimmy wore anyway. Georgia never complained. Jimmy always ripped the knees out and needed replacements. She was sure to buy him new pants so that he looked good and it was clear he came from a good family.

It was a regular day, perhaps early in the school year, because he wasn't wearing a jacket. They drove the family car downtown and Daisy chattered on about her latest conversation with Agi, the talker his dad detested. Laughing and going on about what, Jimmy could not fathom, they arrived at the store that had it all. She picked out his new dungarees for him. Just a little big to grow into but not too big as to look bulky like farm pants. They were away from all that.

She took a moment to look for a blouse for herself, or perhaps a hat to wear to church Sunday morning. Something Gerald would like. While she happily looked through the racks, Jimmy wandered off into the vast jungle of clothing. It was his big mistake. He was the kid who wandered off in the woods and never returned.

He saw the mirror attached to a huge post. It was rectangular and stretched to the floor. He'd never seen one so big. At home there were only the small mirror on the door of the medicine cabinet over the sink and the one his mother held before her face when she needed reassurance.

Jimmy had never seen his whole body. It wasn't a thing or an object in his mind; it was running fast and crashing into things and the pain of his brother's noogies to his shoulder and hunger for his mother's food. So when he stepped in front of the mirror that day, he saw the skinny body of an eight-year-old boy. He saw weakness. He saw a sunken chest. And then the hand reached out for him. It was the hand from a horror movie that reaches from the grave to snag its victim. It was the hand of loathing that took him like quicksand. That took over his eyes.

And as Jimmy stood there, transfixed by the body in the mirror, a transfusion of emotion flooded the cells of his flesh. Emotions that would occupy his inner life from that day on, emotions that would bully every perception and experience into submitting to and accepting their pronouncements. It was no longer his body but the body of shame and self-loathing. The body of his ancestors' failures. The body of his mother's humiliation and his father's heartbreak. He wanted to turn and run but his legs did not move.

His legs did not move and he could not get away from the mirror, and from the reflection of his ugliness. And he could not get away from his mother. Because she was his only hope of escaping the hand of disgust around his throat. Only disappearing into her smile provided relief. She was everything.

His father was gone doing God knows what, God knows where. He wasn't out plowing the back forty. Early each morning, before Jimmy was up, he heard his father leave, choking on his insecurities. He wore a white shirt that was stiff and still clean when he returned shortly before supper. He wore a noose around his neck and his breath made Jimmy turn away. It reeked of stale coffee.

That left Jimmy with his mother. And left her to educate him. As mothers do. She wrote the handbook, the laws of living, the shalls and shall nots of being. These were the commandments. She was the director, his father the enforcer.

Her delivery was impeccable, the insistent tone nearly imperceptible. The threat of disapproval adeptly veiled. The commandments were delivered in a style her children could not refuse. The demands were soaked in a smile that Jimmy knew would be gone should he refuse. These encounters with her angry twin became the ground for the one recurring dream of his childhood in which he approached a beautiful woman, a Jane Russell, or better yet,

Rita Hayworth (he loved that sultry glare) only to find at the moment their lips were trembling toward the kiss that would catapult him to the moon, her head transformed into a monster's. Into the head of the giant fly he had seen in the movies. And he fell backward, repelled and terrified. Eager to obey. Fearful of discovery.

Each instruction involved a mirror. An image of sorts. One began in the room with the mirror that talked. The bathroom mirror dared him to look, sneered and hissed when the door shut and berated him for his many failings. He shivered when he looked up at his face, when he saw the mark. Most often he avoided looking. It was his custom now to look down, at the linoleum, at cracks on the sidewalk or at the shoes walking his way. He pretended not to listen to the rebukes and taunts coming from the shining glass.

And so, Jimmy entered the bathroom uneasily and walked quickly to the toilet where the challenge of his mother's command waited. It stood beside the American Standard with its arms folded. Made of iron, it had only one expression. Contempt. Guilty until proven innocent. In this case, accurate. A good boy did not pee into the water but against the porcelain wall of the toilet bowl thereby reducing, or eliminating, any sound that might make its way to the ears of those nearby in the kitchen or bedroom. Actually, it was improper to call it "pee" or "piss" or any word beginning with the letter p that might be associated with that which did not exist. His mother called it "tinkle," or, when in particularly jocular moods, "tinky," "Do you need to tinky, Jimmy?"

But it wasn't the sound of piss hitting water that really mattered, though there was a secondary gain in concealing the fact of body functions, and it wasn't the spray that hit the seat and cascaded to the floor, though these were an unpleasant part of keeping the house clean. No, the purpose of the rule was to give him a task to focus on insuring he was not in there touching his penis. Perhaps fondling it, feeling the pleasure, the soft fullness, the warm pulse of life wishing for more, perhaps...no, not that...perhaps loving the miracle of his maleness, the shudder of excitement, growing weak in the knees. What if he forgot himself, what if he forgot the ugliness beating at his temples? What if he soared into exalted realms of bliss stroking himself and for a moment doubted the authority of the mirror?

But Jimmy did not go against her wishes. He hid from himself any and all erotic suggestion. So thorough was he in self-censorship that when he did have a wet dream, when he did arrive at high school, after a long bus ride staring at Donna Stevens, with a hard on so big and beautiful and exciting he thought it might bust through his pants, he told himself he was a freak and waited to get off the bus until it emptied and the rush subsided.

Walking to class he looked into the glass window panes on the entrance door and saw himself divided into pieces, each one a different shade of pathetic. He was certain everyone would see the mark and turn and point.

Sometime later when Suzie Ferguson picked him out of the crowd to exercise her pelvic thrust, he was dumbfounded to find once more the intrusive force beneath his Jockeys. Fully clothed, the two of them dove to the depths of her couch in the family room before the permissiveness of the television. They kissed and moaned and pounded each other with their hungry genitals protected as they were by layer upon layer of shorts and Levis and panties and proper wool slacks and ignorance, and despite these helpful safeguards the horror of horrors began in a place so deep in his loins, he could not find a beginning to understand the magnitude of the explosion that erupted into his shorts and sent his whole body quaking the length of the poor couch. An eight-year-old part of his brain shrieked, "My God, I'm going to tinky!" And he would leap to his feet, often too late to stop the flood, pretending he had a cramp in his hamstring. Worrying that his reflection might show on the screen of the TV, which was then dark and blank and, he thought, watching him with a menacing gaze.

"What's wrong, Jimmy?"

"Cramp."

"Again?" She was trying to be kind but her hips were still rocking and she found it tough to be interrupted so abruptly, especially when it didn't concern her parents who she was sure were sleeping.

"What do you mean, again?"

"Why are you standing like that?"

"It hurts. Whad'ya think?" It was a poor lie. But he didn't know what else to do. He couldn't risk turning toward her. He was sure the strange white blood would show. She would laugh. The surge subsided at last. Hoping the stiff denim would shield his mistake he climbed back on her. She was not slowed.

He was pathetic. And yet the taste of sex busting loose not only thrilled him, but placed an unfamiliar wedge of doubt and protest in his chest. The rules still held him largely in check. They fulfilled the alternate purpose of all rules, which was the elimination of possibilities. Possibilities were foreclosed. They were as dangerous to the order of things as living next to a colored person.

As a consequence, he continued to look for himself in the large glass windows of storefronts and in the broad, bright smiles of girls and, later, women of all ages. He made a habit of looking for himself in any surface he passed that might reflect back something of himself that he could hold up to the mirror, something that was not marked. He found none but the image of the eight-year-old standing by himself, standing slouched in a dark hallway, depleted of energy, which emptied through the skin that never touched his mother's body.

Over time his body disappeared. The ground disappeared, as did his feet and spine. The faces he looked to for a sign of himself drifted past, pale and disembodied like so many balloons on short strings. He looked to each trying to hide the desperation that filled his lungs and would not leave. He was certain the slightest word or look might tear a hole in his skin and leave him, like one of the balloons, spinning and gasping, madly out of control, to the ground.

∽

Jimmy drove home from Suzie Ferguson's that night in his father's Mercury. A big boat of a car. They were living in Connecticut by then. The flat earth was no more. Trees made all the streets into tunnels. He didn't realize it but he was in love with the hilly, abrupt curves in the road that turned and fell like water racing through rock. Curfew was midnight, which meant he had to gun the horses especially hard to get there just late enough to annoy his dad and on time enough to avoid punishment. The thrill of humping Suzie until the last possible moment was gradually replaced by a gathering dread as he imagined his father's face in the morning and the mirror he would have to pass getting to his room. He could feel teeth dig into his belly, the hand of Captain Hook stabbing at his groin, the stain on his forehead growing.

Suddenly a memory arrived out of nowhere. Jimmy nearly swerved off the road. It is the eight-year-old in his bedroom: a room with no mirrors. Bedtime is near and he is done crashing into the posts and mattress pretending to be Jim Brown carrying the football. He dreamed of being Jim Brown. Brown, with massive thighs and running over tacklers, running through them with muscular contempt. Watching them fall at his feet in disgrace. In a few years he would long to be Chuck Berry, reeling and rocking across the stage, jumping on one leg, guitar in hand and across his thigh like a machine gun mowing down convention. But that night he wanted to be Jim Brown. He wanted to be the great fullback and put his head down and smash through the goddamn mirror. Break it into a thousand pieces, take his cleats and grind it into dust, spit on it and walk back to his life tall as his body reached.

He remembered with shock that forgotten kid lying on his narrow bed, that field of dreams, still sweating from pile-ups and triumph. The kid whose attention then turned to the room, to the walls and ceiling, to fences and barriers, outlines and endings, and a strange thing he'd heard about called "infinity." Somewhere in his brain, unshackled by the mirror, he broke another of the profane laws: he began to think. Infinity? How can it be that this room has an end, the closet that holds the clothes has four walls, the Hardy Boys books have an end. How can there be a story, a something, that has no end? And with this, his forehead wrinkled into a frown and his brain twisted and cramped. What about beginnings? There have to be beginnings. The game has to start. He didn't want to think of the possibility of no endings as long as the mirror was in one piece. But his mind returned to the puzzle that tucked him into bed each night. No ending. Infinity. And without recognizing it, he realized he loved the thinking, the puzzling mystery and above everything else, infinity. He pulled his curtains open and looked for it above the basketball hoop and above the old maple. Is that it? Is infinity black?

One such night, as he was beginning to drift into sleep, the images fading in his mind like distant galaxies, the bewildering attempts to conceive of a world without end giving way to the empty dreamy feeling that followed such efforts, something happened. It may have lasted all of a nanosecond, quicker than a snapshot. It may have sounded like the pop of a light bulb burning out. He wasn't sure. He couldn't say if it was real or a dream or if he made it up but Infinity kissed him good night. And bingo, into the beyond he flew, shot out of a Saturn rocket, expanding and filling the Milky Way, simultaneously here and everywhere and nowhere. And most spellbinding of all, more glorious than the Indians winning the pennant, the mark was gone, completely. Not a trace. As was any evidence of his body. The scars on his knees, the ribs showing through his skin: gone. In their place was something extraordinary, a bigness he could never describe and a feeling greater than any he could imagine even if all the love, joy, and fun he'd known were added up all together. It was better than being Jim Brown in the end zone. Better than beating his brother at basketball. Better than his recurring dream ending with Rita Hayworth in his arms. The nanosecond stretched for light years. And brought him back to bed. The next day he would scarcely remember what took place. But in that instant something happened that began to bring about an end to the reign of the mirror. It would take over forty years, but what happened that night, in that flash, turned the mirror into a piece of glass. It turned the world into a pebble and the stars into candles and Jimmy into a pilgrim.

And thanks to that kiss, that unspeakably loving touch, Jimmy began, quite unconsciously, to wonder about some of the signs scattered about. He looked under rocks for his father's tongue. Put his ear to the wall to hear his mother's nightmarish confession. He picked up the handbook in his mother's cursive and read what was legible: don't touch the penis, don't brag, don't be angry, smile and pretend. Pretend. Pretend each day is like any other. Pretend the past is dead. Pretend that pain is truly banished from the world like smallpox. Most of the laws Jimmy learned as he learned to walk and talk. Jimmy was a good boy. His mother thought he might become a minister. And yet, from the time of the flash, he noticed a new force within that occurred simultaneous to his compliance with the rules of the house. This force was a foreigner. An underground movement. For every time he swallowed hard and did the right thing, the underground resistance pressed against his chest and registered a secret no. And for every no, he felt the no dig deeper. He felt anxiety worm through his stomach. But he could not stop it. He could not evict it. And it grew until it seemed he was against everything. Until he was sure the sign was unmistakable. Surely they must hear the scream. They must see his clenched jaw, the angry thoughts and fantasies. But they did not. "You're tired, Jimmy. You're a sleepy boy. Go to bed, Sweetie." They were accustomed to not noticing. His mother was a master with the paint brush. And so he learned to sleep and dream of war.

Sleep so deep it lasted into daylight. Dreams so strong they sailed past waking. So strong all perception was eclipsed by dreaming and all waking consumed by sleep. So strong that sleep and dream covered awareness like algae over a pond. Such that waking and dreaming and the deepest sleep, usually the province of non-being, bound together like separate bacteria forming a new organism. Bound and braided and so terribly entangled that any sense of Jimmy faded into the paint on the walls. This is how Jimmy came to live in so many worlds. In so many moments. And in some of those moments, quite surprisingly, foolishly, Jimmy forgot himself enough to speak out against what was the most sacred and dangerous of all the laws of the world. The one law that held the entire complex together like dark matter: never criticize your mother. Never.

Rarely did Jimmy launch an attack when they were alone together. The surveillance system was too vigilant. The secret service too well trained. Nevertheless, a stealth part of his arsenal managed at times to strike and pull back. His mother's response was immediate. The mask dropped and rage blasted from her, hot as a furnace melting steel. His retreat was as immediate. Scorched and white with fear, he fled to the cover of a many-chambered house. The house of many gables and all that must be forgotten. And as he ran he only barely noticed his mother adjust herself, as though she were fluffing a pillow, and assume again the pose that made her mirror happy and memory obsolete.

But these encounters were not what Jimmy remembered when he woke decades later. He tended to remember the three of them together. Seated around the dinner table on a Sunday. Frank away at college. The house smelling of pot roast and roasted carrots. The high ritual of Sunday dinner.

∽

Mom has been in the kitchen all afternoon. Dad and I don't lift a finger. Which makes us look important, as though honoring us is the purpose of the feast. But this is all about Mom. She is the alchemist making gold in her lab while the king gets fat and dull sitting on his throne. She is the high priestess of normalcy spinning magic from despair. She prepares the food, sets the table: the linens, silverware, and glassware. And finally, she makes the announcement. With a voice a bluebird would envy, she invites us to her table, which is an altar to the eternal presence of Mother. To the goodness and everlasting abundance of Mother's love. World without end, Amen.

Dad looks me over as I come to the table and disapproval covers his face like a shadow. I have failed to observe and be sufficiently respectful of the Sunday services. I'm not wearing shoes. Terribly rude.

"How many times do I have to tell you? You wear shoes to dinner." This is not a question.

"Dad, come on."

"Don't 'come on' me. Get your shoes on."

It doesn't take much to get him going. Disgust is near. We're just getting going. This is only a preliminary bout.

"Why? It's just us, at home. What does it matter?" This is not a question either.

"You know why it matters. Your mother has been slaving in the kitchen all afternoon to make this meal. Get your shoes on. You weren't born in a barn."

So mother is a slave. Mother is a queen. We must pay her our respects. I get the shoes and return to the table sufficiently contrite. Dad is fidgeting. Mom is smiling. I am looking down. My favorite direction.

Dad says the benediction. It's the same every meal, every Sunday: "This is the best roast I've ever tasted." Mom is suitably humble and appreciative of his praise. He has mastered his lines. Not bad for a guy with no tongue. The tension is tougher to cut than the beef. I can't feel it but I know it's there. Mom is smiling. She has prepared her sermon. Every set of commandments requires a ritual to persuade the followers, and every ritual requires a sacrifice to erase any doubt. Today it is a literary figure whose heart shall be removed. Her laughter is the knife plunging, her judgment is the hand holding the knife plunging, her words are the blade digging; blood is the gravy, is the wine, is the, wait, it's dripping from my eyes, my nose, my lips. Neither Mom nor Dad gasp or run for a towel to stop the bleeding. Mom just rolls on.

"That Jackie Collins! What a nut! I tried to read her book. What's the title? I can't even remember. What a crackpot! Hollywood! My gosh, the things they do there. What a terrible place. Oh my gosh, I couldn't get past fifty pages of that trash!" More laughing. "I won't pick that up again." She said it like it was a turd she had to barehand.

I don't read books. The mirror won't let me. But I can tell Jackie Collins has broken a hundred commandments in the first ten pages.

More than likely it's the sex thing and drinking and something else outrageous that has been outlawed in Ohio. Mom is smiling and laughing and thrusting the knife deeper and deeper like an ice pick into a block of frozen blood. No one notices the tension growing. I only barely notice the flinch deep in my stomach every time she calls her a nut. I don't feel it spreading out into my arms.

"Why do people read trash like that? It's number one on the best seller list again this week! What's wrong with people? Why I'll bet it isn't even true, most of it. I like a good story, with nice people that will make me feel good and make me laugh. I'll never pick up another one of her books. Not that nut." Her laugh is an explanation point. A mockery.

And then it happened. I didn't rehearse it. It just happened; it just flew out of me before I could stop it. It spread from my arms to my throat and then it flew like a falcon. And when it did, everything stopped. For one terrible, wonderful second it all stopped: Dad eating, Mom talking, me fuming, the dog panting, the house calcifying. Had I been someone else, I might have noticed the similarity to the flash, how the gap filled with something bright and startling as the first glimpse of an unexpected moon rising over treetops. Something caught it. I can't say what because of what was happening.

"Mom, stop calling her a nut." That may not sound like much, but it was thunder and lightning in January. The walls tilted inward. Dad dropped his fork and began shuffling the salt shaker. Mom's face dropped an octave. "Mom, you don't know. You can't tell after only fifty pages."

"I can tell plenty." Her voice is stern. Her eyes are razors.

"No, you can't. Not in a few pages; she may be setting something up. Give it a chance." I am staggering like Sonny Liston after a minute in the ring with Cassius Clay. "She's not a nut." It is my closing argument to the jury.

And just like that it is over. The blood is gone. The knife is put away. What's left of me is merged with the pot roast and trembling over the dinner plate. The silence is heavy as a fallen tree. Dad is looking at Mom. His face is red. The dog is gone. Time creeps by with wounded legs. Even Mom's recovery is slow in coming but once she does, once she finds her pose, her smile signals to all that we are to go on and what happened is not really what happened but some aberration, an unexplainable goof that doesn't deserve to be remembered.

I am looking for the escape hatch, a lifeboat, anything. Time is breathing again and I am in the driveway shooting baskets. I am dreaming of being the hero in the big game. Long-range impossible jumpers, double-teamed, from the corner, last second, GOOD!! I can't be stopped. The crowd is going nuts. I drive to the top of the key, head fake, pull up twenty-footer, GOOOOD! Nothing but net. Nothing but cheers. The fans are going wild. I am Clyde Frazier. I am too much for anyone to stop. I am in trouble. Here comes Dad. He's muttering to himself. He looks like he wants to hit me. Fists are clenched.

"You better not ever talk to your mother that way again."

I'm holding the ball staring at my feet.

"I'm going to floor you. Your mother is the best mother there is and you'd better treat her like it."

"I just..."

"Don't 'just.' What's wrong with you? Your mother does everything for you and then some and all you can do is be..." He stammered something under his breath and walked away shaking his head. But he didn't need to finish; I took care of that for him. The mirror smirked in the upstairs window. Mom dictated the commandments, but Dad was the enforcer. It would be days before he looked at me. I dribbled the ball off my foot. Idiot. What a damn idiot! The crowd boos. Shot after shot bangs off the rim.

∞

"Dad. Dad." Jimmy's plea is barely audible to his own ears. His father is gone. The air is suddenly cold. Before he can take a step toward the house and toward laying himself down in apology, the ground gives way and he is falling, falling through a dense cloud. Falling wildly, terribly fast, head over heel, no visibility, no idea when he might hit the ground or if there is ground to hit. Falling, no parachute, no James Bond super stunt to save him, annihilation waiting patiently.

Jimmy realizes the only way to end the fall is to follow his father into his dream. Yes, into his dream, where he finds his father walking a golf course without clubs. He is walking ahead of Jimmy, always keeping his back to him. Jimmy uses a driver made from a cabbage head. The ball buries in the folds of the cabbage and goes nowhere. His father watches and turns away in disgust. Gerald walks into woods where the fairway should be and Jimmy follows silently but quickly loses sight of his father.

Trees give way to tunnels that furrow deep underground. Water oozes from the walls. Walking is nearly impossible; the base is so slippery and bumpy, the ceiling so low. Darkness hides rocks and holes, and he stumbles and falls, stumbles and falls. It is not pain or fear that brings on the sobbing. But he is sobbing uncontrollably. His tears collect and begin to fill the cave, rising to his knees and quickly to his waist. There is panic. He tries to run but cannot. His legs are heavy and weak. The water rises to his chest. The water turns colder and colder and begins to freeze. He is a wooly mammoth caught in a field of ice. He prays for his legs to work, to be able to run. To run out of time, out of the woods, out of his father's dream, but he can't feel his legs. He can't feel anything. He closes his eyes.

What he sees next is green. Green everywhere. Green of a thousand different shades. And sounds. A trillion voices. Chorus upon chorus of celestial sounds urging him on. Urging him to go forth, to open his eyes to the world. Urging him to sing along, to dance and play. The jungle calls his name, green parrots and howler monkeys and butterflies larger than melons, calling his name and urging him on. They are chanting now, "Stay, stay, stay here, Jimmy." And he wants to lie down. He wants to eat the fruit.

But he reaches a clearing and from the edge sees a swamp. The swamp pulls at him. He is close. His shoes are sinking into mud. A strange glow catches his eye from the far side of the swamp. It is drifting toward the center. The glow is a merger of maroon and gold. The color is so captivating he feels compelled to move toward it, not noticing he has entered the swamp and its waters have now risen to his knees. The glow moves closer and begins to pulse. Something stirs in his stomach. What is this?

Then, as though the sun burned through a thin fog, the glow dissipates and spreads slowly across the water's surface like a carpet inviting him to take off his shoes and feel his feet on the plush wool. Inviting him to walk toward the heart of the swamp, which now reveals, in all the exquisite detail and proportion of a Persian miniature, a separate world, a world within a jewel, and sitting in the core of this world, no larger than his hand, is a middle-aged woman. She is wearing an old-fashioned lace dress. She has deep creases in her forehead and black coiffed hair. Her eyes are closed and she is stroking the hair of his father, who is curled in a ball on her lap. What began as astonishment to Jimmy is now a trembling throughout his body. But he can't take his eyes off the expression on his father's face. Something he's never seen. A contentment. He realizes the woman is Ruth, his grandmother, the mystery that cannot be solved.

A surge of desire floods his limbs and he longs with all his being to go to his father. And as he is about to throw off his shoes and take to the magic carpet, Ruth opens her eyes and looks at him and his father does the same and they smile what would seem to be a loving smile except that her eyes are entirely black and his father has no teeth and suddenly Jimmy is fighting terror and the feeling that he is being smothered. Faster than a prairie dog, he turns and tears from the swamp. He runs for the jungle but it is gone. He runs blindly. Terror is a snake where his spine once was. He runs and runs until all there is running. He runs beyond the swamp, beyond the memory of his father's toothless smile, beyond the longing and terror; he runs until there is nothing left of him, until the whole of the dream collapses into nothing. And nothing else.

∾

Jimmy stands by the basketball post he and his dad built. It took them three hours to dig through the rock of the Connecticut earth and make a hole for the post. Neither spoke a word the entire time. Jimmy wondered to himself if he would find his father's tongue under one of the ancient stones. He stood there now, leaning against the wooden post, and felt his body return to its shape. He felt winded and wondered why. His head was tingly and clouded like when he woke from a nap that lasted too long. The ball felt large in his hands or was it that his hands felt small and young? He wondered how his shoes could be muddy and wet.

Anxiety pulls at his sleeve. He might have asked himself, "What is happening to me?" but a memory came to him he couldn't ignore. He is 12 and returning home on a summer night in Ohio. The air is pleasant and free of humidity. Fireflies are flashing here and there. A handful of stars returns the signal. Jimmy thinks he hears the molecules of space say hello. Without knowing it, he senses something near. Something inviting. And for no real reason, he begins to run. And the dark gives way as he moves through it. The sea parts, and his body effortlessly builds momentum. He is running, running without a thought of any kind. Running, the fireflies observe, like a deer. Running, they would say, free. There is no resistance from this black body of wakefulness or his own warm muscles propelling the bones and flesh of his story through a timeless night. He is running and a dim place within notices the quiet, the quiet that surrounds him, the quiet of his foot landing on the summer lawn, the quiet of his stride and breath. That breath, which is effortless and perennial as water. That enters and leaves, enters and leaves. Fills and empties. Soon only breathing moves. His feet and legs have disappeared. His arms and chest have fallen away. His head and shoulders have dissolved into the sea the fireflies swim in. Only his breath remains. And it is not breath. It is opening and closing. Opening and closing. And then it is gone. Gone, as though it were never there. In a seamless flash it is all gone. Everything. Except something magnificent and nameless. Something impossible to remember and never forgotten. That was always and never. That was him and not him and everyone and no one. That made the mirror laughable, impotent. That made the sun bow and the moon sing. What was left was joyful. Was space and motion making love, their formless bodies wrapped together, inseparable as sea and salt, erotic as virgins on a beach. All in the fold of nothing: not this and not that. Jimmy ran and ran. He returned to himself like a pale moon in a bright morning sky. Transparent. His body returned like birds in spring. He ran until he reached home. The lights were on in the house. He looked at his house standing under the stars on the banks of flat Ohio. It looked like a box taped shut.

The memory left Jimmy dizzy. He stood there in the fading light of that Sunday afternoon wondering if he could move. Not sure why his body felt like it wasn't his. Not sure why he couldn't just walk in the house. Not sure if it was getting light or getting dark. The ball in his hands felt dead. He dropped it and it bounced twice. When he picked it up, it felt small and silly. He threw it at the hoop and it bounced off the iron rim down the driveway and toward the street. Jimmy chased after the rolling ball and thought how odd it was to run. His body seemed to move reluctantly. Each limb seemed to have a mind of its own. The cold damp air stung his lungs. With the ball once more in his hands, he turned toward his house and walked alone to the garage, which was open but dark. Anxiety returned as he remembered his father walking through that door moments before. He grew weak when he imagined opening the door and seeing him sitting in his chair. Jimmy hoped he wouldn't look up from his television program. He hoped he wouldn't see that look on his face. That was the sign he dreaded as much as any. The sign that he was a disappointment. The sign that he was ruining something. Reminding his father of something bitter he could not swallow. That he was taking him down into fields of gloom. This he could not bear. This he could not forgive. Ever.

# CHAPTER 4

# A Birthday

∾

All is ready. The moon is in position, as are the heavenly bodies. The sky is black, as it was in ancient days, and dusted with starlight. Waves of light have crossed the universe to be here for this moment. Capricorn has climbed the rugged cliffs from the south and arrived at the eastern horizon as planned. Pushya, greatest of all the stars and crown jewel of the muscular goat, shines brighter than Venus in the blue hour. And that radiance touches every jewel and particle in the great web surrounding and penetrating the sphere of what is his welcoming.

Three minutes remain under the watch of the Goddess of Spring. Maia bows to primordial Juno, who has lifted her lengthy dress and walked onto the stage of seasonal theater. She makes her appearance and the air turns still. Birds that once sang every note and song their throats could proclaim are now quiet. The curtain is up on life. And seated at her loom in the shade of an oak, wide at the trunk as an old man's life, is the mother of this unlikely flux, Maya, spinning all the magic and mystery of this world from common thread. Old and wrinkled, the hint of a smile on her lips and sad lines beneath her eyes, the elusive one brings what is dreamlike to life. Her art charms and bewilders those passing by. Her magic delights and dumbfounds the children playing at her feet. Too quick at hand is she. They behold nothing but the rise and fall of her handiwork and still less of that which is immovable.

All is ready and moving with the precision of a clock. His body and that of his mother are near the port where fate will take Jimmy by the hand and compel him to follow her winding way. Georgia has held him in her womb these forty weeks. For over six thousand hours, he has shared the warmth of her blood and listened to the lullaby of her breath. For those many days and nights, her voice has whispered affections to the growing presence she has come to know as his alone. They have traveled together as one passenger the nearly five hundred million miles of elliptical flight around the blazing star that is mother and father to all that has lived and may still. As one they have looked out onto this land of beginnings and felt both large and small, both happy and frightened by the marvel of what is. And as they did so, Maya patiently wove together silk from Georgia's long line of ancestral bodies. Wove those glistening strands into the tender nakedness of he who would enter the world as Jimmy. She who touches all that moves, who transforms trillions upon trillions of cells into bones, and blood, and neurons and pink lungs that will expand and contract with the cosmic breath until death calls his name. She is Maya, the magician. So intricate is her work, the pyramids look like a child's wooden blocks piled high in a sand box. So precise is her craft, the knowledgeable fall to their knees faint from astonishment.

And so it goes and goes, readying for another life to come tumbling into existence. Thrashing and tumbling into this wild, wild kingdom of tumult and the sublime. Into this improbable intercourse of the divisible and indivisible. Into convulsions of becoming, cataclysmic finales, into the speck and enormity. Tumbling into the thunderous makings of epoch upon epoch, universe upon universe; tumbling, free falling into the arms of a silence greater than the sum of all the worlds ever spawned and into the mix of a people still hiding in caves. Readying, never stopping. Opening. Opening yet again. Opening yet again, to something never seen before.

∽

But Georgia is not opening. She is not moving. Her breath is shallow. The drugs have taken her away. A net has been cast over her water. She is frightened, remembering the pain, lying there alone under a fluorescent sky in the cold. Gerald is absent. Hurrying back from a business class in Cleveland. Her mother is at home caring for Frank. She feels the cold steal her body. Surrounded by masked men and the sounds of metal meeting metal and such terrible smells, once again, she is taken over; her body paralyzed, her voice extinguished. She is a dry, empty cloud. A blanket of ether is laid over her breath. Panic breaks the cold into pieces. She disappears.

What is auspicious to the stars is lost. Beauty has been vanquished, the river bound. Strangers are the first to see the crown of his head. The shiny black hair. Georgia is gone. She can't help him. He is stuck. A deep sleep binds his arms and legs. He is a cork in the neck of a bottle. He cannot feel his mother's will, he cannot hear her breathe, nor feel her muscles coaxing him from her body into outer space. Deep sleep. Heavy and dreamless sleep. Waking in a stupor. Trapped beneath a mud slide. Can't move. So heavy. Waves of fear. More fear. Then nothing. Angry, loud sounds. Nothing. Strange voices. Not hers. Nothing. No soothing breath. Nothing. Gagging on cold blood. Nothing Blank A masked man in a white coat puts on his rubber gloves. He calls for the tray of instruments. A masked woman, more obedient than a dog, hands him the steel forceps. Her eyes are large and admiring. The man adjusts his grip and jokes about the catch. She laughs appropriately. Georgia is motionless. He maneuvers the forceps around her flesh. She stirs. He places the cold fingers at the temples of the still hidden infant. Pressure is applied. It is cold and hard. A hollow forms on the tender walls that will leave a permanent dent. More pressure. And he pulls the baby from his mother. Extracted like a tooth.

Jimmy is taken from her. Taken and delivered to the cold, clean room. Held by cold hands under the buzz of a white night. Their common flesh is severed abruptly with large scissors and thrown in the trash. Georgia sleeps like the dead. She does not feel the frantic. She does not see her black-haired baby boy taken away. Frantic invades the drugged slumber. Her small hands struggle and instinctively grope for her baby. The doctor holds Jimmy upside down and slaps his bottom. His lungs fill with air but he does not cry. Georgia sleeps but does not dream. His soul fills with original sin.

The nurse takes him from the room. She takes him to another room just as cold and just as blindingly bright as the last. Another masked man waits for him with knife in hand. She places him on a tray and the white ghost raises his blade to the baby's maleness. He cuts it off like fat on beef. Blood flows from Jimmy's penis. It is his blood that stains the towel. It is his penis that feels the razor cut through his flesh. Now he cries. He screams. He writhes from side to side trying to escape. The good nurse holds him down and tells him he's all right. He cries and struggles, rages and twists his little body under her cold hands. At last he gives up. She bandages him and takes him to another room further away from his mother. There he is put in a box next to a dozen other fresh souls equally bewildered, drugged, and throbbing with pain. Left alone to sleep and wrestle with something that can't be seen or understood. A ghostly feeling all the motherless children will come to know and dread. A mood that will take up residency in their permeable psyches and color each throughout their lives with the engulfing and perplexing sense that something is terribly wrong.

He will sleep but not with his mother. He will sleep but not in her arms where he might hear her breath speak his name. Where he might listen to the call of eternity. To the song of welcome. The stars weep in disbelief. Helpless, they strain to see him but cannot. Georgia is their vision and she is far away. Cleaned and dressed and alone in her own room where she will lie dead to the world for hours. Where she will strain to emerge from the density of her sleep. Where her breasts will fill and long for the mouth of her little one. Where franticness will have its way with her defenseless mind and etch its harsh signature on her brow. And she and the stars and the precious baby will be isolated from one another. And the light that traveled a billion years to be there on time, as well as the light of mother and son, will not shine on this first day of the fair month of June.

Gerald arrived shortly before 10:00 PM the evening of his son's birth. He was tired from work, the night class, and driving. They shuttled him to a waiting room with other expectant fathers. No one talked much. They sat and smoked cigarettes and read the newspaper. They fidgeted and smoked some more. A few dozed in their chairs. One by one they were called to speak to a doctor. Gerald's turn came and he received the news of a boy with relief. He feared the idea of a little girl for reasons he could not explain. The doctor asked if he'd like to see his son and he said yes. He was the first to lay eyes on Jimmy. And thus, in the strangest twist of fate, the man with no tongue was handed the honor of telling the first story in the book of Jimmy. A story that would be repeated in such a way as to become myth. He had his opportunity the following morning when Georgia finally came back to life.

"Hi doll." He called her his doll and she was. It reminded her of her father calling her baby. She felt annoyed but ignored it.

"Hi sweetheart." She took his hand and smiled. It was a lovely smile even then with so much fatigue pulling her down. Gerald felt warmed in a way he relied on so completely, he nearly forgot about their baby.

"How is the baby, Gerald?"

"Fine. The baby is fine. It's a boy, Daisy. You have another son."

"Oh good, we wanted another boy, didn't we?"

"Yes, we did."

"Have you seen him"

"Yep, I saw him last night, I mean this morning really."

"What does he look like, darling?" And with this question the world stopped spinning.

"Just like Frank, blue eyes, blond hair."

And the moon cried out, "No, stop, not so. Not so."

"Just like Frank, really?" Imagining it to be true, she gave in to the fatigue and closed her eyes.

And the twinkle left the stars to the east.

〜

Which stories survive and which are cast out into oblivion, which are crafted into another story all together, which are repeated again and again, and which ones have to be pried out of forgetfulness like an old rusted nail from a board; these constitute the riddle that is the family testimony.

The story of Jimmy's birth was one of the survivors. From time to time it returned to the conversation like a dog to its bone. It held a curious place in the family portrait, one that perplexed Jimmy and left him, as the years went by, increasingly uncomfortable. It was the same with each telling. The laughter. Always laughter at the same moment in the story.

Georgia dozed with the image of her child securely in her mind. Gerald sat down in a chair and watched his wife sleep. Each felt relieved and a bit anxious with the news of the newborn's likeness to his brother. Frank was a handful and brought out an angry side of Gerald Georgia had never seen. It created an unwanted conflict between them. An uneasiness stirred beneath the happiness of the birth of their second child, and, as it turned out, their last. Would this new baby be as difficult as Frank? Would that cause more strife between him and Georgia? Gerald quickly forgot all of that gazing at Daisy. She was so lovely and dear. He forgot all his anxieties looking at her face.

The door opened and a nurse entered the room. Georgia stirred from napping and opened her eyes. "Would you like to see your baby, Mrs. Brennan?"

"Oh yes, please." She was reminded, without clearly remembering, of the frantic that just hours ago had raced through her body. Her muscles stiffened slightly to protect her should it return.

"Here he is!" And the nurse entered the room beaming, carrying in her arms a baby boy with thick black hair covering his head and neck.

Georgia instinctively drew back. She laughed a low nervous laugh and said the punch line to the story, the words that gave it a kick and produced the laughter that made Jimmy cringe and his own laugh contract. She said the words that echoed through much of his experience in life, that communicated something incomprehensible. She looked at Gerald puzzled and alarmed and spoke for the first time in Jimmy's presence: "Oh, there must be a mistake. You must have the wrong baby."

And the moon sagged. The wind lost its wings.

"My husband said our boy is blond like his brother."

The frantic feelings zig-zagged through her.

"Oh no, Mrs. Brennan, this is your baby. Here, you hold him."

She placed the infant in his mother's arms so he could see her for the first time. But it was not the radiant smile of Georgia Daisy that Jimmy glimpsed when he looked up. It was not the smile that made everyone feel better. Georgia's warm green eyes did not look down upon her son. It was the face of a confused and tired woman, torn between trying to accept the infant lying in her arms and rejecting the child her mind insisted did not belong to her.

"Gerald?" Her plea went unanswered.

"Mrs. Brennan, is something wrong?" The nurse had given up on enthusiasm.

"Well, it's just that my husband told me this morning that when he saw our baby last night..." Her voice trailed off and she looked again at the new life in her arms. Her mind began to clear from the collision between her expectation and the very real infant given to her at this moment. She looked into his dark brown eyes and felt her heart give way. She felt the weight of his body in her hands. He squirmed and a bubble emerged from his mouth and when it popped, a smile slowly rose from the doubt covering the most beautiful face he had ever seen.

"It's just that I thought there might have been a mistake..." But again her voice trailed off. She was no longer convinced of the image of the baby in her mind, since taking in the features before her eyes.

"Oh no, Mrs. Brennan, no mistake. This is your baby all right. Isn't he a beauty?"

Georgia nodded. By now she was lost in a world unfolding before her like a rose from a bud. She smiled and cooed with the baby. She marveled at the size of his head and the depth of his brown eyes.

As she took him in, he turned his little head, ever so slightly, to see which face was there to meet him. The first mother had startled him. And the newborn, all eight hours of a life, tensed the muscles in his neck to move his large head and see for himself who was there. And in that one gesture, the questions of the next decades began their own period of gestation. Impossible questions. Questions his naked body would never forget: Who is my mother? Why is she frowning? Why does my father not recognize me? Must I be my brother? What is so damn funny about all this? What is too frightening to look at?

∽

Stories are made of exclusions. Remember the curious matter of the dog that did not bark?. But in post-war Ohio, history is fact. Stories are wallpaper that hides cracks in the plaster. An oral history evolved in the Brennan household that could be repeated and forgotten. It was possible to laugh at life, to have the last laugh, as it were, knowing full well the contingencies of the world would prevail in the end. Knowing full well a swerving truck-load of loss could be coming around any corner of the road. A stranger had entered their midst. Sadly, the family needed a story to distract them from realizing they were all strangers to one another. So it went, from the hour of his birth until the years surrounding Georgia's death; Jimmy became the leading character in the drama of estrangement. A drama that allowed the family a focal point for the many tides of emotion threatening the mainland. And one that allowed for the dismissal of all thoughts pertaining to the worst of fears: the return of memory and, along with it, the pain that would not die.

Everything dies. What is it that is not born? Gerald did not take his son in his arms. Instead, with love and dread he said to him in the tongue of his grandfather's father and the language of dust, "I give you death." Georgia held him close without allowing him to touch her body and found herself saying silently, in the language of longing, "You are my precious." And while doing so, she recognized what she thought was something old and trustworthy in the black window of his eyes. Until that moment she had not been aware of an angst floating inside her world. A new measure of comfort spread across her life and smoothed the edges of loneliness like a warm iron on linen.

The moon, already sleeping soundly, dipped beneath the plains to the west. The sun climbed the steps to its throne and peered into the heart of the future. And all the blessed starlight of the ages entered the waters of the Great Lakes to the north, Erie and Heron, Superior and Michigan, for the day's bathing.

The story of Jimmy's birth baked slowly in an oven made from memory and longing. Each memory held a secret written in a language too old to translate. Each longing reached beyond the moon and the stars for its birthright.

As it warmed, the story rose and released an aroma none could identify that was, nevertheless, pleasing and inspired hunger. And the pleasing vapor drifted over the fields of Ohio carried by a silent wind. It drifted over the Lakes and over the past and into a future some twenty years removed, finally settling in a wooded farmland where a dark man in a cloth robe is singing and walking slowly from a stage high above a multitude of motherless souls wandering through mud and trees and yearning to be found. The man's thick fingers pound on guitar strings, his shoulders dip and rise, his hips rock and sway as his body slowly fades from view. But his voice can still be heard, echoing out over the land in a language older than any story, chanting the ballad of every heart, chanting the song of freedom and motherless children far, far from home.

And the song of songs reached the baby. It reached for him and found him. And having found him, it snuggled into his soft flesh and made a home and went to sleep. But though it went to sleep, the song of freedom never forgot the boy and he never forgot how to sing.

# CHAPTER 5
# Matricide

∾

J immy sits at a wooden desk and chair in his sixth-grade classroom. Desk and chair are all of one piece and, consequently, especially restrictive. He is a tall boy by now, and there is no room for his long legs under the belly of the desk. Squirming only gets him in trouble with cranky old Mrs. Hudson and provides no relief from the experience of being trapped in a bird cage. He steals a glance at the large clock above the door and groans when he sees the minute hand has scarcely moved. It seems to crawl like a banana slug up the steep west face of the clock. He listens to the tick and the tock of the second hand, which easily laps both the hour and the minute, but does nothing to alter the interminably slow pace of either. Another twenty-five minutes will drag by before that black arrow reaches the north pole of the clock and sets off the bell, like an explosive, announcing the release of the cheering students for the night.

Twenty-five minutes is enough time for the nightmare to hit. They attack by day and by night. Awake and asleep. Jimmy understands the experience of Gregory Peck in his favorite movie, *Spellbound*, when those three lines on the table cloth trigger his psychotic spells. Waking or sleeping, he is powerless to fend off that bewitching dream state. It strikes like a seizure. As it does today when the classroom full of his friends turns into a courtroom full of gossipers, neighbors, and a jury of his peers.

Standing before the court is the imposing figure of none other than Perry Mason, the undefeated heavyweight champion of the world. He is dressed in his only suit, a smart, black, three-button that is nothing special but sets off those relentless, black eyes. Jimmy shudders as Perry turns, peers directly into his soul, and says, "The defense calls Jimmy Brennan to the stand." The crowd gasps and all eyes turn on the boy. District Attorney Burger looks at Mason with that bewildered look on his face that signals he is about to get creamed again. Jimmy freezes in his chair and looks to his father. His dad stares straight ahead. Mason is still looking at him. He is bigger than Jim Brown. And patient. He waits like a lion for its prey to enter the clearing.

The judge calls Jimmy's name again, and he slinks toward the bench trying somehow to be invisible. The bailiff extends the Bible to him and begins administering the oath. Jimmy notices it is a Bible very similar to the family's, the same one he recently took from the bookcase to swear his undying hatred for Frank. This leaves him in a panic, fearing he has just handed over his soul to the devil for eternity. That same panic rises swiftly in his chest when he sees the Bible staring at him and the devil grinning from the blood-soaked impression of his hand on the cover of the Good Book. A deep trembling, more like a tremor in his head, begins as Perry Mason approaches the stand. "Mr. Brennan, were you familiar with the deceased, Georgia Daisy Brennan?"

"Yes."

"Please tell the court how you knew Mrs. Brennan."

"She's my mother." By now he is shaking and a tear is forming in his eye. He looks to his father but Gerald is looking at the floor.

"Mr. Brennan, please tell the court where you were on the afternoon of Friday, June 12th."

"I don't know. I guess I was home."

"And what were you doing at home?"

"I don't remember."

"Let me refresh your memory." Mason turns and strides to his table. Della Street is watching his every move. He returns briskly, a covered object in his hand. When he again stands before Jimmy, he pulls the object from the bag. The jury strains to see it.

"Mr. Brennan, have you seen this silver hammer before?"

"No."

"Mr. Brennan, surely you heard your own brother testify that you were playing with a silver hammer the day your mother died. Now let me ask you again. Have you ever seen this silver hammer?"

Jimmy shoots a glance at Frank, who is smirking in his seat, one fang showing. "Yes. It's mine." The audience is shaken and a murmur spreads throughout the room.

"Your Honor, I'd like to submit this silver hammer to the court as Exhibit A."

Lieutenant Tragg is visibly upset. He's missed another crucial clue. Burger will have his ass one of these days.

"Now Mr. Brennan, isn't it true that you have, in the past, been known to fly into a rage toward your mother?"

Burger leaps out of his chair like a Jack in the box. "Objection, Your Honor! The defense is leading the witness."

"Sustained. Mr. Mason, you will please limit your questions to the actual evidence before the court."

"Of course, Your Honor." Mason smiles as if this were just part of the plan. The big trap. His eyes are big as walnuts in the shell. He turns from the judge and fixes them on Jimmy. They are boring into his forehead like a drill.

"Isn't it true that on the afternoon of your mother's death she was upset with you for using bad language and had you write fifty times 'I must not be so-o-o-oo?'"

"No. I don't know. I don't remember."

"Mr. Brennan, your own brother has testified under oath."

"Yes, all right, but it was a hundred times, and with my left hand."

Mason is charging toward the kill. Smoke billows from his nostrils. He is a stampeding bull and Jimmy the matador without a red cape. Burger watches in awe. The crowd is stunned, not wanting to know what they already are thinking.

"And isn't it true, that as she turned her back, you crept up from behind and brought that silver hammer down on her head. And didn't you then bang the hammer again and again until you made sure that she was dead?"

With that, Jimmy broke like a little boy. Stammering between sobs and gasping for breath, he confessed to one and all, "Yes, yes, it's true. I meant to do it. I couldn't get her to stop calling me Jimmy dolly. I loved her, I did, but she was too nice all the time. It was sickening. I couldn't take it anymore. I couldn't." With that he collapsed into a ball of self-hatred. Condemned before the world.

"No further questions, Your Honor." Mason almost looks sympathetic. Jimmy watches him walk to his table. His shoulders are as wide as the Cleveland Browns' front line.

Everyone stares at Jimmy lying on the floor, except his father, who is walking toward the exit. Jimmy watches his narrow back pass through the opening and the door close behind.

∽

Ohio in 1960. Dwight Eisenhower is on his way out; Jack Kennedy is on his way in. The country is teetering on the cusp of changes that in a short seven years will make the coming generation unrecognizable to the survivors of the Great Depression and the Second World War. It is a mere fifteen years since the end of that episode of slaughter and bravery. Millions have been successful in forgetting the nightmare their fears require them to remember. What they have mastered is a numbing of emotion, a hollowing out of interior life.

Ohio in 1960 resembled 1953 more than the present day, which had just elected a Catholic to the White House and would soon see Negroes breaking down barriers to the white world. Gerald was certain it marked the end of civilization. He had by then moved his family into exile from Indiana and the known world. They arrived in the suburbs of Akron along with scores of others fleeing poverty and the reach of memory. Immediately they set about blending in and not drawing attention to their origins. Despite the loss of his tongue, Gerald was a successful accountant in the city of numbers that was his calling. Blessed numbers that went unchanged day in and day out. Daisy made certain they dressed and looked like everyone else. And no one spoke a word, or dared ask a question, about the place and people left behind. Not even in the confines of their home, which was one of thousands of ranch houses sprouting in the suburbs like mushrooms. No one explained to Jimmy why it should be called a ranch. Weren't they part of the wild, wild West? There was nothing wild about Ohio in the '50s. But it was new and it was clean and it was easy. And that made all the difference. Because, while for much of the world, still staggering from the impact of fifty years of war and losses too monumental to count, still barely able to lift their heads up much less their hearts, God was dead and nausea was ruler of the free world. But not in the suburbs of Ohio. Not in the core of the country. For these emigrants from the farms and small towns to the new America, it was not the Heavenly Father but the past that was dead. The past and every stinking load of sorrow. Banished, like tax collectors from the temple.

A new era had indeed begun but it was not the vision of the young senator from Massachusetts that they saw in their dreams but a life in which work and sweat no longer followed them every hour of the day. They came to worship something called leisure. And the ranch house was the temple. Although the interior life of the individual had been abolished, as it had to be in order to keep the past in its grave, the interior of the ranch house, what was called the family room, became the sanctuary for the life of the family. It was a radical retreat from the outdoors. Exposure to the seasonal changes was far too risky for the architecture of a world without loss. Each season brought along its own harkening of what was. The time capsule of suburban life in the Midwest had to protect its citizens from the kind of stimulation that could evoke associations, good or bad, with the life left behind.

In order to satisfy instinctual cravings for the natural world, the golf course was invented. And a charismatic leader named Arnold Palmer was chosen to lead the people on weekend walks through well-manicured green highways carved from the living hearts of forests and the defenseless bellies of meadows and pastures. The streets slowly emptied. The front porch disappeared altogether. Neighbors became strangers to complain about. And the weekend became the guardian of sacred time. It provided something to look forward to which insured the residents would never look back.

While the past was continuously, though not consciously, buried alive, the future was the new idol in the religion of ease. Nearsightedness dominated the visual and psychological field. Looking forward so occupied the thoughts of the suburban tribe that soon the present atrophied and took its place with the past in the forgotten archives of American life. So without realizing it, an almost type of living evolved that existed somewhere in mental space poised between the disembodied past, the unwanted tensions of the present, and the longed-for ease of a future perpetually promised. Without knowing it, without the aid of evil, they courted death. They courted the cessation of tension and memory: the enemies of peace.

And, quite predictably, the perfect instrument was invented to assist every family residing in the security of its own home. The television. The magic of the TV was their enchantment, capable of unscrambling waves and constructing images on a flat screen that gave everyone the opiates needed to complete the arrangement. And while this modern miracle unscrambled certain waves and gave families Walt Disney and Rin Tin Tin, it quite successfully scrambled the brain waves of the weekend worshippers and eliminated the threat of any reflection that might disturb the new equilibrium of the soul.

☙

Jimmy's house ran like clockwork. One day mirrored another. No backward or forward, better or worse: it was a perversion of continuity. This allowed for the elimination of differences, which made it possible for them to believe they had escaped the field of loss, and it fed the dream of complete satisfaction, which made it possible to believe in a constant source of goodness. That source was Georgia, who spun the whole illusion out of her mothering love as effortlessly as creation spins its web: it just appeared. Effortlessly.

However, the weekend posed a problem to the order of things. What to do with the yawning gap between breakfast and the evening's entertainment? Chores were for farm kids and so Jimmy and his brother were rarely asked to perform any jobs around the house. Gerald was not to be disturbed after a hard week at the office. (Where was the office? What did he do all day in that suit and tie?) It was crucial to prevent hunger, and thus the days were organized around three square meals and assorted snacks. Then the boys could play catch, or war, and the hours floated by like summer clouds. It was seamless. Uninterrupted by want or fighting. Each, on his own, found a way to forget about time until the main event of the week: Friday and Saturday night television.

Gerald and Georgia sat down like a king and queen awaiting the court dancers. Georgia smiled as though she were a little girl at her birthday party, and Gerald sat in his chair intently staring straight ahead as though his mother might appear out of the screen at any moment. Conversation was forbidden. Rapt attention was given to the world of black and white. Although there was some laughter, a solemn mood settled over the room. A spell.

Friday night was the warm-up. It was the same each week: an hour with Mitch Miller and his band. Mitch was not exactly Ohio. He sported a goatee and his hair grew over his ears. More than likely he'd changed his name to hide his Jewishness. The music was good but it was his main singer that captured Jimmy's attention. Leslie Uggams. Jimmy was secretly in love with her. Her features were as fine as Grace Kelly's and her skin was the color of warm cocoa. And that voice! She took him to far-away places where desire still lived.

He couldn't say anything out loud because they would laugh at him. But in the privacy of his imaginings, Leslie Uggams was his.

His body filled with a strange warmth. He had to be careful because it was the time of the mirror, and he risked great shaming for straying outside the parameters of normalcy. And wanting anything, especially a colored girl, would reflect badly on the provisions of his mother and require a suitable scolding to get him back in line. But his powers of secretiveness were growing, and he looked forward to Friday nights and that strange warmth that found him curled into the corner of the couch. Luckily, the others were so occupied with the music and images on the screen they never noticed the illicit affair going on within.

Friday night was good, but Saturday night was the main event and the climax to the week's banality. Mitch Miller was a suitable warm-up act; however, he was only that and Saturday belonged to the King and his band, the Lawrence Welk show. Families all over the country were treated to non-stop, wall-to-wall smiles from the opening notes to the last melody. One happy smile and happy tune after another, each bigger and brighter than the last. A chorus line of happiness that would never end. It was the pinnacle of post-war American triumph: the total evacuation of suffering. So complete was this purging, some wondered if so much suffering had been a dream. Lawrence Welk waved his baton like a magician, and every molecule of evil and unbearable heartache just disappeared so thoroughly that the king and queen of every household could go on with the confidence that those terrible things were forgotten and gone, never to return. Lawrence Welk, and his family of good men and proud virgins, told them so. They were mesmerized by the show, by the irresistible dream, by the feeling of safety from feelings no one could find words for.

Jimmy never liked Lawrence Welk. In fact, he developed a huge loathing for him, his voice and that smile that seemed every bit as coercive as the mirror. Jimmy spent a good portion of the show thinking of ways to get him to stop, of grabbing the baton from his hand and cramming it down his throat. Wondering if the smile would go on while the maestro choked on the stick. Wondering if his own life was any more real than the box that had taken control of their minds. But most of the hour he thought of Leslie. He took her by the hand, and they snuck away to the bomb shelter and lay on a wool blanket kissing and whispering into each other's ears and, without so much as a grin, gave each other all the warmth and delight the vessel of his yearning could hold.

The world of entertainment was not without its version of balance. At some moment in the '50s a new and necessary component was added to the lineup. The murder. Murder captured Jimmy's attention. It was curious how similar the feelings evoked by a good killing were to those engendered by the image of Leslie Uggams. Both, simultaneously, melted and charged his entire self with an energy he thought foreign to life. Both found a place to be and to hide in the storage rooms he carved into the woodwork.

Shakespeare had yet to make his way to Akron, Ohio. Hamlet and Macbeth were unknowns to the Midwest psyche and without those, and other great killers of the past, the people had to content themselves with movies and TV shows that brought blood back to the veins and death back to the shadows. Jimmy's favorite movie was *Ten Little Indians*. Ten murders in less than two hours. That was a Saturday night to remember. Whether in a movie or on a TV show, his favorite victim was the one discovered stuffed in a closet by an unsuspecting family member. Everything in the lead-up was ordinary enough to lull both the discoverer and the audience into a false sense of ease. This ended abruptly when the door opened and the deceased, eyes bulging as if from thyroid disease, slowly leaned forward into the long, spellbinding fall to the feet of the horrified observer.

So taken with this image was he that Jimmy decided to reenact it with his mother. He thought she would think it was as funny as he did. And so one dull summer afternoon, with his mother off shopping, he visited the refrigerator and grabbed a bottle of ketchup from the shelves. When he figured Georgia had to be close to home, he took to the closet and poured the ketchup over his head and face.

It was perfect. Right on schedule she arrived. As was her custom, she put the groceries down on the kitchen table and merrily made her way to the closet humming or singing a song she'd no doubt heard on the Lawrence Welk show that week. She paused at the door, perhaps intuitively wondering where Jimmy was, thought nothing of it and opened the door to the sight of her son, covered with blood, staring into the great abyss with eyes big as 50 cent pieces, free falling into her arms. Georgia shrieked loud enough to wake a bear in hibernation. The ketchup splattered over her blouse and onto her neck. Jimmy hit the floor like a fifty-pound sack of flour. She would have fainted had it not been for the laughter coming from the carpet.

Was she going crazy? No. It was true, he lay there laughing. But she did not enjoy his prank. Her face burst into flames and every particle of outrage kept in cold storage for the last twenty-five years flew at him in such fury that both of them were surprised and frightened. In one colossal assault, she incinerated the little man with the red hair, her mean and insensitive father-in-law, and her own husband, who had kept her in solitary confinement since the day he severed his tongue and took a vow of silence. She was aghast with what came from her. Of course she blamed Jimmy and his unspeakable behavior for her loss of control, but deep within she had to admit, what she could not tolerate, that she was glad to have erupted as she did. Jimmy suffered third-degree burns. But he didn't mind because something better than expected happened, something he could not have predicted. Something far better than his sadistic prank and the delight he felt in terrifying Georgia; no, this was different, something satisfying and strange in the feeling of having at last found his mother.

"He what?" Gerald exclaimed over a drink after the boys were in bed. "What in the world?" Disgust and his own brand of rage oozed from the pores of his skin, which had been sealed to prevent any sweat and odor from permeating that slim membrane. His feelings were too strong to hold back. The gilded queen had been attacked and the entire glass menagerie threatened. "Something's wrong with him."

Daisy had debated telling him of the day's event. She most certainly did not speak of her own dramatic role. Since the time Frank had been little and provoked so much hostility in his father she was careful to censor what and how she told Gerald at day's end. Regrettably, she felt she had no choice but to divulge a transgression of this magnitude.

"Gerald, please don't get angry. He's a boy. I'm sure he didn't mean any harm by it." Daisy had become so accomplished at stripping meaning from life that she was up to this challenge, particularly after the jolt of her own participation and an afternoon to prepare.

"He'll get the belt for this one."

"No. Please don't. He's already upset enough with himself. Maybe it's partly our fault for letting him watch all those movies."

"That's ridiculous."

"Come on, let's go to sleep. It will look better in the morning."

Had it been 1980, they would have dropped Jimmy at the doorstep of a psychiatrist for the duration. As it was, the incident was never mentioned again. It receded into the vault of untouchables.

And so it was that a special place was reserved for murder in the life of families. And because irony had yet to be invented, no one thought twice about devoting Sunday night to homicide. As if ordained by God, the Perry Mason show arrived with a weekly killing and a lesson in the consequences of the great passions of greed, jealousy, and envy gone awry. By revolver or the blade of a knife or strangulation by the killer's own hands, another victim met his or her end, and the weekly diet of blood and death was satisfied.

For Jimmy, twelve years old, slave to the mirror, living under the tyranny of forgetting and niceness, it was all about the murder. But to the nation it was all Perry Mason. At the dinner table they called him Perry. It was Perry who helped them sleep at night and remember the gaiety of Lawrence Welk throughout the day. What he did was take the Holy Day, the resurrection, into a secular world the people of Ohio could understand. Enough of this mystical Gospel of John, they needed the messiness of complicated relationships and ordinary life to be redeemed in order to feel secure. And Perry never let them down. Without exception, week in and week out, he took in the falsely accused, the innocent, and vindicated them. He took the dangerous world by the neck and shook it like an old rug until the good and the bad separated out. And most of all, he revealed the truly evil and sent it off to the gallows, allowing the free and the innocent to live their lives in peace. He was a hero to all. A savior. He had no wife, no children, no interests, it appeared, other than prevailing over the might of evil. What a force he was: that huge barrel chest, the penetrating eyes, the deliberate and unwavering pursuit of the truth and the real villain. Everyone loved him. He was humble and kind. A servant of justice.

The world made right by Perry Mason enabled Gerald and Georgia and all the others like them to go on without thinking of murder and evil or much of anything besides numbers and grocery lists and, perhaps, learning the new game of golf. Jimmy thought about it a lot. Along with Leslie Uggams and infinity and, in the coming years, rock and roll, he thought about death and dying. Never having heard of Raskolnikov, he became a study in crime and punishment. The initial flirtations were benign enough. They were the product of experiences that came unbidden in his youth.

His first recollection was sitting with the family in the screened porch at his grandparents' house in Pittsburgh. The house he loved despite the angry spirits flying about he could not yet detect. Perhaps one of them landed on his shoulder and invaded his body because on one particular afternoon, as they all sat chatting about nothing in particular, Jimmy looked across the room at his mother and saw her laughing and enjoying herself, but her legs were crossed and the shorts she wore did not hide the varicose veins ranging like rivers up and down her bone-white calves and thighs. The sight filled him with disgust and shame that quickly turned to anger. He wanted to scream at her to cover herself. So bewildered was he by this flood of emotion that he left the room quite suddenly and headed for his grandfather's study where the old man kept a jar of peppermints. He took a candy, unwrapped it quickly, and sucked on the sweet hardness until the feelings subsided.

Another event stayed in his memory and returned for unknown reasons from time to time. It was Halloween. Georgia had made cookies and late that afternoon she and the boys made a snack of them. Jimmy loved cookies, especially the icing, and wanted more. His mother refused, saying it would spoil his appetite. He pleaded but she denied him. Suddenly anger flared like paper catching fire and before he knew what was happening he slugged her in the face just below the cheek bone. They were all too astonished for words. The moment froze. The cookies melted. Georgia's face grew red and hard as cement. "You get to your room immediately, young man, and wait there until your father comes home." Her voice quivered and her body stiffened. Jimmy fled to his room and tried to reverse in his mind what he had done. He counted the seconds until the executioner arrived. And even without the coercion of the mirror, without the disgust of his father beaming down on him, he knew what a bad, dirty boy he was.

He was a serial killer with one victim. Following the incident in the closet the attacks were largely mental. There were exceptions. The most satisfying opportunities came when they were driving a distance and he noticed Georgia dozing in the front seat. If he put just the right amount of alarm in his mouth and spit out loud and sharp, "Look out! We're going to crash!" he could make her wake up screaming in terror. The punishment was worth the amusement.

Otherwise he struck in the anonymity of his mind. From his room when she called for him in the mornings, "Jimmy dolly, time to get up, you'll be late for schoooool," he could feel his hands around her neck. He hated the sing-song rhythm, the high pitch, and, for God's sake, he wasn't a doll. It made him feel like a girl, like he should be wearing a dress. Sometimes he wondered if she wanted him to be a girl. If she was disappointed and longed for a little girl to make dresses for and cook with.

What he hated more, was what took place in his heart, even in the grand moment of walking slowly down the stairs in his pajamas, walking toward her with his hands outstretched, seeing her smiling face grow gradually more and more alarmed, placing his eager hands around her throat and squeezing until her eyes bulged and that damned canary voice gurgled, just like he'd seen in *Ten Little Indians*, even then, he could not escape feeling sympathy for her. And it was more than a sympathy for being the only female in the house. More than a sympathy for putting up with his father, for the loneliness she wore when no one was looking, for the ghostly fears that followed her doggedly. It was the perplexing fact of love that he could not kill, no matter how many times he went to the electric chair for her murder. It was the neediness he felt. The warmth that tingled in his chest when she brought him food or scratched his back while they sat on the couch and watched a show. What he could not escape, no matter how elaborate his fantasies of being Jim Brown or running off with Leslie Uggams, was the tender feeling he had for her. She was kind. She was good to all of them. She never complained about standing alone in the kitchen and baking the butter horns while they played in the family room. It gave her unending delight to watch them devour the entire batch at breakfast. If he got sick in the middle of the night, she was there comforting him, making sure he was warm and bringing him broth as his health improved. He thought each murder would cut through at least a strand of the rope that tied them together. But that was not the case. To his dismay, it tightened the knot rather than destroying it.

And so he entered a *Twilight Zone* dream world. A story of loving and hating that had no end. A tale as unreal as any he and his friends made up in the wooded gorge at the edge of the neighborhood where they routinely mowed down whole battalions of German and Japanese soldiers. As real as the losses and tragedies that shaped the lives of his parents, the multitude of events, major and minor, sealed and buried deep in the no-man's land of their collective amnesia. Evacuated like nuclear waste from population centers. Confusion did not describe the state of his thoughts. At least murder brought some order, some cohesion, to the scramble of competing selves he knew and did not know. And to this he gravitated. Not just thoughts about murder. But of his own death. Of annihilation. Buried alive. An eternal fall into oblivion. He dreamed of his funeral and a throng of people mourning his absence. He marveled at the strangely comforting melancholy that came upon him as he thought of others singing his praise.

By the time they moved to Connecticut in the fall of his ninth year, death stood in every closet. They were near New York, and when he heard of Sing Sing Prison, he looked for escaped prisoners on the roof outside his window every night before bed. Most days he looked under his bed for the murderer, but one Saturday he came in from playing near the swamp at the edge of the neighborhood and began undressing on the side of his bed, completely innocent and free of murderous thoughts, when a hand grabbed his bare foot and pulled foot, leg, and body toward the floor. This was it. He could see his eyes bulging. He could feel the hands around his neck. Murder seemed utterly random and inevitable. The fact that it was Frank under the bed, and now in hysterics over the sight of his terror-stricken brother running from the room screaming for his mother, and not the one-armed man who had throttled Sam Sheppard's wife in Cleveland, was of little consolation and did nothing to dissuade him from his conviction that a force in the world existed that wanted him dead.

This certainty grew to include his brother and father and every anonymous shadow darting past his window. Hadn't his brother tried to kill him two days after he came home from the hospital? Hadn't he flipped his baby carriage and sent the infant Jimmy flying through the air? But why? He'd made no attempts on Frank's life. Admittedly there was the Christmas morning Santa brought Jimmy a new bow and arrow. He went immediately to the basement where he shot the rubber-tipped arrows into a target for hour after hour. Frank soon tired of his gifts and began to taunt Jimmy from the top of the stairs. For hours he ignored his brother's provocations and focused on shooting at the bull's eye until finally by mid-afternoon, fed up with his antics and anticipating his head coming around the corner once again, he turned and let the arrow fly. It struck Frank clean on the forehead directly above the eye. It stuck and quivered. Both boys were stunned. But Frank ran for his parents crying and yelping like a puppy bit on the ear. Gerald descended the stairway with heavy foot. He took the bow and arrow, broke them over his knee, and threw them in the incinerator. Then he gave Jimmy a sound spanking.

But that was one event. It was intended to drive Frank away, not to kill him. Nor did he wish to kill his father. He stole from him. It started with a dime and a nickel. With two-bits here and two-bits there. His father came home from work and went directly to his bedroom to take off the suit and tie he was required to wear. Jimmy usually followed him to his room and tried to talk while he dressed. When he was changed into his casual clothes, Gerald went back downstairs to Georgia and his dinner. Often Jimmy lingered in their bedroom or his own room. Sometimes he went to his father's wallet and the pile of loose change on the bureau and fondled the coins in his fingertips. Eventually he was emboldened to steal from his father. It started with small change and worked up to a dollar. The most he took was a five-dollar bill. He had a purpose and that was to buy a ring for Mary Jo Bellinger, a sixth-grade crush. He was the last to ask her to go steady. She had taken nearly the entire year to work her way through all the boys in the class. She let it be known that it was his turn and he phoned her up on a Friday night during a commercial at the half-way mark of *The Flintstones*. She accepted and that was that. Back to the television and time to get ready for the Mitch Miller program.

But Jimmy was not content to split hearts as was the custom of the times. So he stole the five dollars and bought a silver signet ring at the pharmacy and gave it to Mary Jo one Friday night just before school let out for the summer. She was so impressed she kept it for an entire three weeks before sending Emily Herman and Joan Likener to his house to return the ring. Three weeks was a record.

Trouble lay ahead when his brother discovered the ring and told the parents. They demanded to know where he came up with the money to buy such a gift. Jimmy stonewalled and was still holding out when the dog ate the ring. By the time it came out in his stool several days later, everyone had forgotten and the matter was never brought up again.

So he stole from Gerald but never thought of killing him. He desperately wanted something from him but not his life. His was not a Greek tragedy. It was born in the USA. Similarly with Frank. He wanted to be him, not kill him. He wanted to be confident and capable of talking non-stop for an hour. Yes, he competed with his brother as if his life depended on it, and yes, he swore his hatred on that Bible. But kill him? Never. For reasons he could not fathom, only his mother brought out the killer in him.

And what about his brother and father? Hadn't they, each in his own way, taken her life as well? Hadn't Frank taken a machete to the bonds of love? Hadn't he stood before the mirror flexing the muscles of his neck until they bulged like Charles Atlas, until the barrier between his head and body rivaled the Berlin wall, and not a drop of need could pass what was as strong as the Hoover Dam? It was his own version of stubborn and it proved every bit as tenacious as their father's. Didn't he sever every indication of softness and the feminine? Didn't he declare tenderness and surrender acts of treason? Weren't these violent actions against their mother?

And what about his father? Hadn't he put Georgia in a glass jar like a kid catching a firefly? Wasn't it murder when he sealed the lid on that jar and placed it on a shelf in the pantry? What would Perry Mason, or Edgar Allan Poe, or Sigmund Freud call it? And when he exhumed his mother's body from her grave in Wheeler and brought her home to sit near him on the couch while Lawrence Welk sang and danced humanity out of the cycle of birth and death, what was that, Doctor?

All the while the light in the glass jar flickered and faded. It took all the tricks of a million years of evolution and a thousand years of forgetting to keep it from going out. And though it wasn't extinguished altogether, and while Georgia discovered a will of her own, a will that rivaled that of her husband's and would keep her spirit alive despite the shrinking world she inhabited, Jimmy knew in his bones it was murder. It wasn't a pinch of arsenic in the tea cup. It wasn't a pillow over the face. It wasn't any of the usual methods he saw on television. It was something more insidious. Like nerve gas.

But the effects were as lethal. They all suffered from it. And they all pretended the dead acre of land where a soul once lived was not. It wasn't that they were cruel and evil. And yet it wasn't an aberration. For each, in their own way, it was a daily practice of numbing and killing any feelings that might get by the sentries: it was an end of all beginnings. What did Perry Mason tell them if not that murder was commonplace, happening in our homes right before our eyes?

 ∽

And to this end they courted death. They held the hand of death and called it maturity. They slept with death and called it reality. Banality, resembling a corpse, was cultivated with the same deliberateness as the bank account. They made themselves numb and capable of subduing the schools of emotion swimming about in the pool of consciousness. Gerald welcomed in depression, constant as winter cloud banks over the Great Lakes, because it was preferable to facing the ghastliness of a past that would not go away. Daisy sang popular tunes to herself and chose the death of denial over drowning in loneliness. Frank made his body into rock and then fought his entire life to break it down, perishing before his time as a result. Jimmy succumbed to the heavy spell, to the pull of non-being, much of his waking life, and struggled to free himself from its grip like a child trying to awaken from a bad dream.

But life was harder than cancer to stop. Fire can't be extinguished with rules. This is what truly baffled Gerald. He thought he'd put an end to it. Like a child who blows out the prank candle on his cake only to see it leap back into full flame a second later, Gerald did his best to subdue and, if necessary, crush any uprisings of energy and delight. This required a daily vigilance and a far-ranging plan. Vacations were curtailed and finally stopped. He said the boys fought too much in the back seat of the Pontiac. Parties were outlawed. He said the men flirted too much with Daisy. Conversation was kept to a minimum and all but a few chosen stories were censored. Sadly, they drew the shades on what light there was that made day other than night.

He led them on a long walk from Indiana to New York. Georgia agreed whole-heartedly on the destination. Each believed it was a straight road, an interstate highway system, to a land beyond the graveyards of their ancestors. Gerald was sure Ruth would be waiting for him. Georgia was certain she deserved a life with fine dresses. Neither recognized the trap they entered passing through Ohio on their way east. They saw it as the promised land and not the box canyon that it was. Death row. Their already broken hearts further atrophied in an atmosphere of stale air. Their already troubled psyches never questioned the path of endings: the path of no return. How do you kill life and stay alive? How do you forget the past without contaminating the future? How do you keep out the light without going blind? And worst of all, how do you do these things that you are convinced will ensure survival and success without sacrificing your children on the altar of security?

Jimmy was confounded by the unexpected twists and turns of life in this narcotic maze, this climate of idealized amnesia. He staggered and stumbled like a boxer before the knockout. His legs broke and then crumbled. He fell and couldn't get up. Fell and kept falling. Into deep sleep, he fell, disappearing and falling through an infinite night. A bottomless hole. Head over heel, backward and forward, his arms flailing, his scream instantly swallowed by the dark. He fell into the silence, which seemed to be watching and was lost. With the scream went his only hope of waking. The falling stopped and he drifted through emptiness like a moon without a planet. Without starlight to orient. Without a body to give outline to himself. He drifted into dust. Into massive nebulae floating in the ether, aimlessly floating and expanding, celestial clouds, star wombs. Anxiety overwhelmed what was left of his mind. The only thought still beating was how to make it end. Understanding was impossible. Make it end. Make it end.

Jimmy woke in a sweat shouting the command that would instruct his life. The command that would accompany him through his years in the many battles to come. That would fight alongside the others, those his mother had written, those his father had ordered, and those of his own spirit's impulse; stand next to those like an undetected traitor in the midst, loyal to no cause other than the one: make it end. Make it end. The solution that answered all paradox; living and dying made into one.

And so it went. With welding torch in hand, he forged love and hate into one. A third species of emotion. Not simply one or the other but a marbled fifth chamber of the heart that confused and uplifted his spirit in the same moment. What looked to be coupling with a primal death instinct was that and more. It was true that Jimmy wanted an end to experience; no sooner did pleasure make its way to his skin, and he was finding covert ways to close it down. He looked for things to be over. Events, good and bad, even kissing, which he hungered for, brought with it a tension that necessitated a conclusion.

His father was a master at endings that trumped beginnings. But Jimmy's was more of a tightrope act. He flirted with experience and denied it in the same breath. It appeared the death instinct had taken over his soul because he developed an erotic affair with the morbid. Not only did thinking of his own death and funeral satisfy him in an odd way but he secretly hoped for things to go badly for others. He sought out natural disasters and could not restrain the desire for more and more casualties. He looked at photos of the concentration camps and felt a fascination and appetite for more. News of a relative's ill health prompted a wish, a hunger really, for that life to end. A feeling similar to, but more than, melancholy leached into his everyday moods that he seemed to pursue and desire. He polished ill fortune until it glowed like a gem. It all added up to what Freud would have insisted was his death wish, his need to eliminate all tension, all experience of aliveness. His compulsive need to choose a flat line of existence over the texture of living. To dominate and kill goodness in its infancy.

Who could argue with the evidence? Wasn't it true that even many years into his adult life he felt the same inner demand? Wasn't it true the day he walked into his supervisor's office and found two young sparrows trapped in the fireplace at the base of the chimney? Didn't he feel the surge of Raskolnikov's blood even before he reached down to pick them up? There they were perched on the grate, young and bewildered. Frightened and helpless. Jimmy looked at the tiny black eyes and the heads that tilted to the side and felt a fear of his own intentions. One by one he closed his hands around the bodies of the little birds. He felt the trembling warmth of the plump young life against the palm of his hand and his fingers wrap around their frozen wings. The tenderness was unbearable. The birds did not struggle. Their eyes glazed over. Certainly they did not perceive the strength of the adrenaline racing through his veins and the power of the command pounding in his head to crush them, to squeeze with all his strength until the tiny bones shattered in his grasp.

The forces driving Jimmy were not ones he could feel. Their power came from a source he could not identify as originating within himself. And as he received the compelling surge to kill, another force exerted its influence and demanded he disobey the order. For a moment that spanned an eternity, the two forces met on a wire suspended over a mile-high cavity in space. This razor's edge was the ground for a battle between being and not being that consumed the greater part of his psyche. And even as he released the baby birds through the window to the great blue awning, even as the little ones found their wings and returned to the air, to worms and branches, he knew the battle was not won. In that moment, freedom and love prevailed but he was convinced only because he lacked the courage and will to do what was really in his bones. The mirror had the last word even then. And as he walked away from the window, the mark on his forehead stung and shame once again crept up his spine like a spider.

And he felt as he had as a child. Wanting to disappear. When awake wishing for sleep. When asleep wishing to awaken. He grew dizzy, unsteady. A vertigo not even Kim Novak could save him from consumed his thoughts. He was the rope in a tug of war between equals. He sought out life and turned his back. He loved his mother and cared for her while he fought her and railed against her. While killing her, he tried desperately to find her. When he found her, he hated her. Despair dug his hole deeper. Shame filled it in. Even as the grown man in the middle of his life saw the dear white petals begin to fall from Daisy and the yellow center of her flowering fade, even as Jimmy cared for her through her dismal decline, the same battle waged its ugliness and pitted his love for her against his disdain. He suffered greatly seeing her vanish, and he suffered just as greatly feeling the familiar fight against what was vanishing.

Jimmy pleaded with the gods for relief. He pleaded with himself and scolded the intractable slant. He threw himself at the feet of medicine men and wise men alike. Threw himself into drink and drugs. Played the fool again. He would have thrown himself overboard but the vertigo was too strong. On the few unforeseen days when a calm interrupted the storms, he found himself crying out under his breath, "Why? Why?" But the quiet of midnight was the only response. God didn't answer. Books didn't answer. "Why" was not a question but an exclamation of helplessness. It did not breed more questions. Deeper questions. Complexity had been defeated, as had inquiry of any sort, so that most questions were stillborn. Others were perversions of what puzzled him. A few were never asked.

Once he had asked Georgia what "fucker" meant and she had threatened to cut off his tongue, like his father's, if he ever said that word again. But most of the survivors, those who would certainly spark a revolutionary fever, were held hostage in a dungeon at the foot of a long and winding stairwell. A dungeon every bit as dark and forbidding as those of the medieval tyrants he'd seen on the television. Skeletons hung from hooks on the mold-covered walls. They were matted with cobwebs, but when he looked closer, he could see each was himself in a different age and posture. There was the rock star holding the broken shell of his guitar. There was the artist, his paint brush protruding from his neck, his eyes stapled shut. On a table covered with ashes were the books and ideas that had been arrested and never seen again. Tolstoy and Melville. Even Mark Twain was too subversive. Georgia had once caught him reading Herman Hesse and reminded him that authors don't really mean what they write and he shouldn't take it seriously. And there was the king, Fyodor Dostoyevski, lying beneath them all, the pages torn from their binding. Unsafe, even in the depths of the dungeon. Gutted and left to rot. The titles all that remained of the master's work. And Jimmy's favorite, *Crime and Punishment*, lay at the bottom of all the rest, shredded and spat upon. Nearby stood a large steel canister, sealed and marked "dangerous," with skull and crossbones painted on the side so as to warn the jailers to stay away. The steel drum held all the questions that would bring down the house. Poisonous snakes that must not be released, the asp that would take Cleopatra.

❦

The phone rang and rang but no one answered. The caller recovered his dime and furtively darted through the streets of West Los Angeles looking for the next phone booth. Again the phone rang off the hook, but Della Street did not pick it up. She was flat on her back draped across the massive mahogany desk of her boss, Perry Mason. Her stockings and shoes lay in a pile by the doorway. Perry Mason stood over her half-naked body. He wore his suit coat and tie but nothing more. Della pulled him toward her with all the smoldering lust suppressed throughout the course of the trial but now free to devour her snorting bull and hero.

"Oh yes, Perry, yes! You're the best Perry, the best." She lived the life that millions of American women secretly longed for sitting next to their grey flannel husbands on Sunday night. They were celebrating as they did at the conclusion of each trouncing of that moron Burger. They celebrated the triumph of good and innocence.

"Oh God, Perry, oh God, yes yes! I'm so close, so close. One more, yes, one more probing question, Perry. Please give it to me, one more."

And he did. With the same contained erotic rage she'd seen a hundred times in the courtroom. "Miss Street, are you familiar with Exhibit A?"

"Oh yes, yes!"

"Isn't it true, Miss Street, that you love Exhibit A? That in fact you crave it? Isn't that true, Miss Street?" As he probed, his voice grew louder and showed signs of coming unhinged.

"Yes, yes, it's true! Yes, yes, oh God, oh God, yes yes yes yes, Perry, yes!" And with each gasping, screaming affirmation, Della Street confessed her true self for all the women of Ohio. In one breathless instant, she confessed, with every ounce of her being, both the guilt and innocence of her desire.

"No further questions, Your Honor."

And with that they each blasted into a billion particles of joy, leaving their earthly forms and ascending into that great realm beyond the flesh. They soared past the moon, becoming one being and only after a season of bliss did their spirits begin to lazily drift back and forth, back and forth, floating down to the waiting outline of their bodies, the way a garden of rose petals might fall from the sky and ever so lightly settle to the ground.

Huge longhorns receded into Perry's skull and his eyes rolled forward. Della sang the song of willows. Neither had fully come into the state of a personal self when the phone rang again, this time more frantic and persistent than the last. The pair startled and clumsily reached for their clothing. Della got to the phone and answered, trying to compose her breathless voice.

"Mr. Mason's office, may I help you?"

"I need to speak with Mr. Mason immediately. It's very urgent." Indeed the voice on the phone was as breathless as her own.

"Who may I say is calling?"

"Jimmy Brennan. Please, it's important I speak with Mr. Mason right away. There isn't time to waste."

"I'm sorry, Mr. Brennan. Mr. Mason is not currently available." She smiled warmly as Perry finished buckling his belt.

Perry Mason looked at her quizzically and then nodded to Della.

"Just one moment, Mr. Brennan."

Perry took the phone and paused a few seconds. The receiver looked small in his hand and even smaller held against his head, which was statuesque and calm as he gazed into the unknown. "This is Perry Mason."

"Mr. Mason, thank God. I must talk to you now! I'm in terrible trouble."

"What seems to be the trouble, Mr. Brennan?"

"I can't talk here. It's too dangerous. They're after me."

"Who is after you?"

"Tragg and his bloodhounds. They think I killed my mother but I didn't, Mr. Mason, I didn't. I swear."

Perry shot a glance at Della. She looked sympathetic. "All right, Mr. Brennan, come straight to my office immediately. But come in through the back at Palm Street."

"Thank you, Mr. Mason. I'll be there in five minutes."

Perry hung up the phone and looked up at Della. His face was thoughtful. "It's the Brennan boy. Della, get us something cold to drink. I have a feeling Mr. Brennan has a lot to tell us."

In less than five minutes, Jimmy was pounding at the back door. Della let him in and showed him to the office. Perry stood at his desk and offered Jimmy a seat. Perry sat and slowly folded his hands on the very spot where just moments before the head of Della Street had rested as her spirit ascended to the heavens. Perry took his time and looked deeply into the eyes of the boy seated before him. Was he looking at a killer, a liar? Della watched the boy as well and each in a flash came to the same conclusion: these eyes were too soft, too bewildered to belong to a murderer. They exchanged glances and silently affirmed an eagerness to hear the boy's story.

"All right Mr. Brennan, now suppose you tell me everything you can about this trouble you're in."

Della picked up her pad and pencil. Perry took one last look at the legs that had so recently wrapped around his back and pulled him in. Then he turned his attention to the boy and waited. And for the next ninety minutes Jimmy told him everything he knew. He told him about the closet and the bloody ketchup. He told him about the silver hammer and his bare hands. About love and confusion. What he couldn't tell him because he didn't dare, or because it was out of reach, Perry had to listen for in the gaps, the unintended confessions. He listened to the stories within stories, to the words beneath the words. Over the course of those ninety minutes, he put together a history based on the reported fears and desires of this strange boy seated before him. Perry Mason was a master. In the span of one and a half hours, he found his way to the dungeon and went directly to the steel barrel of toxic questions. There was little time. During the telling of his story, Lieutenant Tragg had called on a hunch and was on his way to make the arrest. Perry was a bull and in no time had broken the seal and removed the questions from the container. He held them in his hand and looked through those that were still legible. When finished, he paused, as he always did, and looked up from what had been held in the unknown, which was now, at last, returning to its rightful place within the known world. A modest, satisfied smile, characteristic of his moment of realization, spread evenly across the face of Perry Mason and in that same instant the dungeon, that chamber of unbearable and unwanted holdings, began to crumble and fall from existence.

Della and Jimmy watched as the large man sat with his hands folded and his eyes blank. They watched as those same eyes blinked twice and he returned from what appeared to be a trance. He smiled again that faint, reassuring smile.

"All right, Jimmy. I'll take your case."

"Yes! Thanks, Mr. Mason. Jesus. Thank you." Jimmy looked down as was his practice and tried not to cry. He looked about the room for the mirror and was relieved to find none. How could he have been here so long without checking? Despite the emotion of the moment, he felt oddly lighter than he could remember. An image of running through the dark of night flashed through his mind.

"You do realize the risk you are taking by facing a court with this material." Perry was serious now. "You're too young to face the gas chamber, Jimmy, but if the jury finds you guilty, you'll be condemned to life in prison."

"Yes, I know. Will the cell have mirrors?"

"We won't think about that now. But I must tell you that juries do not take kindly to any thought of a boy murdering his mother."

"But I didn't kill her. Don't you believe me?"

Once again Perry let a pause become the moment. He let it fill the room. The pause reached into the tangled thoughts of that late afternoon and the generations of questions freed from the dungeon and spread them out like jewels on a white cloth.

Perry smiled again. He liked the boy. He glanced at Della. A subtle pleading met his eyes. Looking back at Jimmy, he said in a kind and confident tone, "Yes, Jimmy. I believe you. But the question is will a jury believe you? We haven't got much to go on. We'll have to work hard between now and the date of the trial. Della, call Paul Drake right away. We've got to unearth Gerald's tongue to have a chance with the jury. Jimmy, I think we can make a case that you never touched your mother's body, but you'll have to work very hard to help us put together the few pieces of evidence we have. This is a very perplexing case, Della. Mrs. Christie would be delighted."

Perry looked inward and wondered aloud, "Who did kill Georgia Daisy Brennan? Or what? Was it the Alzheimer's that took your mother or was that a self-inflicted study in amnesia? Or will the jury believe it was caused by the bang, bang of the silver hammer on her head? Did she suffocate in the jar Gerald held her captive in? Were the screams you heard Georgia scratching against the glass walls, growing short of oxygen? It might have been her own mother who cast that hateful, and perhaps fatal, curse upon her daughter with her dying breath. Or her father, who demanded she remain little and adorable, leaving her unprepared to survive in the world. Was it your brother Frank, who broke everything he touched, and, having been deprived of her softness, did he then bring his hard head down upon her fragile brow? And what about her brother, the carrot-topped predator? Did he not steal her soul and leave it in the sewer? And we shouldn't forget the times we live in and those Georgia lived through that exposed her to mass murders, the Great Depression, and enough human misery to destroy any faith in Jesus and Mary in the strongest of us. Not to mention the '50s, which coerced your mother into the death sentence of being mindlessly pretty and subservient to her man. And lastly, and certainly most tragic, perhaps it was your mother's own hand that did her in, Jimmy. Perhaps she was unable to face remembering what she had never been."

Perry grew silent, puzzling over the string of suspects. Absorbed in the pause, he allowed the questions to roll around his mind, avoiding the temptation to pounce on any one solution. He considered the possibility that Jimmy had been involved. In feeling trapped and caged by the tyranny of niceness could he have struck out at his mother? That having lost her to her shame, had he sought to find Georgia and free her from the porcelain mold cast around her being? Perhaps that was his motivation for taking a hammer to her head. How could he hope to break through to the real? More sinister still was the likelihood that Jimmy's father, in a state of delirium, had hired his son to commit the crime. Not against Georgia, but against Ruth. Having succeeded in making Georgia into Ruth, Harold found an unexpected rage growing in his stomach. He could never face how angry he was with his dear mother for leaving him when she did, so Jimmy was enlisted to do the dirty work.

Perry Mason closed his eyes and felt a frightening vertigo pulling at the edges of his brain. He felt swirling currents of chaos surrounding and pushing down on his capacity to think. And, barely able to keep his mind from submerging into unconsciousness, he heard the shouts and cries of many generations hurling past. The revolving dramas of a cast of thousands spinning and gobbling up whatever lay in its path, like a Kansas twister. And for the first time in his life, Perry felt a murderous instinct rise up in his chest. For the first time ever, he shuddered at his own desire to take a human life in his hands and end it. He saw the frailty of human beings overcome by forces unleashed by the countless acts of generations of individuals desperately trying to make life bend to their will. He wanted to reach out to them. He wanted to dive into the turbulence and plead with them to stop, to pause and allow the sea to quiet on its own.

He was interrupted by a knock on the door. He shook his head trying to free himself from what seemed like a monstrous dream. The great Perry Mason had been overtaken by the drama of a thousand years running. His eyes blinked and he glanced at the clock on his desk.

"That will be Lieutenant Tragg. Jimmy, you'll have to dig deep to win this." He looked like a boxer that had taken a big punch. "You can, and I'll help you."

The door opened and Lieutenant Tragg walked in the room with two bloodhounds following behind.

"Perry."

"Lieutenant."

"Mr. Brennan, I have a warrant here for your arrest in the murder of Mrs. Georgia Daisy Brennan."

Jimmy's heart fell through his stomach. Knowing what was coming made no difference when the words were finally spoken. He turned and looked over his shoulder at Perry and Della. They were standing now and smiling toward him with affection. Perry nodded. He was all confidence again. Though inwardly he worried there was too little to go on and that the jury was likely to draw emotional conclusions in the early going of the trial, outwardly he showed only calm assurance that he would add Jimmy to the list of falsely accused defendants he'd served. He nodded, and Jimmy turned and followed Lieutenant Tragg into the hallway.

# CHAPTER 6
# Brother

∾

You and I are brothers, which means we are different. We are opposites, which means we are alike. We duel like swordsmen over politics and laugh like boys over past antics. You are the strong man in the circus; I am the boy who never left home. We envy each other, we adore each other. You cried twice in your life. When they took you in to remove a stone from your heart, some joked out loud, "I didn't know he had one." Of course you do and it breaks just like mine every time a discouraging word comes at you. I am Mr. Melancholy. Crying is my pleasure. I live in a mountain lake where the sun doesn't shine. You are a man of the world and never venture into the wilderness looking for me. I dislike the world and stay away from battlefields where I might find you. You live in a vault. I live underwater. We are opposites, which means we are alike.

I love you Frank. This makes you uncomfortable, I know. Too bad. Other than Mom, you are the person closest to my heart and your voice is as familiar to my ear as a robin's song. Not that I was ever comfortable next to you. I was caught in a web trying to be you, better you, look down on you, a lousy moon to your huge planetary life. You were everything. Really. Not that I understood you. Even today, you are a mystery. What makes you so fierce? Why do you break things? How can I tell your story with so many unanswered questions lined up like cars in a traffic jam? Shit. What do I have to go on? While my life began with the strange story of mistaken identification, yours seems to have begun at the age of four. Why is it there is no record of your birth? It is as though you were never a baby. Is it true you never cried? Were you born with a full set of teeth? Did you ever sit on Mom's lap? I have searched everywhere and all I can find is the four-year-old boy running about the house driving his father nuts. But all I have to go on are a few tattered stories. Photos don't talk. Those stories named us, Frank. I am different and you are difficult. I never moved and you never stopped. Good and trouble framed us like school pictures on the mantel. Whose dreams are we trying to escape?

This is the first of your biography: Dad is painting the living room in Loraine. Mom is in the kitchen, big surprise; I am in her womb and you are running circles around the ladder Dad is standing on to paint the ceiling.

"Frank, for the last time. Go in the other room." Dad is fuming. "Georgia, get him out of here before he spills the paint." A solitary can sits on the drop cloth by the wall. It is open and full of paint and possibilities a four-year-old could make a mural out of. Frank is orbiting two stars: Dad and the paint can. Occasionally he collides with the asteroids floating about the room and careens dangerously close to temptation's way. "Get out of here." Dad is yelling now.

Mom hurries out of kitchen, "Frank, come, sweetie, Dad is trying to..." too late. The paint is spilling over the cloth onto the carpet like water from a dam.

"For crying out loud!" Dad is stammering, furious. Climbing down the ladder and taking off after Frank, who knows he's cooked and is streaking for the front door. "Damn that kid."

"Gerald, don't. He didn't mean to." But Mom's plea can't catch up with the two cats who are by now out the door and tearing around the house like a good cartoon.

"You get back here right now."

But Frank isn't coming back until he's lassoed and tied like a calf at the rodeo. He's fast and nimble but only four and in short order Dad catches up to him and grabs him by the arm which brings him to a screaming halt.

"Let go! You're hurting me!"

"I'm going to hurt you more after what you did." And right there on the spot, in front of God and neighbors, Dad pulls down Frank's pants and whales on his butt until it is red and raw and he is crying for Mom. By this time she has shed her apron and caught up with the pair of mismatched wrestlers.

"Gerald, stop. You'll hurt him. Stop, he's just a boy. What will the neighbors think?"

But Gerald wasn't stopping. He was enraged and more so now that Georgia had sided with the menace over his knee.

"He's got to learn." And he gave Frank a final round of swats before shoving him away in disgust. "Go on, get in your room and stay there."

But Frank didn't learn. What he did learn was how to make trouble connect him to his father.

Gerald didn't learn either. Despite Georgia's attempts to reason with him later that night when Frank was in bed, "You can't treat him that way. He's your son and you hurt him out there. He's only four for goodness sakes."

Gerald turned from her. Anger flooded his body. He couldn't stop it or the wish to hurt someone, which frightened him and caused him to retreat faster than Georgia's critical words. All links between his feelings and his past had been severed, leaving him bewildered and helpless to understand his reactions. He did what he knew how to do when overwhelmed: he shut down.

"Gerald, you have to talk to me. Please, darling, please." But it was too late. He was gone and would not return for two entire weeks. Fourteen days of silence. Solitary confinement. Georgia turned inside out trying to bring Gerald back but he was too stubborn. Too humiliated.

Her unborn baby turned over and over and she feared a miscarriage. The baby heard the foreign sounds and floated in anxiety.

∞

Frank said to his mother, in a thousand ways he would repeat over a lifetime, "I'm tough, Ma. I can take it." And he set about to simultaneously fight his father and please him. To be like him and to better him. By the age of seven his fangs were showing, the steel walls of his vault were set, and his world was stripped of anything sacred. And all the play, all the exuberance and dynamic energy of that four-year-old boy, compacted and fused to a single track that plowed through and knocked down anything in its way: every obstacle, every emotion, every injury from an unsettled past constantly attempting to invade his life, to the one goal in his sights: success. Not the success of his father, which enabled him to burrow into the manicured world of golf, secured by gates and privilege, but the success of the Baby Boomers, which elevated him and his loved ones to a different class where they roamed free of ugliness and pain. Free and transcendent of the dreaded humiliation that stalked them all like the most relentless of predators. Free of the heavy, heavy pain carried by legions of the dead stretching back in time far as the eye can see.

∞

That episode with the paint can and ladder and the great chase that followed through and around the house past the garden and the neighbor's fence was just a prelude to other skirmishes between you and Dad. You know the one I'm thinking of. Remember? We've laughed about this one a hundred times at least. You were 17 by then. I admired you more than the president. More than Bob Feller.

Certainly way more than Dad, who was such a deadbeat. Did you know? No one was as strong as you or as smart. The weight-lifting really paid off because your neck was as wide as a bull's. As wide as Jim Brown's. No one could bring you down. You wanted the car and Dad said no. You didn't back down.

"Come on, Dad. Why not? You're not using it."

"No. I said no."

"That's not a reason. Give me a good reason." As the tension mounted, Mom began to sing one of her popular songs in the kitchen. I watched from my chair at the table.

"Just because you never go out doesn't mean I should stay home and watch stupid TV all night."

"You're too hard on the car. What do you do with it? You're turning it into a piece of junk."

"It's not my fault. It's just normal wear and tear. Have I had an accident? No. You just don't want me to have any fun."

Couldn't you see Dad's face getting red? Didn't you know to stop when he started moving the salt shaker around?

"Come on, Dad. Sue's waiting for me."

"Sue? Again?"

"What?" Frank's fangs are starting to show. His neck is bulging and red. Dad has insulted his girlfriend and he's going after him.

"You don't like Sue, do you? You don't even know her. You don't like anything. I can't stand being in this house with you, I can't wait to get out of here, you bastard." These were not foreign sounds to Dad's ear. They were sounds that reverberated like a bell next to his eardrum. Sounds that tore through the layers of sediment between 1962 and 1936. They proved the past was not the past. Dad was out of his chair charging and sputtering,

"Goddamn you, I'm going to floor you."

But Frank was quicker and off he dashed through the dining room, Dad on his heels.

"Get back here, damn it."

I was ringside when Frank passed the table and deftly took one of the chairs and back-handed it in front of Dad, which tripped him up just good enough to allow Frank time to make it to the bathroom and lock the door behind him.

"Open this door right now!"

Dad pounded on the door and swore at Frank and the gods and this damn world that stole what was precious and irreplaceable. Mom cowered in the hallway and cried, "Gerald, stop!"

I sat in the chair bemused and frightened and swore to myself I'd never do anything like what Frank had just done. That was the good boy. The other one was eager to be a teenager and find a way to drive Dad nuts just like Frank did.

I don't know how long Frank stayed in the bathroom. Long enough for Dad to give up and retreat to his chair and build a stone wall that lasted more than two weeks. Mom and Dad didn't like Sue. She was Jewish. She was sexy and the one time they met her, she had garlic on her breath, which was just about the worst sin a person could commit. Being sexy was probably the worst. Frank loved her. That was another violation. Dad was firmly against any of his boys getting attached to another person. When I made the mistake as a junior in high school and found my heart broken for the first time by Gail Holtzman, he did not congratulate me for braving the world of love but said in a dry self-critical voice as I sat on the couch crying, "I shouldn't have let it happen." Frank cried alone when it was time to say goodbye to Sue and move to Connecticut. No one went to his room to comfort him. I heard him through the thin walls of the ranch house sob for the first of the two times he would do so in his lifetime. I was dumbfounded.

You are so hard on things. Dad was right. That '53 Ford was in pristine condition when Grandpa gave it to us. What, only 11,000 miles in eight years? God, it was beautiful. That creamy white top and the jet-black body. Those huge white walls. It was gorgeous and in less than a year, it was a beat-up wreck. The Pontiac wasn't much to look at but it suffered the same fate. What were you doing? I guess there were drag races. Okay. But what was it in you that made everything break? I don't get it. And my Schwinn racer. God, I loved that bike. Brand new shiny silver rims and mud guards. The most beautiful crimson frame and white tape around the handlebars. Three gears even. You borrowed it to do the paper route and then you took it over and bent it out of shape in a summer. There is even a story, a fragment of a story, one that wasn't told often and when it was, the tone was hushed and secretive. They say I was home for less than a day when you flipped the carriage and I landed on my head. Were you trying to kill me? Your drive is relentless. Why? Why do you work so hard? You never rest. Your body is so tense it feels like a board. Talk to me. Talk to me.

∾

"Jim, the doctor is here. Jim, did you hear me?" Sally is standing in the doorway to the waiting room. Her face is drawn and exhausted. She's been in the hospital for eight straight days. It's 10 o'clock at night when Dr. Mundal enters the lobby of the surgical center. He is a young doctor on a fellowship at the hospital. East Indian, terribly smart and calmly methodical in his speech.

"Hello, Mr. Brennan. The procedure went well. Your brother is in recovery now and should be in his room in an hour or so. As you know, the tumor had grown into the wall of the intestine and caused extensive bleeding. We stapled a graft over the area and it held quite well. However, we can't say how long it will hold; the area is very compromised."

"Did he do all right?" Sally is grim. They've been married nearly twenty-five years. Their two babies are now young men and standing next to her. We all have bloodshot eyes. The sound of their world collapsing threatens to defeat the numbness that has crowded out any real feeling.

"He did fine. Didn't lose too much blood. His blood pressure is good. Hopefully they'll be able to take him to radiation in a day and shrink the tumor away from the intestine."

Hopefully. We stare at him. He is young and handsome, a picture of health and success.

"Thanks, Doctor Mundal."

"Good luck." He turns and disappears into the bee hive. We look at one another reluctantly. Hope does not shine from our eyes.

An hour later we enter his room. Frank is writhing on the bed, twisting in anguish. He is only awake enough to mumble but it is all too audible, "Get me out of here." He is begging. My brother is begging. His body is acting as though they are cutting on him without anesthetic. "Get me out of here. Get me out. Pain is terrible. Do something." He is frantic. The nurse is tending to his instruments. Like he's setting up for a concert.

"My brother is in pain here. What are you going to do for him?"

He turns to me reluctantly. "I've given him 10ccs of morphine. It should stop the pain soon." He looks away to the machines, which are beeping and engaged in a digital fireworks display.

"Well, can't you give him more? It's obviously not enough."

"I can't give him more now. Too risky. Maybe in 30 minutes. I'll check with the doctor."

"Can't you check with the doctor now? Look at him. He's in terrible pain."

The nurse shoots a glance at Frank and walks to his side. "Mr. Brennan, Mr. Brennan," he is nearly shouting now.

"Don't yell at him."

"Mr. Brennan, can you hear me?"

"His name is Frank."

The only thing Frank can hear is the emergency alarm ringing in his brain. His head is twisting side to side. His body is thrashing like a fish on a hook. He is screaming but with rags in his mouth that smother the sound and make it all the more horrible. "Help me. Gotta help me."

"Go talk to the doctor." The nurse picks up the phone outside the room.

Until that moment I had never held my brother's hand. He is a hand-shaker. A man from Ohio uses the handshake as his signature. For a San Francisco attorney the handshake, the hard look in the eye, these are signals, primal statements minus the growl. They all add up to one unmistakeable assertion: I can take you. Now I'm standing over Frank at midnight in this crazy hospital room holding his hand. I'm nearly blind with anger and drowning in fear and guilt, certain I'm failing him, certain he would know how to get it done, fearful he won't last another hour. And in the midst of every terrible emotion possible is another one I didn't expect. A stranger. A good feeling hiding in the corner. This feels good. I like holding his hand. I like feeling his hand holding mine. Holding on to me. I like it.

"The doctor says he can have more medication in an hour."

"An hour! What the hell! That's nuts! You gotta do something for him now. Look at him! Let me talk to the doctor."

"We can't risk giving him too much medication, Mr. Brennan, he might suffer respiratory arrest."

"Can't risk it? Shit, he'll be lucky to last the night. Do something now and get the doctor."

"I can give him another 5ccs but that's all. The doctor is on his way."

The 5ccs don't do shit. The doctor doesn't show up for 90 minutes. Frank lives his nightmare in the hell between sleeping and waking. I am ready to scream with him. Sally and I stand next to him and watch helplessly as the pain has its way. As his face contorts, like a Francis Bacon painting coming to life. As his voice chokes and pleads. As he fights his last fight.

◦∾◦

There we were, after all the years, the games of catch in the back yard, the arguments over Vietnam, the distance, hippy vs. fraternity, the distance, emotion vs. reason, distance; here in this room, holding hands. Holding on for dear life. Linked together at last. Touching, needing, our common blood closer than it's been in fifty years.

I don't remember you touching anyone. Except when you walked by and noogied me in the shoulder. And the handshake. I never saw you hold Sally's hand. Did you?

I'm a sucker for touch. Without it, I seem to fade away. Like I only exist when I'm touching someone. My body seems porous and energy leaks out the holes in my skin. I can't stop it. Touch is a sealant. I should have been a Siamese twin joined at the back. Sometimes it strikes me as odd that I never feel my back. What self I own seems to live on the surface of my skin and face.

This probably sounds nuts to you. You're so strong. And thick. And tough. How did you get so hard? You're body is a brick. The rest of us are softies. Even Dad. I guess you just braced yourself against life for so long you forgot and went on knocking into things and people and made yourself a living contraction. You exiled rest and relaxation from your home.

What did you run on? What was the source of your fuel? Now we're holding hands like a couple of old wires spliced together.

The first time I remember holding hands was with Kathy Saunders on top of the ferris wheel at the Kiwanis' Labor Day carnival. Must have been the summer after you started college. Jesus, I was lonely. When you left, you have no idea how quiet the house was. You were the only life in the place. Of course, Mom chattered a lot but eventually her string ran out. The place smelled of doom. When we dropped you at the airport, a cavern opened in my chest. It swallowed me. You probably didn't know. How could you? Sure, Kathy and I held hands as the big wheel rose and dipped through the summer night. Around and around we turned and it was bliss. You probably held Sue's hand and loved it. You probably did a lot more than that! I remember the stories you told; my favorites were the ones about the fraternity parties at college where bare tit was kid's stuff. I wasn't sure what a tit was but it sounded good to a 13-year-old infatuated with skin.

You always told a good story. Most of the time you laughed harder at the punch line than anyone else. If a crow could laugh, it would sound like yours. It demanded that others laugh just as hard.

I believed every word you said. Every great event. I didn't understand exaggeration. You embellished life. Packaged it up and magnified the glory. I was a master of disappointments. Nothing in life compared to the portrait you showed me. You were an air-brush master. I was a flop. Did you really experience life this way or did you manufacture stories to make it seem so great? Maybe both. Seems you were always trying to convince the world of something. No wonder you were so good with a jury. I remember your pal Joe, the private eye, saying you were undefeated. No one worked a jury like you did. And no one worked harder to prepare.

Once I read a copy of your closing remarks to a jury and I was amazed at the language, at the relentless reasoning of your argument. It was spellbinding. Not in a dramatic way but in a forceful way, as though you got a grip on the intelligence of each jury member and wouldn't let go until they succumbed to seeing things your way. You practiced on me when we were kids. You rode in the front seat and I sat in back. We listened to the latest hits on the radio and you turned and looked at me with the eyes of a hawk and said, "Don't you think that's great!" It was never a question, was it? It never allowed for a different opinion.

I can imagine the jury bending under the pressure of your presentation. Bending, bending and bent into a position of agreement. Agreeing on one reality. One reality and one truth. What was your case? What was the verdict you drove home again and again? Who were you representing? I see how brilliant your game plan was. You turned the tables, didn't you? Every ounce of your life energy went to defending Big Daddy: Trans-World Airlines, Lloyd's of London, US Air. You made them into your best friends! Brilliant! All the aggression that drove Dad to reject and humiliate you was now yours to win the riches and favor of your clients. They loved you. You were loyal to the end. You won them over and redeemed yourself. There is no pain. There is no victim. The victim is a fraud. Not guilty. And the humiliation that might have crippled a weaker soul became your spear. A harpoon to the heart of the case for mistreatment. Objection overruled.

While you made mince-meat of the injured, your brother healed their wounds. You seemed to delight in telling me, sometimes within the first hours of a visit, of the latest shrink you'd destroyed on the witness stand. I was no match for you either. How could I be? I carried the Brennan curse. I had no voice. Mute. Oral circumcision. I was everything you wouldn't allow: wounds, emotions, and defeat. Opposites in a field of likeness. You left behind Akron and Loraine, Ohio. Wheeler, Indiana, ceased to exist. The Big Daddies promised you riches and prestige. They asked you to believe you were the one who could do the impossible; who could win what had never been won. The invincible one. Indestructible. All the while, life went on all around you, without you, lonely for you, fearful for you, and longing for you.

Meanwhile armies of the past joined forces with the blasphemies of wealth and organized on the hills of Marin. There they readied for what resembled a medieval battle. A battle that would begin the tragic downfall of your dreams. That left you naked and bleeding. Powerless and alone.

∽

"Stop it! Stop it! I can't take it." We could barely hear his cries for help. The nurse refused to hear. I was ready to hit him.

"Where is that goddamn doctor? You've got to help him. He's dying in agony. You have to give him something to stop the pain now."

"Mr. Brennan."

"No, don't put me off, damn it. You can give him something. This has gone on too long."

"Mr. Brennan, the doctor is on his way."

The doctor is on his way. The doctor is on his way. This is a giant hallucination. It can't be real. But then I feel that desperate hand grabbing mine.

"Mr. Brennan." The doctor enters the room silently. Sally is off her chair in a flash, eager to escape the unbearable sight of her husband. Her face is white.

"I'm Dr. Henley, head resident for the night. The procedure seems to be working. The most recent blood work shows the bleeding has stopped. His vitals are pretty decent for what he's been through."

"But Dr. Henley, he's in so much pain." Sally isn't asking yet. "We've got to do something; he's in misery. Can't you give him more morphine?"

"Certainly. That's not a problem." Dr. Henley signals to the nurse. What was the problem? I'm dying to swear and tear into them both.

"We'll keep monitoring the blood level and if it holds, perhaps they can try to radiate in the morning and shrink the tumor back."

"How long until he's not in pain?" Sally is pleading.

"It won't be long. We'll give him a good dose to make him comfortable. A few minutes at most." The nurse is fast at work. Frank's protest can be heard from behind the curtain. The doctor seems oblivious to the cries and moans.

"Do you have any questions?" He seems to mean it but who has a brain left to think with? Sally and I are destroyed. The boys are down in the lobby draped over vinyl chairs trying to get as far from this place as sleep will take them.

"What sort of chance do you give him?" Sally doesn't want to know but has to ask.

"We really can't say, Mrs. Brennan. Right now he's holding his own. We'll get him calmed down so he can sleep and hope the patching holds. That's the best we can do for now." He looks sympathetic.

After a few last instructions to the nurse he turns and leaves. Dread takes his place. Fighting the urge to go away we return to Frank. The increased dosage is working. He is quieting. The torture is over. His hand is soft.

∾

The phone rang mid-afternoon on a Sunday. I was old enough to have developed a fear of phone calls. Past the age of 50 all too many bring news you'd rather not hear. Dad's liver cancer. A dear friend's prostate cancer. We were used to the calls from Mom's nursing home. "Your mother has fallen." I hate that ring tone. This time it was Frank on the other end talking from the speaker phone. His voice sounded small and far away. It was unusual for him to call on a day that was not a birthday or holiday so I felt surprised and happy that he wanted to talk to me for no apparent reason. That lasted maybe ten seconds. I shouldn't have answered the phone. Should have hung up. Something is wrong. Big wrong. Maybe his son got his girl pregnant. Maybe the firm is in trouble. Divorce? A particular vintage of anxiety had been waiting in the cellar for this moment. The house of cards swayed in the wind generated by a sigh that met my hello.

"Hi Jim." His voice strained to sound normal.

"Hey, Frank, how are you?" Don't tell me, please. I'm already worn down from taking care of Mom for eight years. We just moved her into a skilled nursing facility, and she's somewhat stable but I don't have much in reserve.

"Hi Jimmy." It's Sally. This is unusual. She typically joins the conversation after we've talked for a few minutes. That probably rules out divorce. When Frank separated from his first wife, he broke the news by himself. I never spoke to Karen or saw her again. Not because I was angry with her. I actually agreed with her. Who can be emotional with him?

"Hi Sally, what's up?"

"Hi Uncle Jim." Oh Christ, it's Eddie. All three of them lined up. This can't be good. Maybe it is a pregnancy. No, they'd keep that to themselves. Everyone loves Eddie. He's the youngest. The funny guy. His greeting is grim and as void of good tidings as his parents'.

"Eddie, hello. How are you, big guy?" I'm praying they are true to form and don't tell me.

Frank laughs but it is dead wood falling. His voice comes out shrunken and apologetic. The barrister is absent. A crow with a broken wing huddles close to the ground.

"Well, Jim, I'm afraid we have some bad news." No. Stop. No bad news. "They say I have a tumor on my pancreas." The world stops spinning. The cards are tumbling in slow motion like autumn leaves.

Frank will be silent for a while. Sally takes off at break-neck speed. Dear Sally, in shock, fills me in on the details of the doctor's visit. She talks faster than her handwriting. The tumor is advanced. Inoperable. They're doing a liver biopsy Monday to confirm the diagnosis. The facts spew from her mouth like water from a punctured hose. Space collapses. My body turns to lead.

"The doctor said to plan a trip to Bora Bora." An attempt to laugh. Silence.

"Sucks, huh, Uncle Jim?" Eddie is shaken to his roots. We all are. The invincible one has taken a hit. Sonny Liston is down. Life is standing over him snarling and shaking its big fist. Eddie is looking to me. We're already positioning for that time.

"It sucks, Eddie. You're right. It sucks."

"Right."

"Jesus, Frank, how are you doing?" Oh, oh. Your Honor, I call Mr. Emotion to the stand.

"I don't know. I guess I'm in shock. Don't know what to think." The witness is unprepared. He stammers and gropes for something to make sense of. Sounds more like Dad than my big brother. He gives up. Weakened by the effort.

"He has stomach pain and back pain." Sally rescues him and turns it to the somatic. "That's how we found out. He had this back pain that wouldn't go away. It started up when we were in Portland for Christmas. I guess pancreatic cancer is like that; the symptoms don't show up until it's too late."

The words were out of her mouth before she could catch them and stuff them back in the box that held all the ugly fears. Too late. Too late. Those words echoed on and on through the remaining conversation. They didn't dissipate and merge with the canyon walls. They created a permanent stain.

"Frank, how can I help? You tell me what I can do. I'll do whatever I can. You call me whenever you need to talk. You too, Eddie and Sally."

The earthquake was over and the plates settled into new positions of instability. But wait. The world had shifted. My voice found a new range. Without intent or volition, I stepped into the seat of strength. The head of the family. As silently and unceremoniously as buds forming in March. It happened. A silent transfer of power. And just as quietly came a stirring. What was it? It couldn't be. Not now. Surely not now. A thrill rising in the spine. He needs me. We'll be close like never before. We'll talk. Like brothers.

It is April. Frank won't see Thanksgiving.

૯૭

The night is endless. You are sleeping easily and then fitfully. At least the pain has stopped enough for you to go under. Still, you look anything but peaceful. My hand is on your arm. The hair on your forearm is soft. Your skin is warm and the muscles relaxed. Breathing is rhythmical and steady. Inches from death you feel so alive.

I have to remind the nurse to give you the pain medication. He is so reluctant. I want to punch him. But I haven't punched anyone since sixth grade when I took on Joey Hubbard and he beat me up in front of the whole school. Wonder if he got in trouble. You and I fought here and there but I was no match for you. I think you took it easy on me. That was nice of you. But you saved it for those awful noogies to the shoulder. Damn they hurt! You were such a sadist hitting me with those pointed knuckles and then laughing the crow laugh. Do you know your fangs showed and your lip curled up in a snarl? The crow covered your tracks, but I knew how mean you could be. When we were older and you were mean, I got angry and you said that stupid thing about Winnie the Pooh: "If you can't take a joke, the hell with you." The hell with you. You beat me down like the bike and the car. I still loved you like crazy. You were my hero. And then I turned 18 and realized, shit, I'm bigger than he is, and promised to give you four noogies every time I passed you in the hallway to make up for the past bruises. You laughed and pretended to cringe.

Jesus, you seemed to like the pain. What about that? Now I'm sitting beside you on the eve of your demise holding the hand that hit me so hard. I'm holding the hand that threw the baseball to me. That threw the chair in front of Dad. That stroked Sue Corsin's bare tit. If you knew I was holding your hand you'd squirm and pull away. Or hit me. Now you like it and I like it. We are united. I like holding hands. Touch is salvation.

When I visited Mom, I'd hold her hand. We'd go shopping and walk along the bay and I'd hold her hand and she'd seem as happy as a clam.

It was different for me. I felt uncomfortable with being so special to her. Half the time I was so annoyed. I just wanted to get away. All the questions, repeated and repeated. But it was more than that. Obviously. There was always something in me fighting closeness with her. Wanting it and fighting it. Caring for her and rejecting her. Did you ever hold her hand? Did you ever feel those bony fingers clinging to your strength? I felt so uneasy with her neediness. So disgusted when she turned into that cute little Daisy girl holding on to Daddy's hand. She seemed pathetic.

Sometimes it did feel sweet and good to be taking care of her, to give her moments of happiness and security. God knows she had few of those in her last five years. But other times I reacted as if her neediness would swallow me. As though it were quicksand. I suppose it did.

But when I try to remember the two of you holding hands or being close, I can't. Even when she was so unstable during those last visits, you let her step down from a curb by herself. Usually I ended up escorting her to the car or into the restaurant. I held her arm and anchored her to the world. You didn't seem to want to touch her. Maybe that's why she fell leaving Eddie's baseball game that spring. Hit her head on the curb and spent the rest of the evening at Marin General. Lucky it wasn't worse. Where were you? Why didn't you help her down?

I remember watching you greet her. You always called her Ma. It looked like an effort to muster up a little bit of tenderness for her. "Hi Ma," and like an old black oak fighting against the wind, you bent forward and gave her a hug. You held your breath. It was a quick hug. Not an embrace and not repeated again until the goodbye hug at the end of the visit.

I understand not wanting to touch her. Not wanting to feel her fear. Whenever I was near Mom I had to fend off disgust and contempt for my own mother. How terrible is that? I was the worst offender. Bad to the core. Are you avoiding that? What are you afraid of? You successfully banished emotion long ago. There isn't a dependent bone in your body. That was my inheritance.

You never rested or surrendered to fatigue. Prepared for trial until midnight, up at 4:00 AM to finalize the plan. You are the pinnacle of self-reliance. Or are you? Perhaps the dam has broken and the reservoir of repudiated feelings has flooded the lowlands. Do you lie here flattened and crushed by the weight of your own needs come back to claim their sovereign land?

On Sundays you left early to do the paper route. I remember Saturday night at dinner you'd ask Mom if she would make a double batch of pancakes for breakfast. You devoured them along with a plate of bacon and half a bottle of syrup. Your appetite was voracious.

What else did you ask her for? I can't see you sitting on her lap. Or sinking into her arms. All the pictures show you looking out from that damn stroller. Never touching. Never held. When I was hurt, I sobbed uncontrollably. I choked and gasped for air. Did you cry? It was shocking to hear you the night you kissed Sue good-bye. You went on and on. Was that the first time? Were you shedding those tears for yourself?

It wasn't until you got home from Vietnam that I saw you cry again. Home only two weeks when you got word George had been killed in action. Your best friend gone. Was that the last time? Was Mom a comfort? I guess what I'm saying is I don't understand you and Mom. Dad I get. You talked business and told your stories of the strange events that passed across your desk. You brought him your triumphs. He listened and shook his head in admiration and incredulity. It confirmed his belief that the world is a crazy place. But he was proud of you. You won him over. It was a man's world you inhabited. The fraternity, the army, the firm, the golf course. You lived with men and came home to your wife and boys for a time out. But early the next day you were right back at it.

It seems you worshipped success. Everything was an investment to that end. Material success and the success of the individual self. The inflated self. Not that you wanted to be King of the Mountain. Not the greatest. But among the greatest.

But what about Mom? She was so peripheral. Part of the admiring gallery. The role-player no team can be without. I can't see the two of you together. Am I blind? I felt too important to her. You held her at arm's length. I couldn't get away from her. You couldn't get far enough away. I don't understand. Why are you so uncomfortable? Are you afraid? Of what? Is success another word for fear? Of this? Of the whole remarkable tower crumbling? Of breakdown? Was all that breaking of stuff you trying to beat life into submission? Trying to beat down your own weakness? And what is weakness if not the wanting, the yearning, for a mother to come to for a little tenderness.

୧୨

This is the End. "I'm sorry, Mrs. Brennan, but the bleeding seems to have started up again." The doctor is back with bad news. "The stitches didn't hold."

"How much time does he have?" Her words are grim but Sally is numb. We're all numb. The boys have returned to the room to hear the news delivered as the sun comes up on another beautiful day in San Francisco. Their faces are blank.

"It's hard to say. I'm sorry. We can move you to another room for more privacy if you like."

"Good. That would be good. Thank you."

Frank does not participate in this decision. It was his choice to try the procedure that caused him five hours of terrible suffering. Now it's over. He's sleeping. Odd how even when sleeping, he looks as though he's working hard. But the fight is over. The procedure was crazy. Everyone knew there was no chance of it working. But Frank was fighting all the way. Any mention of getting his affairs in order was taken as an act of treason.

"What, are you giving up on me?" We all got hit with this accusation at one time or another. Even his doctor the night she recommended hospice was subject to his cross-examination. He battled and battled the way he had throughout his life. He never said goodbye. Or I love you. How terribly lonely it must have been those last days. Staring into the face of death and thinking it was calling for someone else. Thinking that death would not come naturally to he who had made a world to his liking. It was unbelievable. This smart man, this strong man, holding on and refusing the honesty of dying.

"That's it? What do we do now?" Eddie is starting to panic.

"We go with your dad and say good-bye."

"Shit. Is he in pain? Does he know what's happening?"

"I don't think so, Shawn. I think he's past all that. Come on. Let's go."

And we did. We made the long walk to the ninth floor. The last stop. A room with a view. A suite really. Very thoughtful. Very California. Looking out onto a beautiful panorama of the city in all its radiant vitality waking up to another Friday of prosperity. Not a shadow in sight. Frank's beloved San Francisco, his adopted home. A long way from Ohio.

᭤

I love you. I wish I didn't. I wish I didn't have to say what I'm saying. If you can hear inside the coma, you're probably cursing me and want to cut off my head. I'll bet you wish I'd never grown a tongue. I'm sorry. I don't want to hurt you or place fault on anyone. No one is to blame. It's all so big. I'm a fool to think I might understand but I can't help myself. Something is pushing me. What is it? I hope you'll forgive me. It's November 2. The day of the dead, El Dia de los Muertos. An auspicious day for your departure. Your spirit is so dynamic it deserves a big day. Don't be afraid. It's all right. It's all right. Has anyone come for you? Mom has been gone four months. Everyone thinks she left when she did in order to escort you to the other side. Sweet. I can see her smile now, free of the conditioning of her time and full of the best of her love for you. Are you dreaming? We never shared our dreams. I suppose you thought they were bunk. Maybe that changed with the dream that woke you last month. How did it go? Mom is singing in a grand opera. She is dressed in the robes of a queen walking toward center stage where she turns to you and with all the passion of Maria Casales delivers this aria: "I am coming for you, I am coming..." You woke up trembling in cold sweat.

When you told me, I shivered and goose bumps covered my neck. A few weeks later she returned. This time it was her unadorned voice calling your name; "Frank, Frank, Frank." You woke up on the floor.

When Sally told me what had taken place, first my eyes closed of their own accord and then a silence stepped forward replacing all worries. We are taken care of. I was tempted to be skeptical. And jealous. You couldn't possibly be that connected to Mom. But of course you are. Who can undo what has been woven by the invisible? Not you and all your victories. Not me and all my failures. Not the mudslide of Dad's depression. Not the violence of shredded memory and thwarted love. It's life and not only life. We are perversions, lost in high grasses, chasing after gold but endowed with a spiritual heritage that outlasts evil and human folly alike. We belong to awe.

You and I are brothers, which means we are different. You and I are different, which means we are alike. Born of one mother. Born of a thousand mothers. Born of the unborn one. You and I are a story carved in rock. Our pages turn backward and forward. Should we laugh or cry? Should we dance for joy or fall to our knees in despair? You and I are brothers. Be in peace, brother. Be in peace.

෴

Frank arrives shortly after we do. A new nurse rolls him in and parks his bed by the big window. She is beaming. The room is bursting with light. We have come from the underworld and the radiance hurts our eyes. Our nurse promises to return shortly with new bedding. She asks if she can bring us anything. No one has an answer. We are dazzled by the light, by the beauty of the day intruding on our anguish. The morning could not be more oblivious to our moment. Death could not be more irrelevant to the world's agenda. We are tempted to stare at that brilliant world. Tempted to lose ourselves in the architecture of the urban carnival opening beneath a blue, blue sky, empty of pain. Where life appears unstoppable. Never ending. We are afraid to look at him. Afraid to see and feel. Our minds, exhausted as they are, eagerly assist in avoiding Frank. Suggesting we still have time. Suggesting that death is still approaching. Maybe caught in a traffic jam. We have time. Time to watch the scintillating November light fall on his face. Time for the ancestral spirits to arrive. Time for a few stories. The hooded one couldn't possibly steal him from this golden shower. Certainly death waits for nightfall to slip in the back door. Surely we'll have another day with him.

The nurse has barely closed the door when we dare to look his way. And the moment we do he sits up in bed. His eyes open wide and a ground swell convulses through his body. His torso rises and falls. He struggles to breathe and raise himself above the flash flood of blood but fails. It lasts thirty seconds and ends. And when it does, his body falls back on the pillow. Motionless. Breathless. It ends so fast, it is as if the Pacific has heaved its last wave upon the shore and then lies flat and quiet forever. Impossible.

We stood beside the body expecting him to return. We stood there empty and speechless. With no goodbye on our lips. With no "I love you" on the tongue. We stare at him and feel robbed. Just like that, taken, by the magician's sleight of hand. Gone. Gone from this world. The day never blinks.

๛

The pain was brutal. His absence surrounded my lungs and wouldn't let me breathe. His silence was so loud I couldn't hear anything but those last terrible sounds: the muffled scream. I felt certain I had failed him. Certain he had descended into hell. A week went by. It felt like seven years. I was afraid to sleep. Afraid not to sleep. I was afraid to sleep and not be near him. Afraid not to sleep and be without a bit of his presence. Depression rolled in. The pain didn't budge but at least it was obscured for moments and hours. I walked about in a daze. How could I comprehend what had happened? Under the gaze of starless skies I cried out loud, "Where are you?" and walked on without a response.

I feared he was continuing to suffer trapped in an afterlife of fear and pain equal to his last hours. I worried about his boys and Sally. Sleep was hard to come by and made little difference to the exhaustion occupying my body. Some nights I slept on the couch to protect my wife from my restlessness. The Saturday after Frank's death was one of those nights. I left our bed around midnight, tired but unable to fall into a deep sleep. On the couch I thought of Mom. She died in July when I was so worried about Frank that I barely made room for the grief that belonged with her. I missed her that night. Once again I thought of things I should have said to Frank. Ways I should have gotten through to him. I felt responsible for his battle with death. For his failure to say goodbye to his kids. I should have written him a letter. A letter that would have convinced him not to fight. Convinced him to surrender and say goodbye. And say I love you. Something.

I fell asleep thinking I was weak. I had backed off out of fear. Fearful that history was repeating. Fearful that he would call me "traitor" and turn his back just like our grandmother had with Mom. Fearful that our lives were nothing but an echo, endlessly spinning backward and collecting shreds from the past to weave into the present. Endless repetition. The unwanted, endlessly returned from the dead.

It was a drop-out-of-existence sleep. The first in months. But at 3:00 AM I woke abruptly. Immediately wide awake and aware of something extraordinary happening in the room. A presence was with me. A presence that was vibrating, almost singing, from every corner of the room. It was Frank.

The room was full of Frank. Pulsing with Frank. Radiant. Frank was touching me, calling me. Outside, the morning was still and dark. "Can this be real? Is it all a crazy dream?" No. It was you. I know you. It was your presence waking me from this deep sleep. It was your motion, the rippling energy, the vibrancy of your being.

I could feel you even though I could not see you. You were here in all your bigness. In all your beauty. The entire room was shimmering. I had no breath. I had no arms or legs. Awe and joy took the place of fear and a ravaged body. You revealed yourself. At least for this moment all the doubts and anxieties fled. The experience was overwhelming in the best possible way. It was a strong wind. It was death and death only. The spiritual realm exists! We were swimming in it together. It was lovely.

We have believed in stories with sad endings. What made us into believers? I guess we were tricked into believing in nothing but this nose and face, nothing but these shoulders and limbs, these feet moving a body through space. Duped into believing in biographies, in personalities shining by their own light. What fools. Oedipus blinded by his own hand. We believed in the testimony of others and overlooked the evidence of radiance dancing by our sides. Yes, Frank was here. But not the little boy running circles around his broken father. And not the teenager lighting a fire to his ambition. And not the attorney stalking the world like a hungry grizzly. A trace, yes, a trace of him was here. A pinch of salt dissolved in broth. But it was the you that belongs to a vast expanse that visited that night. The you of splendor and grace that came to say what cannot be said. The word is love. You and I are more than we ever dreamed. More than starlight. More than we can know. Because we are more, we are less. Because we are less, we are the same. Inseparable.

# PART II

# Radiance

# CHAPTER 7

# Daisy

∽

Truly, nothing could be finer. Finer than Carolina mornings near the sea whose soft breezes, rolling over the scattering of islands along the coast, added a fresh salty smell to the perfume of those lovely early hours. And when the sun rose above the broad Atlantic, spreading its warm touch over forests of tall southern pines, great colonies of yellow jasmine, and the rich mix of ancient wetlands, an aroma so delightful it could never be forgotten permeated every living particle of the earth and seemed the very sweetness of being itself.

So delicious and satisfying were these smells that the mind quite involuntarily traveled back and back through ages of memory to a place as fresh as the scent of lilac. A place of ease. From there the senses opened to the grand symphony of a day. And little difference existed between the sight of cardinals and blue birds flashing from tree to tree and the actual flight of those winged wonders. And even less between the sound of mourning doves and towhees and the birdsong coming from every surrounding tree and bush. Nothing could be finer than a Carolina morning because it softened the edges of separation like a river smooths rock. It dissolved the furtive pain of self and allowed the bluest of blues to bathe an unfettered soul with all this splendor. All this wonderful life. Showered by blue. Carolina blue.

Daisy stands at the kitchen sink readying for breakfast. She rinses the few dishes left over from the night before and puts them in the dishwasher. Since every breakfast is the same (Special K and a banana - you have to have your potassium) her attention is free to gaze out the windows above the sink and lining the breakfast nook, free to drift over the pastoral landscape and its many delights. Daisy loves the view. She loves the tranquility of the lagoon and the slender reeds that grow from the edges. The water lilies sprinkled here and there. She loves the snowy egrets who come every morning to search for a traditional Southern breakfast of raw crayfish. She loves the camellia and azalea bushes bordering the dark water, the crape myrtle trees behind these and the giant pines pointing like the steeple of her Presbyterian church to the grand domed ceiling of uninterrupted blue. A blue like no other.

Though she would pretend to be frightened were Gerald around, she secretly enjoys scanning the muddy banks of the lagoon for the motionless body of their resident alligator lazily basking in the warm Carolina sun. The whole scene makes her heart sing. She tunes her ear to the chorus of birdsong filtering in from the yard and bursts into song herself with that old familiar melody rising from her lungs like a goldfinch in full flight: "Nothing could be finer, than to be in Carolina, in the mooorning, Nothing could be..." There is a bounce to her voice, a delightful flutter like she's heard in the music of the Broadway musicals she adores. Daisy thinks of them now; *Hello Dolly, My Fair Lady, Sound of Music.*

Oh, how she loves this musical world; and once again, overcome with feeling, she launches into another favorite celebration of beginnings and glorious light, the tune from *Oklahoma*, "Oh, what a beautiful morning! Oh, what a beautiful day! I've got a wonderful feeling, everything's going my way." Life is a happy song she tells herself. An unbroken string of fine mornings, with unlimited new days and enchanting melodies that light up the heart and make a girl sing along like Judy Garland under a rainbow. This new life in this new world. This dream come true.

Daisy was born in Milwaukee but she was destined for the South. By the time she arrived in Savannah and drove the bridge over the boggy marshland to the outbreaker island known as Hilton Head, her friends called her by her given name, Georgia. Georgia Daisy. Though she lacked the sweet-flowing Southern accent of her dear friend Millie Thompson, she compensated by calling everyone darlin' and by talking, walking, and dressing with the impeccable taste of a Southern Lady. On her visits to the West Coast to see her boys, she made regular appointments with her favorite sales girls at Nordstrom's and shopped with great joy for new clothes to wear when she returned home to Hilton Head.

She called the girls "Doll" and they thought she was adorable. Gerald sat on the sideline in a comfortable chair tailor-made for husbands waiting the hours it took to try on the latest fashions and decide on something just right. Something stylish and elegant. Not too flashy but noticeably lovely. Daisy bought fun shorts and shirts for the golf course and always more than one pair of comfortable Italian leather shoes. Georgia went for the St. John suits. Made from the finest wool, a St. John suit was tailored just right to show off Georgia's petite figure yet be ever so modest despite the occasional gold buttons accenting the pretty colors - periwinkle, coral, midnight black - of the elegant wool.

Georgia pulled her shoulders back as she always did when preparing to enter a room where she might be seen. She walked with perfect posture and pace. It all spoke of a grace she'd perfected somewhere between Akron and New York. Without hesitation she walked right up to the mirror and admired what she saw.

The girl said, "Oh, Mrs. Brennan, that is such a great color for you!" Georgia smiled. She felt no trepidation looking into the mirror. They had made a pact together years before. A treaty. The mirror on the wall promised to reflect only the best and brightest light and Georgia promised her undying loyalty in making the mirror happy. They spent hours together. Making her hair just right, working the makeup so that it was lovely but not obvious, painting lipstick on her lips the way she'd seen Audrey Hepburn do a hundred times.

Sometimes she sang a popular tune for the mirror. "Hello Dolly! Well Hello Dolly! It's so nice..." She kept the mirror happy and the mirror told her what she wanted to hear and allowed her to turn toward the world with the confidence of finding acceptance. When she turned from the full-length mirror in Nordstrom's, it was Daisy who met the admiring eyes of the sales girl. It was Daisy who beamed her approval. Daisy who looked a little shy after all. A tad uncomfortable for a second before she caught herself, made a little fuss about spending all the money, and then gave in to the moment, to Gerald's look of approval and to the tide of plenty that had swept their generation into the golden years. When she returned home to Hilton Head, Millie would exclaim, "Oh Georgia, darlin', aren't you the prettiest little thing on God's earth?"

Daisy would smile and look appropriately humble. She was a picture of grace. And the world of Southern charm took Georgia in like a true daughter of Dixie.

∽

They were young, not yet sixty years old, when Gerald and Daisy drove through the gates of Hilton Head Plantation to begin their retirement years. Gerald saluted the former Marines minding the security station at the front entrance of the plantation, which spread out before them like a new continent of tranquility. Everywhere they looked, their eyes fell upon beauty: gardens of hibiscus and jasmine, lovely wetlands and manicured lagoons without a trace of algae, and flocks of giant snowy egrets and blue herons. The lagoons were artfully placed within the outlines of the numerous golf courses populating the landscape of the Island; one more beautifully sculpted than the last, these green pastures of America's favorite hobby were the drawing card for the popularity of Hilton Head and other resort communities across the South.

Gerald's business for the thirty years of his working life had been purchased in 1978 by a mega company out of New Orleans. These years marked the beginning of a period of acquisitions and mergers and a frenetic expansion of corporate monopoly. Neither Gerald nor Georgia thought twice about accepting the tidy retirement package offered by the "snakes," as Gerald called them, from New Orleans. They sold the house in New Canaan for a hefty profit and drove to Hilton Head without a care in the world. It was for them, as for many others of the "Greatest Generation," an opening into a life they'd never known: a life free of the toil and the demands of work. A wave of retirees, veterans of WWII with silver hair and wives adorned in flowering dresses, migrating toward a land without winter where the only sweat came from playing a round of golf under hot sun and humid winds. Air conditioning blessed their days and nights, and they lived off the fruits of success in complete comfort.

Georgia was happier than she'd ever been since she was a college girl in the sorority. Of course the early years of motherhood were the best but that was different. Nothing compared to babies. She relished being the mother of two handsome boys. For all those years she gave herself completely and without complaint to mothering Frank and Jimmy, to providing for their every need. Moving to New York and taking up a home in the wooded hills of Connecticut delivered her from the pedestrian strains of Ohio and from brushes with the past. The success of Gerald's career completed the exile from poverty and brought her to a place she could admire with all the stature the mirror had promised she deserved. She joined the women's club and went to Broadway musicals and plays. She played bridge once a week and shopped at the best stores in town. To her astounded delight she even persuaded Gerald to attend the opera. When he enjoyed it and agreed to try another, she thought it was all a dream.

But living in New England around old sophisticated money and women who were not about to relinquish their rank to the immigrants from Ohio and Illinois was hard on Daisy. An insecurity crept into camp under her radar. The mirror lost the edge of conviction it had held. More and more was required of Daisy to assume the pose of the happy, carefree girl at home with the world.

So Georgia emerged as the leading lady in her climb to the summit of respectability. And Georgia was angry. Angry at the competitive snobbery of the ladies in the country club who ignored her and let it be known she would never be one of them. And angry at the women at the Presbyterian church who dismissed her Midwest education as intellectually and spiritually inferior. Georgia fumed over the dinner table as she told Gerald and Jimmy stories of the rudeness she encountered. They were taken aback by the rancor that came from her mouth and the ferocious glare in her eyes. They only knew her as Daisy. The princess of kindness. They only knew the smile.

But Georgia wasn't smiling from morning until nightfall the way Daisy had. Frank was away at college blazing his way toward success, and Jimmy was off with his friends and his basketball more often than not. Gerald was cloistered in his office in the city twelve hours a day or on business trips for two to three days out of the week. Georgia was alone. She had friends and she had the women's club, but the evenings were long and lonely. She had the popular songs to sing while she stood in the kitchen preparing dinner. But she felt something wilting inside. More and more effort was required to bring on the smile that her family relied on. She did so faithfully but automatically with less and less of Daisy involved. Even on the evenings when Gerald was home on time from New York, she could not keep the loneliness away. She smiled more easily and had someone to talk to but Gerald was increasingly remote.

He was frustrated with his work and exhausted by the grind of commuting. His small rural self was no match for the hustling bravado of most New York executives. Though his will was strong, his social ego was not. Gerald had no voice to counter the fast-talking maneuvers of his colleagues. He stammered and protested what he believed to be errant judgment but without a tongue he failed to influence anyone and left the office each day frustrated and wishing he could find a place to escape to. So while others used the hour-long train ride home to drink and play cards and laugh away the tensions of Manhattan, Gerald retreated to the *Wall Street Journal*, further isolating himself from everything but Daisy's smile.

They stopped going to neighborhood parties because too many men were flirting with Georgia. Gerald became furious and refused to ever go to another when one smooth talker kissed Daisy on the cheek as they left a particularly saucy night. No one kisses on the cheek in Indiana, for crying out loud. Had Gerald not lost his tongue in the war with unbearable grief and had his emotions not been stifled by the Midwest version of Irish Catholic repression, he might have resembled Jackie Gleason pacing around the kitchen pumping his fist and threatening Audrey Meadows, "One of these days, Alice, one of these days, Pow, right to the moon!" As it was, he sat at the table turning his fork over and over and shaking his head. Daisy pleaded with him but it was as futile as reasoning with a three-year-old. He hated parties more than funerals but at least in church people were respectful and didn't talk about themselves and art and the latest trip to Europe.

"Gerald, these are our neighbors. They don't mean any harm." Gerald did not reply but moved the salt shaker to the other side of the pepper. "Come on, dear. They're just being friendly."

"I'll say they're being friendly," Gerald said mockingly. "That was a pretty friendly kiss last night all right."

"Oh stop, that's just the custom. We're not in Indiana any more. We didn't want that, remember? He didn't mean anything by it." Daisy could deny an eclipse of the moon when necessary. In fact, it hadn't occurred to her that there was anything to the kiss on the cheek Dick Winslow gave her as they were leaving the party. She wouldn't know how she felt about such a thing. Were they really flirting with her? The mirror promised approval and that was all she hoped for. Why would they flirt with her? She was a married woman.

"We can't just stop socializing with our friends. What will they think?"

"I don't care what they think." And he didn't. And they never returned.

Daisy's social life came to resemble life in the sorority. She chatted on the phone more each day and grew lonelier at night. She went up earlier to prepare for bed and took more and more time caring for her teeth. At times she sang non-stop from the song books of *Oklahoma* and *My Fair Lady*. She took more to dreaming of being on stage before an audience of admirers singing happy tunes in the company of other fair voices. As the years went on, she had more to hide as resentments and an uncomfortable restlessness grew and grew, threatening to break through the smiling face of Daisy, which had become more of a barricade and less a beam of light.

Georgia was bored. She found this unflattering and tried to talk herself out of it the moment she could identify the wrinkle in the cloth. She tried wrestling with something she couldn't see. Something she found selfish and unbecoming. Not once did it occur to her that her spirit was calling, urging her to step out of the restrictions of her domestic role and the pleasing persona so carefully crafted all these years. Georgia talked to Daisy, and each took a turn rebuking the promptings of this foreign voice growing louder by the day. Not knowing if she had accepted the logic of this alternative presence or simply acquiesced, as she was accustomed to, Georgia Daisy found herself moving toward something so unexpected it would throw her and the family into a temporary tailspin.

The confusion she claimed as to the agency responsible for this uncharacteristic show of personal desire was betrayed by the determination with which she left the house that Saturday morning. She revealed no clues as to her intentions but left straight away, as usual, for her weekly appointment at the beauty parlor. When she returned home two hours later, no one so much as glanced up from the autumn football game on the tube. The expectation of the familiar was so strong, the necessity of repetition so ingrained that it took several moments to notice that while Georgia had left the house in the morning it was Daisy who returned in the afternoon having done the unthinkable, what amounted to a revolution: a change to her appearance. She walked in the door from the garage and said nothing. Frank was the first to notice, "What the..." his incredulous exclamation drew the attention of Gerald and Jimmy.

"Mom!!" Jimmy's mouth hung wide open. "Mom! What? Geez!"

Gerald said nothing but chuckled nervously under his breath. He was shocked by what he saw. It wasn't his doll who walked through the TV room and up the stairs. Daisy was different. Her hair was done up like a giant bee hive. But that was only the beginning. It was now frosted, a platinum blond, like so many women were doing. Daisy looked like Kim Novak walking up to Jimmy Stewart. She could have passed for Zsa Zsa Gabor except that she was too thin in the bosom and too delicate in the cheek bones to pass for an Eastern European.

Sadly, the boys of Ohio and Indiana failed her. They were shocked and speechless. None of them knew what to do with change of this magnitude. Or, to be precise, they knew to reject it. To belittle. And while the boys laughed, Gerald said nothing. He never told Georgia he loved her dark chestnut brown hair. He never mentioned that he thought of her as his own Ava Gardner. That wavy brown hair with the deep auburn accents falling to her shoulders the way the girls wore it in 1940 when they met on campus. He immediately thought of Ruth and her dark hair. He remembered as a little boy running his fingers through Ruth's hair and smelling it when she held him in her arms and carried him to bed. When Gerald looked up to see Georgia marching up the stairs to their bedroom, he saw only her back and the twisted mat of hair that to his untrained eye looked a lot like cotton candy on a stick. He wondered what could have possessed her to do such a thing. But he did not follow her to their bedroom. He simply shook his head and went on watching the football game.

Daisy was deeply hurt. She wasn't sure why she was making such a fuss but that didn't stop her from feeling very disappointed by her family. Her insides were tossed around like a small boat on a stormy sea. One second she was feeling she'd made a big mistake and had been a silly conformist to do what she'd done. The next she was furious with all of them for being so stuck in the mud. Especially her husband, whom she very much wanted to sock in the nose.

Georgia could not have said why she was so upset nor where the determination came from that led her to continue coloring her hair for the next thirty years. The mirror was waiting for her when she reached the bedroom. When she looked at herself that afternoon, a bit of a shock went through her body. What had she done? What would she do next? Was Dick Winslow really flirting with her? Were others and she hadn't noticed?

Georgia got hold of herself right then and there. She shook herself and drove those thoughts from her mind with the same ferocity she'd drawn on in the past to rid herself of unbecoming ideas. She would not allow there to be a next. With a force most people did not recognize in her, she pulled herself together and resumed her pleasing ways. Taking care of others. Rarely challenging Gerald. Being the perfect mirror to friends and family. She was Blondie to Dagwood. When the Donna Reed show was popular, the boys said, "Hey, that's Mom." But she kept her hair as it was when she left the beauty parlor that Saturday in November. Every two weeks she returned to have her hair done by the stylist, who adored her. She kept it as an implicit threat that was lost on Gerald. She kept it as a ticket to fit in with the fashion of the times, to be one of the girls. And she kept it without really knowing why but dimly sensing, each time she looked in the mirror or received a compliment, a quivering deep inside her chest. A quivering she was unacquainted with but that, in a mysterious way, felt more her than anything she had known or could remember.

Daisy would feel that strange quivering sensation again on the day she and Gerald drove through the front gate of the Hilton Head Plantation. Flowers surrounded the entrance. Lovely Carolina sunshine fell on one and all as if the rapture were now and forevermore. Georgia Daisy drove into her new world with a smile on her face and a song in her heart, "I've got a wonderful feeling...," and unlike Connecticut, which was far and away superior to Ohio but made her feel slightly out of place, South Carolina made her feel like Cinderella trying on the glass slipper. Ah. The perfect fit. She was a meadowlark bobbing over a field of wild roses.

Nowhere she'd ever been matched her graciousness and friendliness the way the South did. Nowhere she'd ever been made her feel so special. She felt not a hint of self-consciousness being served by black women and men. On the contrary, she expanded into being catered to. "Yes, Ma'am, certainly, Mrs. Brennan." Gerald and Georgia weren't rich but they were extremely comfortable and settled into a life of ease.

For the first time in their lives, they had parties and friends over for dinner. Not once did one of the husbands flirt with Daisy or kiss her on the cheek. They made cheese and crackers for their guests. Gerald fixed cocktails and laughed at the stories his friends told. Three times a week they played golf with the same friends and laughed at the poor putting that never seemed to improve. Gerald wore ridiculous plaid pants and a straw hat and was forever frustrated with an incurable slice, but he loved the challenge. Daisy wore stylish shorts and tops, a cute little sailor's hat and was forever trying to learn a game she hardly gave a hoot about. But they were happy on the links and most of all they were together. No more business trips. No more loneliness like in New Canaan. In fact, they never once spent a day apart during twenty-three years on the Island. Daisy even talked Gerald into taking walks on the beach. There they developed a fondness for the brown pelicans flying inches above the tame waves of the southern Atlantic. They held hands and walked in tennis shoes over the crusty sand on the harbor side. Georgia talked and talked, and Gerald listened to the voice that to him was like no other music.

Daisy made friends immediately. Making friends was a specialty of hers. She was a great friend, never critical, always ready to laugh along with the stories of others, always ready to help or be sympathetic and encouraging of the plights of her friends. She liked joining groups and being a part of something. In college it was the sorority, in Connecticut the women's club, and in Hilton Head it was the golf club, and later, when Gerald was ill, it was the church group. Really, they were all another form of the sorority she loved in college. There she made life-long friends and met the first of the great talkers in her life. She always had a best friend and she was always as loquacious as the last. Millie Thompson was the first of the friends in Hilton Head. Sophie Lestus was the last. Millie was vintage Southern Belle, born, raised and groomed in Atlanta. She talked like she just came from the set of *Gone With The Wind*: "Why Georgia, I just made up some lemon pound cake for you and Gerald. I just know you're going to love it, Darlin'. Mm mm it is sooo good. Lord in Heaven! I'll drop it by real soon, honey. You wait, I'll be by in just a minute."

Sophie was Greek, raised in Alexandria, Egypt, and had a laugh that resonated half-way to Bermuda. She was opinionated and loud, utterly lacking in the genteel manners of a Southern Lady. Daisy loved her immediately. They met at the retirement home one week after each took up residence as the new widows on the block. Sophie called Daisy every morning, "Bonjour, Georgia. Bonjour, comment allez-vous ce matin? Je suis tres bien. Tres bien, merci." French was her favorite language, the most beautiful language. The language of love. They had dinner together, told stories one after the other and laughed until their sides split. Sophie was the last of Georgia's great friends. The last and the loudest of the long talkers.

Gerald would have hated her. She was boisterous, her laughter shook the chandeliers, and she had opinions by the dozen. Political opinions. Gerald would have died a thousand deaths in the company of Sophie. Nor could he tolerate Millie, whose voice was sweet as a canary and said nothing but pleasantries over their dinners together. Millie and Daisy went on all evening weaving their stories together like a Rodgers and Hammerstein duet. Gerald sat to the side grinding his teeth and counting the minutes until he could pull Daisy away without being too obvious. He loathed them all. In Connecticut it was Jan Rupp. Daisy and Jan ate up hour after hour on the phone in the kitchen while Gerald watched the Knickerbockers twenty feet away in the family room. He could hear that goddamn voice going on like a train passing in the night and it filled him with such annoyance he couldn't contain himself: "What in the world do you talk about with that woman?" he demanded, knowing full well no answer in the world would suffice.

"Oh, you know, just girl talk." Daisy wasn't taking it seriously. She'd heard it all before.

"I can't stand it. Why do you like her?"

"You don't like anybody who talks. I'm surprised you like me. Why do you get so upset by two women talking on the phone?"

"It isn't right. She's a nut."

"You don't like any of my friends. You don't like Jan, you didn't like Agi; what's wrong with you? Who am I supposed to talk to? You never talk to me."

And it was true. On both counts. Even in their happier years in South Carolina they would sit at the restaurant table for long stretches of time without a word passing between them. Daisy oscillated between giving up on any conversation and pleading with Gerald to say something. She sometimes wondered in the thick of silence why she had married someone like him. Words were like music. Stories were songs. Without either she was thrown back on herself and the messy dark rooms of her house of mirrors. And yes, he didn't like her friends. He didn't like Jan and he didn't like Agi. God, she was the worst. Must have been Jewish, he thought. Smelled worse of garlic than the hot dogs at Cleveland Municipal Stadium. Somehow he even let Agi talk them into buying a new Mercury sedan from her husband. What a mistake that was. Never veer away from General Motors. He knew better than that. But that damned fast-talking Agi had talked them into it. Like she put a spell on them. Like she was a Gypsy or something. That damned car never did work right, for crying out loud.

❧

Faye was the first true girlfriend and big talker. They spoke back and forth their entire lives. It was freshman year at Valpo, Valparaiso University in Northern Indiana. A good Lutheran school Georgia's father had picked out for her, being a devout and stern Lutheran of the Missouri Synod. It was there at Valpo she met Faye and then Gerald. It was there she became Daisy.

Prior to college she was "Baby" to her mother and father, whom she both adored and feared. He was of English blood and she of German. They ruled over Daisy, and not just her life, but her identity. Making all her decisions for her and informing the person she would be. She was Baby to them even as she cared for them in their last days. Her father was a successful businessman, a natural salesman, gregarious and witty. He passed on the gift of conversation to her. But he was all seriousness when it came to his daughter. She was his prize. Her mother was mostly kind but odd. Germanic and prone to fits of anger. She was more introverted and looked at times like the slightly deranged baby sister of Bette Davis. Her eyes bulged like she had undetected Grave's disease. And there was something spooky in those eyes. Something unwanted. Many untold stories.

Daisy grew up shadowed by rules. She feared her father's disapproval and her mother's rage. She was as innocent as her name and still her mother looked at her as though she had already done something terribly wrong. And when her brother began visiting her room at night, she decided that was the terribly wrong thing her mother had known all along. It upset her to do so but she decided to keep secret the fact that disturbed her mother so terribly.

When Daisy arrived at Valparaiso in the fall of 1938, she was ready to find herself in Faye. Faye lit up the moment she met Daisy. They threw their arms around each other and talked through the night. Daisy knew instantly Faye would be her best friend, just as she did with Jan and Millie. Free talking was the sign of an unrestricted life. And that is what she searched for without knowing. Her life would be marked by rules too numerous to count and a reaching for openings through the liberator of speech.

She and Faye were inseparable. They stayed up late talking about the new boys they were meeting, what love might feel like, and what heartbreaks would befall them. They studied French together and spoke in florid accents. Dreams of Paris and Marseilles danced before their eyes. They walked back from classes singing their favorite love songs. Each longed to be a mother. No less than four babies apiece. There were parties and books and milkshakes and dances. Daisy could talk to Faye whenever she pleased. There was no one to tell her otherwise.

What happened next was omitted from the narrative of her life, sparse as it was, that was passed on to her children and friends. She seemed to tell everything. But it became another hole in the fabric of her story. Another secret hidden below in her boat. What was remarkable was that no one noticed the gaps. The story of her smile was too persuasive. The power of omission too convincing. Spellbinding. What was she hiding down there with her brother's sin? Who was she protecting? Was her mother the mad woman in the attic?

Not until Jimmy began piecing together the tiny bones unearthed in his psyche did he notice the mysterious omissions in Daisy's life. It had been his father who came from a destitute world. Who had suffered a crippling wound. Daisy had come from that grand stone house in Pittsburgh, from a mother who cooked delicious dinners and a father who smoked a pipe and passed out Chiclet gum to the grandchildren. Hadn't they spent many a holiday there in that house? Wasn't it a happy place?

But when Jimmy rummaged through the closets on Hilton Head, he found photo albums of Gerald's family and nothing of Daisy's but a few scattered snapshots. It was as though a time shredder had chewed up her history and thrown out the scraps.

Jimmy was dumbfounded, and even more so when shortly after his father's death Georgia told him she had left Valpo after her freshman year to attend Marquette University. She never before explained why, but Jimmy guessed it was to study French, never once imagining she had fallen in love. Fallen in love with Larry Mitchell. He was a fine young man. Lots of fun. He liked to do the new dances like she did. And to her astonishment she could talk to him nearly as easily as with Faye. Daisy fell hard, the way she and Faye had dreamed together.

The problem was he was Catholic. Her father must have caught wind and yanked her immediately. He had no love for Catholics. He chewed on his pipe and cursed the damned Catholics for daring to covet his only daughter. A moment later he berated Daisy for being so stupid as to get involved with an Irishman. Her mother, Victoria, glared at her daughter with contempt as though Daisy's infidelity to the Lutheran Church had caused her to remember something too awful to behold. Daisy looked at the floor and wept silently. Her tears fell back into her throat. She did not question and she did not protest their verdict.

Four months later she returned to Valparaiso and Faye with real stories of love and a broken heart. Only Faye would know the truth, the truth and sadness Daisy endured as a result of her parents' interference. But something had dampened in Daisy and that something did not laugh as whole-heartedly and sat cowering in the shadow of her smile.

Faye made it all bearable. She made the day's light shine. Daisy loved her more than ever. They gossiped about sorority sisters and laughed about the strange mannerisms of their professors. They drank cherry Cokes and ate hamburgers, read books and did their studies. They were inseparable. The bond between them grew stronger and would not fade the length of their lives though the time together would be brief.

Faye had stories of her own to tell. His name was Ray. Faye and Ray. They laughed at the silly rhyme and made up more to go with it. Their kids would play with Faye and Ray, all day. They would name them Kay and Jay. It was silly and they knew it and they didn't care. Faye was in love and Daisy approved and that was all that mattered. Ray was the right guy and would stand by his girl throughout their life in California until her lungs turned to charcoal and disintegrated from the tobacco smoke she could never say no to.

Daisy watched them together and felt an ache in her chest. She missed Larry terribly when no one was watching. And as the autumn months passed, she watched as his memory slipped away. As the ache faded and a loneliness moved in. That was the only thing she wouldn't talk about.

She threw herself into her schoolwork and because she genuinely loved Valpo, it was not difficult for her to find ways to forget the hurt and humiliation of her father's hold on her life. She made herself smile and carry on as though this were her life and she was happy with her choice to leave Marquette behind.

Boys asked her out on dates but she wasn't interested. They were fine young men, hard-working Lutherans, eager to have fun and eager to be heroes in the war that loomed over the world like a wicked curse. As they danced and laughed and smoked Camels, as they boasted of their desire to kill Hitler's lousy soldiers in Europe, none of them could have imagined the lives of all those men snuffed out like so many flimsy candle flames. They were given a short time on this earth. But not one of them suspected it on those Friday nights in the glorious fading light of autumn when the trees flamed bright with love and young men and eager girls kissed in the shadow of maples and oaks old enough to be their grandparents. They did not see it as the shadow of death.

Those who survived the Depression could not foresee a worse time than that befalling the country. Certainly not the young men looking to become lovers and fathers. Death sneaked into town unsuspected as snow before Thanksgiving and waited for boy after boy to walk into its jaws. The young Christian soldiers marched onward into the slaughterhouse. In just a few years Daisy would mourn for those she knew who left and did not return. Her heart broke for the girls left with arms outstretched and holding nothing but shrinking memories. She counted her blessings that she was not among the girls whose true love's last thoughts were of her while his blood emptied into the mud of a foreign land. She thanked God that Larry was alive somewhere in Milwaukee even if in someone else's arms.

Faye sensed Daisy's loneliness. She took it upon herself to find a good match for her dearest friend. She scouted the best prospects and consulted with Ray when she was in doubt. By the time of the spring Sadie Hawkins dance, she had a list of possibilities for Daisy to choose from. Daisy had never asked a boy out and she was nervous. It made her think of Larry and how easily they talked and dreamed together. For a second, she thought of inviting Larry down and sneaking behind her parents' backs for time with him. She shook herself firmly with disapproval for even thinking such a thing. Daisy was also picky. She carried her father's high standards within and was capable of severe judgments scarcely anyone knew of, so convincing were her smile and pleasing appearance.

"Boy, you're picky," complained Faye. "What's wrong with Roger Morgan? He's cute, and funny too!"

"I don't know. He's just too short or something." Daisy was thinking of Larry and his tall muscular frame. "I like to look up to a man."

"Well, you may be looking up to the moon next Saturday if you keep on finding fault with all these guys. Let's see, how about Ray's fraternity brother Scottie Petterson? Nothing wrong with him I can think of."

"Oh he's such a nice guy, he really is. I guess, maybe, but..." Daisy paused and Faye pounced.

"But! But what?"

"I don't know Faye. I just can't see myself dancing with him. Can you? He's kind of, well..."

"Big feet?"

They laughed merrily. Faye held her stomach as the laughter grew between them imagining Scottie Petterson's feet growing larger than a clown's. Daisy wiped tears from her eyes.

"I know, what about Gerald Brennan? Great athlete, Ray says he's smart as a whip. Tall but with average feet."

"Oh yeah, the basketball player. I remember him from two years ago. He seems kind of shy, doesn't he?"

"Maybe, but Ray says he's in the TGIF club and his fraternity is known for having good guys."

"Is he Catholic? I heard a rumor once he was. That's out if he is. I'm not going through that again."

"Geez, Daisy, it's just a dance. You're not marrying him. Besides, I think he's Methodist."

"Methodist? Why is he here?"

"I don't know. Basketball scholarship, I guess. I hear his family is real poor. His mother died when he was little, something like that and the father got hit hard by the Depression." Faye had a little bio on most everyone in school. Talkers get the skinny eventually.

"Well, maybe. Hmm. He seems kind." Daisy gave it some thought. She didn't feel anything big stir when she considered Gerald, certainly not the wheels of fate turning into position to carry the two of them into a lifetime.

"He is handsome. And there is something serious about him. I like that." The idea was growing on her. Faye sensed traction and went for the deal.

"Good! Then it's settled. When you gonna ask him?" She was leaning forward, nearly falling off the couch, and Daisy laughed at the sight of her eagerness.

"Calm down, Faye. I'm just getting used to the idea." But Daisy knew of all the possibilities there was something compelling about Gerald. She mulled it over in her mind and then, feeling a need to relieve her best friend of the suspense, she said, "All right. I'll give it a go."

Faye shrieked and leapt into her arms. "I'll be the maid of honor, right?"

Georgia lightly slapped her on the cheek and pushed her over on the couch. They laughed and headed off to the drugstore to celebrate with a cherry Coke, giddy with excitement and ready to plan Daisy's strategy.

Two days later Daisy walked into their room after class and saw Faye on her bed reading a textbook. She looked up at Daisy with the same question in her eyes she'd greeted her with since Saturday's decision to ask Gerald to the dance.

"Well? Today? Did you?" She jumped to her feet when Daisy nodded, though she could tell by her expression something was missing.

"What did he say? What?"

"No."

"What? No?"

"No."

"No, what else did he say?"

"Nothing."

"Nothing? He just said no? That's all? Nothing, no thank you, wow, how nice, I wish I could, nothing?"

"He just said no and walked on."

"A real charmer this guy."

Daisy smirked. She seemed dazed by the whole encounter. As though something else had been said she couldn't decode. As though she'd walked into an invisible Kansas twister and been thrown out sometime later unable to account for the lost time. What should have been a "no" heard round the world was not that at all. In fact, the little girl they called "Baby" found the no strangely compelling. Strangely affirming to some area of her self a very long way from the reaches of awareness. She looked like a person who had seen into the future and then just as quickly forgotten what was revealed.

Daisy sat down next to Faye's book and looked at the floor. Faye sat down and put her arm around her friend, somehow sensing a beginning to the end of their time together.

"It's okay, sweetie. There's always Scottie; so what if he can't dance? Cheer up, Daisy, you can come with Ray and me if nothing works out."

Daisy smiled at her friend with the resigned look of one who is no longer fighting with fate. "Thanks, Faye, you're so sweet. But I'll be fine. I need to catch up on my studies anyway. Besides, you wouldn't let me dance with Ray and you know it." The two friends laughed and leaned into each other at the shoulder.

"Oh, Daisy, you're the best." Faye laughed and held onto Daisy's hand and wouldn't let her go for a long time.

The next day as Daisy walked back from class, Gerald ran across the street to join her. Each said hello like they were 13 and about to ask for a dance. "Sorry I was so rude yesterday," Gerald stammered.

"That's okay." Daisy looked at him. She saw a kind, shy boy looking at his feet. A little acne distracted her at first from seeing a handsome proud Gary Cooper-like face.

"I don't suppose I could reconsider that question from yesterday?"

"I suppose you could."

"Well then I'd like to say yes this time."

"That's a lot better."

"Thanks, and thanks again for the second shot. I'll see you soon."

And so he did. Gerald saw Daisy to the dance and they had a good time, mostly talking with Faye and Ray over Cokes. He said he didn't dance much and she said it didn't matter though secretly she wished he did. Gerald didn't notice the longing in her eyes as she watched the others dancing together. And Daisy didn't pull him out on the floor like many of the girls did with their reluctant dates. They sat together and occasionally spoke of the usual things. She tried to get him to talk about himself and basketball but he seemed reluctant. No fireworks went off but he was pleasant enough to be with so Daisy had no special reason for refusing his invitation to have a Coke the following weekend.

It went that way for the rest of the spring term. Daisy had all the volition of a twig broken from the branch of a tree that falls in the creek and is carried downstream until it is caught in sticks and leaves at a narrowing. That is how she came to get involved with Gerald.

He was crazy about her but she left for summer break without strong feelings or the sense that she would miss him terribly. In fact, she was glad to get away because as they had seen more of each other, he began to talk at length about his mother. Daisy listened with sympathy the first time he told the story of Ruth. She felt drawn to the sad outline of his mouth and the obvious devotion to his mother. Something told her she could make his sadness go away and that would make her smile all the more. However, he was still talking about Ruth when Daisy left in June and she found herself in the quandary of how to tell him to stop without hurting his feelings and without revealing her own selfish motivation.

She tried, over the summer, to compose a letter explaining her feelings and encouraging him to put the past behind him. After all, people would think it strange of a grown man to talk so much about his mother. Particularly his deceased mother. However often she tried to find just the right words, it never came together in a way Daisy felt comfortable with. The mirror didn't allow her to hurt someone's feelings and the cowering little girl lacked the assertion to tell someone what they ought to do. Besides, she wasn't sure how she felt about Gerald. In all honesty she couldn't say she missed him much. Not like Larry. But maybe Larry was a childish crush. Gerald was something of an enigma. Quiet for certain, but also oddly remote, as if he were mostly preoccupied. Neither did he laugh much although she could see that her smile lifted his heart and he looked at her with adoration when his guard was down. Something spoke to her of a goodness within his soul. Someone had loved him dearly. Daisy could also see the determination in his spirit. She knew he would be successful and provide her with security and comforts as her father had.

Each week she wrote to Faye and told her how much she missed her company. She asked Faye if Gerald was right for her. Once in a while she complained about her mother's moods. But the summer passed quickly and before she knew it Daisy found herself back at good ol' Valpo, walking with Faye under the lovely maple canopy and gabbing until midnight about her summer at the lake. She picked up with Gerald where they left off and, despite his continuing to elaborate on his mother's virtues, she felt herself growing more fond of this tall, dark, and handsome man.

"What should I do?" As with everything else, Daisy brought the problem of Ruth to Faye. "He brings up his mother nearly every time we're together. It makes me feel like there's three of us holding hands. It's creepy, Faye."

"Tell him he should live in the present. You're his girl now and he should be talking about how great you are, not the ghost on his shoulder. Tell him to bury her once and for all. Or else."

"Or else what?"

"Or else you'll find another boyfriend who'll make you the center of his world, not some ghost hanging around where it doesn't belong."

Daisy marveled at Faye's bold personality. She envied her courage and vowed to make a stand with Gerald at their next meeting. Her belly whirled with butterflies but she threw back her shoulders and told herself she would do it.

Gerald was oblivious to his obsessive preoccupation with Ruth. He had grown accustomed to her presence in his mind and speaking of her out loud to Daisy felt natural and very much the same as thinking of her. It felt to him like introducing the girl he loved to the most important person in his life. And he did love Daisy. It surprised him how much he felt for the slim brunette with the knock-out smile who, quite out of the blue, approached him on the sidewalk that day after accounting class. What an idiot he must have looked like to her!

Now he felt things he'd never felt for anyone but Ruth. Already, in the bewildering theater of the mind, their faces and smiles were braiding together and merging into one remarkably soothing image that now had an outer as well as an inner reflection. Gerald made up his mind that Daisy was the girl for him. He considered himself tremendously lucky to have found someone with her grace and style. So when she asked to stop and have a little talk that Friday afternoon walking home to her house, Gerald felt a pang of fear lance his throat. He knew he wasn't the most exciting fellow around campus, and he feared she was about to let him off gently but surely.

"Gerald, I've been thinking, you know, how long have we been dating now?"

Gerald paused, fearing what was coming. "Well, I suppose if you count summer, well, about eight months. Why?"

"Well, sweetie, it's just that a girl likes to feel she's special, and the most important person in the whole world to her boyfriend."

"Daisy, you are. Really, you are that." Gerald was breathless to convince her. His heart beat faster than on the basketball court and he thought of the murmur that had been diagnosed that year, effectively ending his basketball life. "Really, Daisy, you're the greatest, I..."

"But, Gerald, sometimes I don't feel that way. Oh, I don't want to hurt your feelings, but sometimes you talk about your mother so much, it seems like you'd rather be with her. Like she's more important and sitting here between us almost. It's not natural, Gerald. It really isn't. You've got to stop talking about her all the time. We should be talking about our life here at Valpo or our dreams or even the future." Daisy was on a roll now. Gerald stared at her and then looked at the ground.

But Daisy wasn't done. "People will wonder about you and me. They'll think we're strange to be sitting at the drug store sipping a Coke and talking about your mother pushing you in the swing and singing songs from the 1800s. For goodness sakes, Gerald, do you want people to think we're odd? You have to put all that behind you now. Please, will you do that for me?"

Gerald sat on the bench in a daze. The normally rational thought process which dominated his mind was scrambled and in a free fall. He blinked to try and bring himself back to the moment and Daisy's request, but he found it about as difficult as trying to wake himself from a bad dream. With all the will at his disposal he pulled himself up from the tailspin and looked into the green eyes of Daisy. Gerald knew how to stop talking. He was a pro. And he was not the least surprised when he heard himself say, "Sure, Daisy. I'll stop talking about her. You bet."

"Really, Gerald? You'll really do it?"

"Sure I will. I'll do it for you Daisy. I'd only do it for you."

Daisy felt her heart surge and she leaned into Gerald and kissed him like she never had before.

"Hey, anything else I can stop talking about?" They both laughed and held each other tight but at the back of his mind Gerald felt the full weight of the Brennan Curse descend upon his soul. As it fell upon him, his tongue severed and, like a frightened snake, slithered away faster than the eye could perceive and took a hiding place beneath the garden rocks. In that instant, Gerald took his place in the long line of Brennan men who would not talk. And from that moment on, a loathing for talkers filled his chest. Agi, Jan, Millie, all of them. Neither of the two noticed the shifts in his interior makeup. Nor did they notice the cobbled bits of his young self break up and scatter to different corners of the world taking with them the four-year-old boy lying on Ruth's lap and vanishing into the swamplands of an impenetrable psychic jungle.

The young couple did not notice because they were now in love and in that very moment of embrace found themselves at the mouth of a great river, a turning point they had not foreseen or asked for. But there they were, sealing the pact that would define their arrangement and carry them throughout a thirty-year journey to the Promised Land of Hilton Head: the Island Paradise.

The pact offered Gerald the uncanny answer to a dream. In Daisy, he had found the perfect solution to the unending sorrow of his life; Daisy would agree to be Ruth, love and comfort him and never leave his side. As he sat in his recliner as an old man and she sat on the couch, and as they gave themselves to the trance of program after program on the television, his wife and his mother would be one. When Daisy smiled and called him sweetheart, the warmth rising from his chest was a response to both Daisy's kindness and, simultaneously, the embodiment of Ruth within that loving kindness.

In return, Daisy would be his Doll, the centerpiece of his existence. He would work hard and remove her from the bleak Midwest pettiness and take her to the land of fashion and good taste. There she would be surrounded by flattering mirrors that, allied with her determination, might easily defeat the nagging residue of disease left in her heart by the strange appearances of the little man with red hair.

Neither Gerald nor Daisy said a word as they walked back to her sorority house that afternoon. Daisy was thinking of telling Faye every detail of the day. Gerald was thinking of Daisy's green eyes and the kiss that made his thoughts stop. They were carried home that evening and the rest of their days by the combined forces of fate and circumstance whose radius stretched at least a hundred years back into the past as well as into the future. But to the young man and woman it was simply the discovery of love.

෨

Daisy stood at the window of the kitchen preparing coffee for breakfast. She watched bluebirds gathering materials for a new nest. Even after twenty years on the Island the sight of bluebirds darting here and there thrilled her. She was approaching 80 years and the youthful response to beautiful things still soared within her spirit. Families of mourning doves walked across the soft carpet surrounding their property provided by the lengthy needles of Southern pines. Another glorious morning greeted her, and Daisy sang along with the goldfinches and tanagers a song she loved and, as of late, found herself repeatedly singing aloud and to herself from one of her favorite shows, *The Sound of Music*. Oh, how she needed that music now. She remembered the words, "Raindrops on roses," and the expression on the children's faces when Julie Andrews sang to them. She tried desperately to transform herself, to lose herself in the beauty of the melodies. But she could not. Gerald lay dying in the next room.

Daisy looked around at her favorite things: the lovely lagoon, the great blue heron, the Carolina blue sky; she remembered all her favorite things and still she felt bad. Her singing was theatrical, emotional. The melody helped to obscure but could not conceal the melancholy line of harmony that accented her arrangements. Not even singing along with Fraulein Maria could lift her completely from the sad feelings and disturbing agitation pressing against her throat. At times she wanted to scream and this frightened her all the more.

"Get a hold of yourself, Georgia," she would say to herself. "Georgia, where is your noggin?"

Stern as she was with herself, the measures of self-reproach were only temporarily effective. She smiled more than ever and people commented on how good she looked despite everything. When strangers discovered she was approaching 80, they were astonished. The mirror had been good to her.

But life did not consult the mirror or succumb to the charms of her smile. Gerald was dying and he was shutting down the few entries left open since his stroke a decade earlier. He had no interest in food. Still a servant of nourishment, Daisy was disturbed by this development. When he wouldn't even eat his Jello, she lost her composure and, nearly shouting, scolded him, "How are you going to get better if you don't eat?"

Never mind that he was a week from the end and the cancer made sure the only thing he could keep down were ice chips. Daisy was desperate. She felt the world both closing in on her and coming apart at the seams. She sensed a terror lurking in the dark, much as a gazelle might sense a predator creeping closer in the bush. Was she afraid of being alone? Or afraid of being? Being which now made itself known, really thrust itself upon her and molested her equilibrium, as the reality of Gerald's condition confronted her every day. She tried to be brave. And strong. But she was neither and when trying to sleep through the night, even with the nightstand lamp left on for security, she trembled.

So little of her remained after the many years of conforming to the specifications of the Doll/Mother that to herself and to others she came to resemble a mannequin. Her face was frozen in the smile that once turned heads. And her eyes betrayed the panic creeping into her daylight hours. Had she ever been alone? Or decided for herself how to live? Had she ever balanced a checkbook or paid a bill? Had she ever cooked for one or come home to an empty house?

Fear, that most loyal of relatives, moved into her stomach like Sherman's Army into the South. She tried to move away from its scorched touch. She thought of her mother and father with terrible longing. She remembered the agony of each passing. The stab in her heart when her mother turned on her.

Remembering and forgetting pushed and pulled at her like playground bullies. Daisy held her breath. Fragments of the past pummeled her like hail. Moments later she stood in an alarming blankness. Returning and leaving. Memories, coming and going. Was she going crazy? She couldn't remember a song to sing.

Gerald. She'd forgotten Gerald. She rushed to the family room where he lay in a hospital bed. He looked awful. She couldn't bear to look long enough to see if he was dead or alive. "Honey, Honey!"

Nearly screaming now. "Gerald." He stirred and she felt bad for disturbing him.

Daisy tried to pull herself together. She threw her shoulders back and left the room reprimanding herself for her weakness. Her unconscious served up a tune and she walked back to the kitchen humming it. What were the words? What show was that? "Climb every mountain..." The lyrics burst from her mouth. For a second she felt relief. A surge of confidence. But it was fleeting as everything else. The spinning returned. The Holy Mother vanished. Georgia couldn't remember why she came to the kitchen. She put her hand on the counter top to steady herself. Should she take Gerald some ice chips? When was Hospice coming? Where is Jimmy? Fear and dread. Such confusion. And then the phone rang. Daisy picked up the receiver hurriedly, fearful the caller might be gone. "Hello." Her greeting was a plea. A cry for help that extended to the Heavens.

"Georgia, Georgia, dear, this is Millie. How are you, my sweet darlin'?" Millie's voice resonated through every chamber of her body. It was the song of a nightingale. Thank God. She sat down at the breakfast table and smiled. Her prayer answered. She composed herself and then chuckled nervously, as if she'd been caught with her hand in the cookie jar.

"Hi Millie. Oh, I'm fine, fine. How are you?"

# CHAPTER 8
# Food and Hunger

୬

It is a few minutes before midnight when Dagwood Bumstead lifts his blankets and ever so quietly slips from bed. Blondie is sleeping on her side with her back to the room and is undisturbed by Dagwood's movements. He tiptoes to the door. The dog watches his furtive gait and follows to the head of the stairway where Dagwood pauses, now confident his departure has gone undetected. A gleam that stretches from ear to ear lights up the hallway, and the two merry companions scamper down the stairs. When we next see Dagwood, he is seated at the kitchen table admiring a skyscraper sandwich, at least a foot tall, and layered with every imaginable leftover a refrigerator can hold. It is a thing of beauty, bulging with tomatoes and beef, pickles and cold cuts. Lettuce and baloney, mayonnaise and mustard are spilling out from between ten stories of fresh bread and the whole thing is crafted with enough care and skill to rival the Empire State Building.

And in his moment of triumph, before he takes that first impossible bite, Dagwood Bumstead pauses and looks us in the eye. The gleam has doubled. The master of the nap is glowing like a three-year-old who has found his blanket. Though he has been secretive until now, he does not feel caught. He does not feel hand-in-the-cookie jar embarrassment. A puppy feels more shame than Dagwood. He can look at us with unabashed delight because he knows we understand and share in his exuberant victory. He can look at us without a trace of self-consciousness and proclaim for every white American man, "I have it all." His is a triumph over hunger. The defeat of longing. He can eat when he wants. As much as he wants. There in the privacy of his kitchen it is all in his hands and nothing can take it away. Not the list of jobs Blondie will have for him in the morning. Not the demeaning blows Mr. Dithers will pummel him with on Monday. He is alone with his catch, ready to devour every last crumb, ready to fill his stomach to its maximum capacity. His jaws will unhinge like a snake's to take in the towering meal. And his mouth, the happiest part of his body, the home of his voracious appetite, will explode with sensations so exhilarating as to satisfy every molecule of his desire. He will eat until the plate is empty. He will lick his lips and sigh. The dog will look at him and smile after scarfing up the last of the droppings. When he is finished, Dagwood Bumstead will walk the stairs to his bedroom. He will tuck himself in beside his unsuspecting wife, roll over on his side, smile, and sleep like a baby. Content with a full belly and the knowledge that he lives in a land of plenty.

&#x6BD;

At another table in another land, Gerald stares at his dinner plate. He stares at the boiled potatoes and the scrap of dry meat. The bread in his mouth is hard, and the chewing required to break it down tires him. He gives up and pushes his chair away from the table.

"Why aren't you eating?" Warren's first words of the night sound like a dog barking at a stranger. Gerald says nothing.

"Answer me." The dog begins to snarl.

"Not hungry."

"Eat your damn food. Do you know what it cost me to get that meat? Do you know what I have to do to feed you? Digging those damn ditches every day to earn a couple of goddamn dollars and then you won't even eat the goddamn food on your plate."

It's January of 1937. Food is still hard to come by. Times remain bleak in the small farm towns of northern Indiana. Ruth has been gone for six months, and Gerald's stomach is sick with loneliness for his mother.

"I told you I'm not hungry."

"You're never hungry. Look at how skinny you are! How can you play basketball when you won't eat?"

"I can play all right."

"You just sit around moping. Feeling sorry for yourself. That won't get you anywhere and it won't bring your mother back either."

It was the first mention of Ruth and her passing since the heat of August. The space between them cringed. Memory of the terrible summer heat must have come back to Warren in that instant. He must have smelled the sweat and the torment of his three sons. It was unbearable then and now and so he shot back at Gerald, "You stink. Go take a bath."

"What?"

"I said you stink. You smell terrible. Take a bath."

"There's no hot water. Besides, who are you to talk? You smell like crap every night after that lousy job digging ditches and crawling around sewers all day. You take a damn bath."

Gerald pushes away from the table and is out the door headed to his room as his father hurls curses at his back from the table. Gerald doesn't stop and he doesn't hear tonight what he has heard so many other nights. He only hears his father's shouts fade into the wallpaper and his own contempt muffled in his throat. "I hate him. I hate him." Gerald is determined to deny his father the satisfaction of his anger. He slams the door to his room and sprawls on the narrow bed in the corner. The room is cold. Mold is growing on the walls. Six months have passed since the sun died. They are living in a boarding house on the edge of town. Edgar and Earl live with their wives on the other side of Wheeler. Gerald is alone with Warren. "That bastard. I hate him." He punches the pillow and repeats again and again what is by now less of a feeling and more a fact. A permanent installation. "I hate this goddamn house. This stupid town. That worthless asshole."

But most of all he hated nightfall and being alone in that room, when the emotions of his dreaded life come out like rats at a garbage dump. When the mold on the wall seems to grow on the back of his throat. And worst of all there is the torment of waiting. Waiting that is unbearable, waiting for Ruth to come back, waiting to escape this rotten place and waiting for the heaviness sitting on his chest to vanish.

He will not eat again until he meets Daisy and they have fled Indiana, the Depression, and the graveyard of feelings that come out at night to haunt him. His is an anorexia of the heart. Hatred is the armed guard protecting a vault containing what love remains in the soul of this 17-year-old boy. As a consequence, Gerald is shrinking. He is unaware of the change, the constriction tightening its grip around a receding inner world. An innerness that more and more each day resembles a narrow lead pipe.

He is unaware because all he can think about, all he can talk about, with his brothers and friends, is Ruth. Her memory is a fish at the end of his line trying to escape. He struggles to hold on, to reel in his mother's face, her presence. He struggles with how to keep her near but not feel the anguish threatening to pull him into the river's channel. And there in the confines of four walls that are closer to a prison cell than a bedroom, in that field of desolation, without really knowing what he's doing, Gerald begins to construct what is not truly a memory, nor a story, but a remarkable three-dimensional image of his mother caring for a child unscathed by the cruelties of life. What the image is made of is a mystery. It resembles a dream but while the dream is made of crepe paper, this idol will endure as though it were made of solid gold. Who made this wonder of the world so impervious to wind and rain that a spider would stand before it in awe? This boy, who later in his life became an accountant, arranging numbers day in and day out, never suspected in himself the presence of a Michaelangelo sculpting a likeness of his mother that would endure for seventy years.

That would be his sole nutrient. The daily bread feeding his emaciated being until the world changed and food began to rain from the heavens and fill the shelves of grocery stores all over America. Until he found Daisy, who would take care of him and make him forget the hunger of those nights and the bad taste in his mouth. Until they found together the land of plenty and were at last free of want and free to want.

∞

Jimmy is sitting at the breakfast table watching Daisy prepare her food. She is chattering on as the wheat bread pops up from the toaster. Though he is not listening, irritation grows in his belly, hearing the jolly laughter that punctuates what to him is the same story told again and again. This morning she is going on about her friend Maryella, a tiny, china doll woman, and their last phone conversation that went on for nearly an hour and left both of them weak from laughter. It is 1966 and the women of suburban Connecticut have that kind of time to visit and laugh at the silly things in life. Maryella is a Midwest transplant as well and they have bonded out of a familiarity born from that experience. Their bond is an alliance against the snobbery of the native women. They engage together in certain rituals on the phone in order to conceal the inferiority each carries into this wealthy New England village situated within the kingdom of New York City.

This is her second breakfast. The first was with Gerald, seeing him off in the early hours to catch the train into Manhattan. Her day is structured around eating, buying, or cooking food. For her second meal of the morning, she has chosen toast and honey. Honey is a recent discovery and it so delights her palate that she begins to act like a little girl with a peppermint candy her daddy has brought from town.

Jimmy has eaten but is keeping her company as he often does when his father is gone. He is 17 and finally adjusted to the change from Ohio to Connecticut. The mirror has its way with him in the privacy of his inner life, but he has found a place for himself in the social world of this vastly different place.

The merry tales of her conversations with Maryella are interrupted by the sound of toast popping from the toaster. Daisy pops up after it, places it on her plate, and carries it to the table admiring the golden brown color evenly spread across the bread. Seated at the table she scoots her chair in and like a little girl at a tea party begins the ritual of preparing her food. The napkin is neatly arranged on her lap. Silverware checked to assure it is in place. Her manners are impeccable. She has been well trained and therefore remembers, just prior to picking up her knife, to include Jimmy.

"Sure you don't want to have some toast with me, Jimmy?" Her voice is like a flute imploring the listener to join its mood.

"No thanks, Mom."

"Are you sure? This honey is so scrumptious!" She is using her endearing, how-can-you-say-no-to-me smile. The one that overrides the wishes of others. He has joined her at the table to dispel her loneliness but resists the temptation to lose himself in this new taste. Asking again only adds to the growing feeling of annoyance he has to hide.

"No, Mom, I'm fine."

"Okay, but you don't know what you're missing!"

And with that the dance of making her toast begins. Her gestures are meticulous. They belie any sense of urgency. Smiling all the way, she slowly spreads the butter across the toast. No, it is painted. Not too much but enough to give the brown a warm glow. None will spill over the edges of the crust. Everything is done between the lines. With that accomplished, Daisy reaches for the jar of honey. Her pleasure brightens. She neatly measures out two teaspoons of clover honey from the Winnie the Pooh plastic bottle and follows up with dabbing it over the surface of toast, which is now dripping with the stuff. Her eyes are gleaming, brimming with anticipation.

"Boy, Jimmy, sure you don't want some?" Daisy speaks in a girlish voice. Coquettish, almost flirtatious.

"Nope."

The moment arrives and Daisy picks the toast up, perfectly controlled, and takes a dainty, lady-like bite. She eats like a bird. This bugs Jimmy to no end. He thinks of slamming his fist on the table but backs away. He wants her to act like a grown-up. But with that first taste, she purrs like a kitten, closes her eyes, and proclaims with immense delight, "Umm, this toast good, Jimmy." It is a family expression originating from the time Jimmy was three and made his way one Sunday morning to the pumpkin pie on the kitchen counter where he carved a hole from the center of the pie with his fingers, and, looking straight into his father's eyes, declared, "This pie good, Da." Even Gerald's petrified heart had melted slightly with young Jimmy's sweet pronouncement. The saying survived as a family keepsake brought out to express innocent pleasures, usually involving food, not comfortably given the voice of adulthood.

By this time, Jimmy can hardly look at his mother. For reasons he cannot fathom, he is seething inside. He cannot stop the images flashing in his mind, the terrible sights he has to live with. Why would he think these things about his mother who is kind and gives so much of herself? Why would he imagine leaping from his chair and strangling her? Grabbing the toast and smearing the honey over her face? Surely, he is a monster.

He can hear the bathroom mirror chortling. Why hasn't he outgrown these awful feelings? What would she think of him if she ever knew what nastiness lived inside his heart?

Jimmy is good at hiding and Daisy never suspects her son's darker impulses. But for Jimmy, it is more than disturbing. Because of it, he is transported back to other moments when such feelings overtook him. This particular morning he finds himself in Ohio early on the same day he turned into the eleventh Indian and fell from Daisy's closet covered in ketchup.

The morning is quite ordinary. Frosted Flakes for breakfast. Buckets of milk. The usual supply of maternal sweet nothings coming from Daisy as he and Frank eat their cereal. No one senses foul play in the air. Least of all Jimmy, who happily consumes the sweet milk at the bottom of his bowl. "What can we do today, Mom?"

"Well, I need to go shopping. We're low on food. What sounds good for supper?"

"Steak! We haven't had steak for a long time." Frank loves tearing into a good piece of meat.

"Baby special. I love that stuff." Jimmy loves the dish named after his mother, who was called by that name by her mother until her dying days when she had become so senile she stopped calling Daisy anything but traitor.

"All right, I'll see what the butcher has. Frank sweetie, steak has been very expensive lately but I'll see what I can do. Okay?"

"Sure Mom. But I hope they have some. I like it rare and juicy."

The talk of food made them all giddy. Food was everything. They believed that as long as there was food on the table, a person didn't really need anything else. The land of plenty was bursting with new houses and automobiles, but nothing spoke to the people like the abundance of food.

Gerald and Georgia had lived through the time of scarcity, when night after night they looked down at their plates and saw nothing but scraps of old food. And little of it. Old bread. Old potatoes. Their bellies did not know the feeling of fullness. Their mouths did not know the thrill of fresh tastes. Their dreams could not imagine what they found in the land of plenty.

"Let's make a shopping list, boys." Daisy took a pencil and paper and sat down at the kitchen table with Frank and Jimmy to make her grocery list for the day. That she could make a list thrilled her to no end. That she could drive to the Acme grocery store in her own car, fill a cart with food, pay for it on the spot with cash or check, and return home with three or four bags filled to the top convinced Daisy she had died and gone to heaven.

"Okay now, let's see, Frank you wanted steak and Jimmy wants the special." Daisy began to jot down the items in impeccable handwriting. She had been an English teacher before Frank was born and never stopped advocating for perfection in grammar and penmanship. The list began thoughtfully and grew like a line of ants after a sugar spill.

## Shopping List

*steak*
*hamburger and buns*
*can of tomatoes*
*macaroni*
*baked potatoes*
*milk*
*baloney*
*hot dogs*
*Wonder bead*
*margarine*
*Velveeta cheese*
*iceberg lettuce*
*mayonnaise*

Daisy said each item out loud as she wrote it. Appreciation outlined each word. She spoke in her sing-song voice. Today she was genuinely happy and her speech came from the love she felt for her boys and the joy of being a mother. They were precious to her. Though she could not let them touch her body, Frank and Jimmy felt their mother's love. And they felt it most obviously in the ceremonies of eating where Georgia was able to give what she believed most important to their lives.

What she did not realize was the emotional and spiritual poverty that had followed them to the land of plenty. A stowaway on their freedom wagon that stuck in the skin like a parasite and robbed the boys of satisfaction despite the abundance of smiles and good food. And into the gap that grew between the given and the absent stepped the genius of American post-war capitalism, delivering unto the masses the perfect substitute: the snack.

"How about some snacks?" Daisy's voice jumped an octave higher.

"Yeah!" The boys shouted their approval in unison. An involuntary craving coated the cavity of their mouths. Images of favorite snacks danced in their heads like it was the night before Christmas. Dr. Pavlov nodded his head. One by one they shouted their preferences:

*potato chips*
*pretzels*
*Pepsi*
*Fritos*
*Kool Aid*
*ice cream*
*peppermints*
*Twinkies*
*Ding Dongs*
*cupcakes*
*peanuts*
*popcorn*
*cookies*

Daisy wrote furiously to keep up. The list grew longer than her arm. The boys ran out of breath naming their favorite snacks. They finished flushed with anticipation. The snack was salvation. Twenty-four hour Eucharist. Food for the perpetually hungry. Anesthetic for the unhappy spirits wandering amongst the aisles of fulfillment.

Jimmy had taken to snacks like an infant to a wet-nurse. Hunger migrated north from the stomach to his mouth and became a constant sensation of lack. Though he loved snacks, Frank gravitated to the quick burger at the drive-ins popping up all over town. His hunger left the belly and went to his eyes where he constantly scanned the world for prey, ravenous for contact. Jimmy wanted to take in and taste and fill himself up. Frank wanted to bite and chew, exercise his jaws, and break life down. Each was insatiable. Each fit his hunger to his personality and his personality became his way of eating. Jimmy took to the couch and TV. His solution was passivity, isolation. Frank took to the car and drive-in. His solution was aggression. Social. Though they were different, they were the same, slaves to a desperate wanting that did not wane. A thirst they could not quench.

Jimmy teetered and tottered between salt and sugar. Sugar and salt. His beloved Yin and Yang. The opiates of his existence. He went for the rush. For the electric flood of sensation that transformed his mouth into a crystal palace. That magically morphed his tattered burlap self into silk. Again and again he tried to recreate the first bite. Nothing compared to the first taste. To the initial hit of flavor. It was like going from black-and-white to color TV. He ate fast and developed a muscle for swallowing. Swallowing made room for another mouthful and contributed to the constancy of oral sensation. He was Rat Boy. Scurrying from cupboard to cupboard sniffing out treats. Tracking down that elusive oral satisfaction.

And of all the great snacks spread on the buffet table for the children of America, two became his favorites. His heroin. Twinkies and pretzels. The Twinkie. The Hostess Twinkie. Brought to him by his mother. The ultimate hostess. Packaged as a pair. Twins, side by side. What could be better, more American, than the Twinkie?

Daisy packed them in his school lunch along with baloney sandwiches. He ate the baloney but he lived for the Twinkie. He loved biting into the firm yellow cake that was so sweet and moist, but he yearned to find the creamy filling buried in the center. Pure delight. He could eat a dozen without coming up for air. A whale dining on carp. Rat Boy. Eat fast. Swallow hard. Another. Another, before it's taken away.

Having exhausted the sugar instinct he turned to salt for balance. The pretzel was perfect because of the abundance of salt sprinkled over its body. He devoured bags of pretzels alone with the TV. With a Pepsi as chaser, he broke them down into parts and cleared them of each crystal of salt before crunching the bits into crumbs he could flush down his throat. When Rat Boy was terribly famished, he took a pretzel and licked the salt with his tongue until the whole pretzel was stripped. When the salt was consumed, he put the pretzel back in the bag and took another and sucked it until it was bare. He did this until his tongue was raw. Until his belly was foaming. Until he was somnolent.

༄

It is a typical Saturday afternoon. Dagwood Bumstead sees that the coast is clear and sneaks away from his household jobs in search of the living room sofa where he indulges in one of his trademark two-hour naps. He is a boy who still needs his nap. Because he is a boy, he does not dream of Blondie in her negligee. Today he dreams of bowling with Herb. He is rolling a perfect game. It is the ninth frame and the pressure is mounting to a fever pitch. Beads of sweat bigger than blueberries rain from his brow. He is trembling but rolls another strike. Herb leaps to his feet cheering for his neighbor. One more strike and he's done it: a perfect game. Dagwood prepares to make his final approach at perfection. His face is all seriousness and more worried than when facing Mr. Dithers for a raise.

All eyes are on Dagwood as he takes the first step toward glory. The bowling alley is perfectly quiet. His ball makes the long, lonely journey down the lane and finally crashes into the horizontal pyramid toppling all ten pins with authority. Dagwood leaps two feet in the air. His eyes are bigger than chestnuts, his smile goes out the door. Friends and fellow bowlers mob him and carry Dagwood Bumstead, hero of the day, to the bar where they celebrate with burgers and beer. And not ordinary burgers. Four-inch-high burgers with onions, tomatoes, and pickles. Dagwood is in hog heaven. By the time he reaches home, the lights are off and his family is asleep. He tiptoes in and heads directly to the kitchen where he finishes off the night with a huge piece of chocolate cake and a tall glass of milk. Both the cake and the milk disappear in a flash. What's left is a white mustache above his lip and chocolate frosting at the corners framing the beaming smile of a five-year-old man who just had the best wish-fulfilling dream a guy could have. Dagwood's needs are simple and he never gets fat.

∽

"I'll have the hot fudge sundae." A broad grin spreads across Gerald's face as the family whoops it up celebrating his love of chocolate as well as the assurance that he can still love something. He recovered well from the stroke that laid him out the night of Daisy's 70th birthday, but his mood is more grim than ever. He feels ashamed when his mind goes blank in the middle of a sentence. Just when his tongue had partially grown back, inspired by the pleasures of retirement and grandchildren, the stroke hit and once again Gerald went into hiding.

It was dessert that brought him out and a smile to his face. Chocolate was available in abundance by the '50s and Gerald took to it like a miner to a gold rush. Chocolate creams. Chocolate cake. Chocolate Dairy Queen. He wasn't picky. By 1980 dessert replaced prayer as the ritual of celebration and gratitude at day's end. And chocolate was the Lord's Prayer of dessert. The Madonna of oral worship.

"Oh my!" Daisy said it for him. Gerald just beamed when the bigger-than-life hot fudge sundae arrived.

"Grandpa! Look at that!" Frank's sons Eddie and Shawn were his biggest fans. He just rolled the perfect game and they let him know it. Sixty years after the Great Depression and forty years after Dagwood's private midnight feasts, indulgence had gone public. Desserts had grown to be huge. Big as a trophy.

Gerald eyed the mound of ice cream smothered with steaming hot fudge. He admired the beautiful spiral of whipped cream and the sprinkling of nuts and tiny chocolate chips that finished off the masterpiece before him. Dessert had reached the level of art that

Gerald could appreciate. That satisfied the hunger in his eyes to see something beautiful and reachable. That satisfied the hunger in his mouth for something so delicious it would carry him to another world. And satisfied the hunger in his soul to forget all that was painful and remember, without thinking of it, all that was sweet.

"How is it, Grandpa?" Everyone knew the answer but wanted to hear it again, in his words.

"Out of this world." Gerald shook his head in awe. "It's out of this world."

∾

"Give us this day our daily bread and forgive us our trespasses, as we forgive those who trespass against us." Lutherans across Ohio murmured these words in unison at approximately ten til noon every Sunday of the year. They dutifully recited The Lord's Prayer while dreaming of the next golf game or trespassing on their neighbor's wife.

But in a time of so much prosperity, the act of trespassing came to be defined as the act of setting foot on someone's property. Transgressions against the spirit of another were largely dismissed as necessary casualties of progress. The trespasses of a people were not recognized, thereby eliminating the need for forgiveness. It was an act of blinding thoroughness. In fact, the collective memory was destroyed with the same brutality and absolute efficiency as the genocide of Native Americans. While Tom Sawyer tricked his friends into white-washing the fence for him, an invisible force seemed to trick the better part of the country into white-washing its past. "History is bunk," someone wearing a swastika shouted. And it was true. Hence, there was no forgiveness needed for slavery. No forgiveness needed for the disappearance of the Shawnee and Potawatomi Indians of northern Indiana. None for the fire-bombing of Germany or the mushroom hell delivered to the people of Nagasaki.

"Give us this day our daily bread." But the people of Faith Lutheran Church of the Missouri Synod could not wait for the Lord to give. They could not tolerate waiting. They could not tolerate uncertainty or an ache in the belly that might resurrect a radioactive past buried without ceremony in the landfill of yesterday. And so they took what they could. Increasingly, that amounted to a manic demand that they never be without. That the comfort of food should always be within reach. Vending machines, pop machines, fast food joints, these were all new species of availability Darwin never imagined. Happiness is a full belly and a mouthful of flavors. Dagwood Bumstead had nothing to forgive sitting at his table. Least of all himself.

∽

Gerald did not forgive the trespasses of his father. He did not forgive himself for not saving Ruth from her sad fate. He did not forgive poverty. Nor did he forgive life for its trespasses, for its ruthless march through the hearts of himself and his brothers.

Daisy did not forgive herself for the trespasses of her brother. She told herself she was a bad girl. She told herself it was her fault for not helping her brother stop the fondling that became their secret. Gerald and Daisy took the vows of forgetfulness together. They agreed the past was dead. The future was bright.

Jimmy did not learn forgiveness growing up in Ohio. He did not learn it at the Lutheran church on Sunday mornings listening to Pastor Sauer scold the people. Four years of catechism only taught him that college would be easier than Pastor Sauer's Bible class. Daisy kept him quiet and still during the sermon by feeding him peppermint Life Savers. Forgiveness and sin vanished sucking on those sugar-soaked pacifiers. They were one of his favorite treats. His mother carried them everywhere in her purse. Never be without. He often raided it when she wasn't looking and made off with a supply for the night.

One after another he sucked until they shrank to a sliver on his tongue. Jimmy did not stop. He was ignorant. Enough was an experience unknown to his world. He ate to forgive. To forgive the murders. To forgive the skinny boy in the mirror. Because he ate to forgive his existence, being itself, or the chaotic thoughts and feelings that pummeled his internal life, his trespasses never ceased. His sorry self was an unforgivable trespass as far as he could tell. And food gave him the ammunition to forgive by annihilating the presence of that which seemed so unwanted and unlovable. It was a preemptive strike against becoming a self he felt certain was trespassing in a world he did not belong in or understand.

Jimmy was not alone in forging an existence out of eating. The family could enjoy his "bottomless pit" as they called it. They rather liked seeing him eat so much. It was a pledge of allegiance. Even though Gerald joked that the boys would eat them out of house and home, eating was the one activity in which excess could be tolerated and even enjoyed. It was a great reassurance to both his parents that never again would they or their children experience hunger.

Meanwhile Jimmy went about his vocation of eating. Bags of pretzels disappeared. Pepsi after Pepsi. On his birthday Daisy made him an angel food cake with a white frosting he found irresistible. The strawberries on top were tolerated, but real food had taken a back seat to the man-made treats bursting with flavor. He ate the cake in a matter of days. Sneaking three or four pieces after school. He ate half a bag of hard candy at a sitting. His pancreas worked overtime trying to keep up. No one said a word. In fact Gerald and Daisy smiled, feeling he was happy and provided for. Truly they had left behind the hardships of their youth.

Only in the hour before dinner did Daisy ever object to her son's habits. "Jimmy, stop drinking so much milk. You'll spoil your appetite." Daisy was as forceful as she ever was when protecting the sanctity of supper.

"Mom, I'm thirsty. Don't worry. I'll eat dinner."

"You can't just eat milk and snacks all the time, sweetie. You have to have a balanced diet."

But balance was as far from their world as the Great Depression. Particularly when it came to milk. Jimmy gulped it down with Oreos, with the birthday cake, with Twinkies and Hostess cupcakes. Milk was the best. The water that tastes like wine. No one drank a drop of water in 1958. Not only did it taste like sulphur, but it reminded them of thirst. Hunger and thirst. And where there is thirst, there is yearning.

No, milk was it. They drank a gallon a day. Half the refrigerator was devoted to the sacred nectar. On weekends they poured Hershey's chocolate syrup in a glass and made it sweet and brown. Not a bite of food was chewed and swallowed without a river of milk to wash it down. It saved Jimmy from the likes of asparagus, which came from cans and made him gag. Linguine had more texture to it. Feeding it under the table to the dog didn't work but enough milk in the mouth could conceal the taste enough to get through the ordeal. Milk. Whole milk. Beautiful milk. The Queen of Hearts. The diamond at the center of a brooch. Their world revolved around milk. The cold creamy liquid splashing up against the interior of his mouth made Jimmy forget the mirror and its list of his deficiencies. Most of all it allowed him to pretend. Pretend that the nourishment in the daily bread of their lives was enough. Pretend that his mother was giving him everything, and more than he needed. That the bountiful supply of milk was feeding his soul as well as his bones.

Jimmy continued to eat in much the same manner into adulthood. He gladly followed in the footsteps of Dagwood Bumstead. At midnight he came upstairs from watching Johnny Carson with a jar of dry roasted peanuts and a Pepsi. At college he and his friends ate Reese's Peanut Butter Cups and a Coke for breakfast. And it was at the university that he learned about marijuana. The sacred weed. The smoke that transformed eating into a religious happening. That transformed food into a miracle and eating into worship. Jimmy and his friends ate more than ever. Chili and strawberry pie before bed. Pizza and beer anytime. They discovered ethnic food.

In Daisy's kitchen most ingredients were white. The flour, the sugar, the bread, and the milk. All of it white as a ghost. White as all the neighbors for as far as the eye could see. Gerald once said in an argument with Frank, "I don't have anything against Negroes. I just don't want to live next to one." And he never did. Theirs was a white world. Littered with white lies and white food.

The closest they got to ethnic food was Daisy's chop suey and her homemade chili. Both were laden with sugar to appease the taste buds and distract from the foreign origins. But college towns late in the '60s were bustling with foreign students and ethnic foods that brought Jimmy and his friends to their knees. They tasted sauces and spices they never knew existed. With gusto and joy they smoked pot and devoured tortillas.

And Jimmy discovered garlic. Garlic was banned from his household. Gerald claimed he was allergic. It made him sick when his dinner was prepared with even a trace of the bulb. He gagged when he smelled it in the air. Frank's girl, Sue, was instantly rejected when he detected it on her breath. His father's reaction was so visceral Jimmy was convinced it was a response to something in his past. Did they use it in Indiana? Was it everywhere in the food when he was stationed in New Orleans during the war? Jimmy recognized it in 1969 as the peculiar taste in the great-tasting hot dogs he and his brother devoured at the Cleveland Indians ball park. Gerald took them to a few games when they were kids. They cheered for Minnie Minoso and ate hot dogs all night. Was his Dad close to throwing up between innings? Gerald went to his grave with that secret.

Daisy adopted the repulsion for garlic and interrogated every waiter in every restaurant she sat down in about the presence, or lack of, garlic in any dish she considered ordering. It became a family joke to her sons who took to sophisticated West Coast dining in their adult years and made a point of enjoying the distinctive seasoning garlic brought to a well-cooked meal. Jimmy even ate it in capsules when the first wave of health fanaticism hit California and Oregon. He reeked of garlic and on the several occasions he and his parents entered an elevator together, he watched with some satisfaction as Gerald turned green and said nothing.

Otherwise, Jimmy and his friends had a merry time eating and drinking as they pleased. One good friend was unsurpassed in his capacity to put food away. Jeff Anderson was fondly referred to as "Animal" by his friends on the football team. He was 5'9", 280 pounds. Jeff was committed to blowing out his heart by the age of 30. He was too smart and too unwilling to comply with the mainstream routine to have a future on this earth. The two enjoyed each other's company and decided to go to Africa by way of France in 1972 following Jimmy's graduation from college and Jeff's tour of duty with the Marines in Vietnam. Jeff became famous at Parris Island not for his bravery and work ethic but for the night that on a dare he jovially downed three chocolate-covered cockroaches. While his comrades cringed and groaned, Jeff crunched and swallowed the disgusting creatures without hesitation. His eating was legendary.

So it was that on the eve of their departure for Paris they went out to celebrate at the local pizza parlor. Jimmy thought he could eat but he was an amateur. That night, with an audience of a dozen or so admirers, Jeff polished off three large pizzas, two quarts of Pepsi, and eleven ice cream sandwiches. With a smile on his face he tromped out of the restaurant, let out an enormous belch, and drove home to sleep it off.

That's the way it was. And though Jimmy could not compete with Jeff, he had a remarkable capacity for shoveling all sorts of food in his mouth. Good or bad, morning, noon or night. Like Dagwood he could eat anything and not gain a pound. Beer, ice cream, popcorn, thousands of calories seemed to burn off overnight and leave him as thin as a rail. He ate like that for years without giving it a second thought until the night of his fortieth birthday when he readied for bed, looked down at himself and was shocked to see his father's pot belly protruding from his boxer shorts. He looked at himself in the mirror hanging above the bureau and saw that it was true. A paunch, exactly like Gerald's, had turned his body into a pear. The mirror laughed out loud and as it did, the familiar stench of shame turned his stomach.

It was the beginning of another secret war. A battle that would last years. Jimmy tried to accept his new shape and actually won some ground by preferring it to the skinny kid in the department store. The weight had filled in his face and chest, which always before looked gaunt and sunken. He liked the big appearance the extra twenty pounds offered. It gave him a short-lived advantage over the slanderous voice of the mirror. Victory seemed possible in those first years of conflict. However, the appetite that once was his ally against unbearable emptiness now turned against him and tantalized every moment like a seductive narcotic.

Jimmy's belly grew out over his belt buckle. His pants became tight in the thigh. When he passed store fronts with large windows he now stole a glimpse at his abdomen and measured out the appropriate amount of self-disgust. The skinny kid and the fat man now sat side by side at the back of his bus. Nevertheless, he was too weak to stop the late-night sleep walking to the modern, double-breasted refrigerator. The urgency in his chest was too great, and his trespasses mounted. And as they did, a new nemesis was born. A different sort of mirror, apprentice to the emperor and its equal in the power to belittle: the scale.

Forgiveness never had a chance. The day Jimmy brought home the sleek Sunbeam digital scale, any hope of kindness left the house like an unwanted guest. The unforgiving scale rested on the floor of the bathroom by the radiator across from the toilet. Completely conspicuous. A clumsy informer. Sitting there waiting like a smug priest for confession. Like an angry father waiting for his child after curfew. It was cloaked in white casing and demanded a purity that ensured his failure. Near the top of the Sunbeam, a black window the size of a pack of Marlboros lay in waiting. Ominous as the dark side of the Force, it dared Jimmy to take the step forward onto its narrow footprint. Then, like an electric shock, the larger-than-necessary scarlet numbers flashed their terrible verdict. A silent siren screamed in his ears. Condemnation. The thing was radioactive. It was the hanging judge from the wild, wild West. Each morning he took the reluctant step. A prisoner of war lining up for the daily hazing. A condemned man walking to the gallows. A game with no exit.

His rulers were food and the scale. One seduced, the other condemned. The numbers in the black mirror went up and down like a blues scale. Jimmy dutifully mounted the scale each morning before breakfast. Inwardly he negotiated something delicate: a cha cha cha with the devil. Backward and forward he moved through the thicket of corruption and redemption. Be good and see what you can get away with. Cheat and disobey but feel bad for the deception and vow to repent and reform your life. Such was the daily script. Repeated like a priest in the monastery reciting his prayers. It did not matter which reform policy he was following; Atkins, low-fat, none. The music was the same. The identical tango with virtue and sin. It occurred to Jimmy to throw the damned Sunbeam out the back door. To clear the area by the radiator of silly notions like redemption. It occurred to him to stand before the mirror above the sink and lay his hands on the body he had never laid eyes on, upon the abdomen rounded and full as the side of a melon, and forgive himself his trespasses. Accept what was unacceptable. Love what was unlovable. Hunger for the quieting of turmoil. But he lacked the courage. He turned from himself and walked to the kitchen table chewing on defeat.

And thus did it happen that the Eucharist was celebrated and the crucifixion enacted. That the emaciated figure hanging above Jimmy's head at Faith Lutheran Church became the prevailing image of an unconscious life. A fresco painted on his interior wall. He saw the protruding ribs, blood dripping from the spikes pounded into the hands and feet. He saw the weathered face and head of Jesus, limp and fallen against his chest, the heaviness of defeat and death upon them. The Lutheran vision passed down from Pastor Sauer's pulpit every Sunday permeated Jimmy's young mind with ease. It was the body of Christ on the cross, not the risen Christ. It was suffering, not salvation, that captured him and held his feet to the fire.

Every meal was the last. Eaten with urgency at a small table DaVinci would never paint. Each morning was the same. Marching to the hill where the cross waited for his sacrifice. Jimmy never knew what sins Jesus committed or how he could have anticipated the sins of a nine-year-old growing up in Ohio two thousand years later. He felt sure his sins were worse. But there was no confusion about the cross itself. There he felt a perfect kinship with the carpenter's son. They shared the identical fate. An aborted Mass that ended only in humiliation. It seemed to be the only road out of town.

Jimmy saw no possibility of exile as his father had. Until 1958. When something happened. Something still reverberating through the planet's destiny. They called it rock and roll. Gerald had moved the family to Connecticut. He was a rising executive in New York and believed the final leg of their journey from poverty had been accomplished. They settled in a beautiful New England town surrounded by lovely old maple trees and large homes built by old money. Daisy was ecstatic to leave behind the depressing fields of the Midwest. Gerald thought they were safe at last from the gravity of 1930. What he did not count on was the seismic shift about to shake the entire world. A shift every bit as powerful as the wars that had preceded its arrival in the latter half of the 20th century. The wind began to howl.

Jimmy's life suddenly found a second track. An anti-Christ. An answer to the figure of despair weighing on his soul. Life surged. He scurried home from school every afternoon to watch *American Bandstand* on the new television set. People were dancing! They shouted "Rock and Roll is here to stay; it will never die." The tired act of Jesus was replaced by the likes of Chuck Berry scooting across the stage on one foot. Elvis Presley discovering the lost continent of the pelvis in front of a national audience. In a short five years, the British would invade and Gerald would shake his head, convinced it was the beginning of the end. Bad enough that that Catholic from Boston was now our president but to see this motley band of long-haired Brits walk into his house screaming "Yeah, Yeah, Yeah" was more than he could stomach. He declared it the end of civilization.

Had he come so far for this? Once again Gerald felt the necessity to flee. When he could, he would uproot and move to a place where it was possible to shield himself from the intrusions of a world that made no sense to him and threatened to undo all that he had built up around his family to protect from unwanted strife.

Jimmy found his breath in the music. He dreamed of being on that stage. In a burst of creative life his parents did not know how to subdue, he took to singing and drawing. For his third-grade class, he walked up and down the aisles singing the hit song "Who wears short shorts?" It was a great success and gave him a taste of the pleasures of exhibition. He made a bet with Frank that by his 13th birthday he too would have a rock and roll hit parading on American Bandstand.

"You will not." Frank mocked his ambitions.

"Yes I will. I'm going to. Little Stevie Wonder did it."

"I'll bet you five dollars you don't."

"Okay. I bet you I do."

The bet was on. And something else was on. Something big. Bigger than Jimmy's dreams of standing on a stage before a screaming crowd of admirers singing "At the Hop." Bigger than Dagwood Bumstead's Empire State sandwich. A crack in the sidewalk outside his door appeared overnight, and a dandelion grew from the slightest of openings. In fact, Gerald was partially correct; a split in the monolithic structure of his world had begun. It was Arctic ice breaking up in spring.

Gerald and his generation would watch in dismay as the great mass of ice and snow parted, and their sons drifted away from everything they valued. The ground rocked and rolled. The quake that hit every neighborhood, that lasted more than a decade and changed the arrangement of American life beyond recognition, swept Jimmy into its currents and carried him far down stream from the known world. For although he lost the bet with Frank and never recorded a rock-and-roll hit, and though his dreams turned to passive fantasies disconnected from real pursuits, Jimmy was different because of it.

A stone thrown from across the river had hit the mirror and caused a crack in the glass. A rival walked on stage. An alternative force vied for his attention. One that challenged the obsessions with food. One that beckoned him to draw wild geese and sing his heart out in the shower. That made him notice the long beautiful legs of his third-grade teacher sitting on top of her desk with her legs crossed and her nylons showing up to her thigh. There were no varicose veins to spoil the view, and there were no words to express the feelings that flooded Jimmy's young body.

He did not realize the awakening for what it was. He could not possibly understand the emergence of a spiritual life so radically unique to all that he understood. But it pulled him along nonetheless. He was like a salmon under the influence of native intelligence swimming upstream to the source of his birth waters.

It would take years and there would be many narrow escapes with death. Spirit would seem to desert him, would seem to disappear altogether and cause him to doubt in the truth of it. He would oscillate, sometimes careen, from fantasies of his well-attended funeral to dreams of concerts packed with adoring fans. From finding life to forsaking it. From binging and purging to singing and dancing: doing to undoing. And though his life was lived largely in fantasy, something the mirror had no trouble denigrating, an undeniable spark had been lit and was doing what it could to become a fire.

All the while the post-war culture, so carefully assembled to provide all comforts and security, was tearing at the heel like an old sock. The marriage of heaven and earth parted like bitter lovers and established separate factions that engaged in a civil war that would last a half-century, past the deaths of both Gerald and Daisy, and show no signs of a cease fire. Vietnam and the Civil Rights movement took the tear and ripped it clean through like an angry bear rampaging a bee hive for honey. Black fought with white. Liberal with conservative. Father with son. Inside every heart and soul and outside in Columbus, Ohio, Berkeley, California, and Montgomery, Alabama, the dual worlds of the individual and society engaged in hand-to-hand combat. The warring parties dueled viciously. It was a standoff between a contemporary emancipation proclamation drunk on electric Kool Aid and a resolute, status quo resistance, hunkered down in bunkers and reading from the Bible as well as the code of trauma, battling for dominion over the world. Red State against Blue State. Should against Want.

∽

Dagwood Bumstead was happy to see the sun set on his day. He was happy to leave behind the black-and-white office work and the tirades Mr. Dithers threw when business was bad. Blondie and a hot meal awaited his arrival back home, and the late night snack promised to smooth out any rough spots from his day. Dagwood was a new man by the time he walked through the door. In fact, he felt a relief from the demands of adulthood and greeted Blondie more as a boy than a grown-up. He ate with a gleam in his eye and slept with a smile on his face; carefree and content.

Gerald was equally happy for the end of the day to arrive. He walked to the train station by himself, glad to be alone and away from the demands of an executive position. Daisy waited to have supper with him every night whether or not the train was on time. When Gerald walked through the door, he looked for her smile. Finding it was like coming in from the cold to a warm fire. In fact, he wanted nothing more than to relax in the presence of that warmth. Nothing more than to sit back in his chair and bask in the silent assurance of a home made safe from neediness.

Jimmy dreaded the end of his day. He worked hard and successfully. He was a model of composure and ate moderately in the years since inheriting Gerald's protruding abdomen. But as the sun went down and the darkness around him grew deep, Jimmy shuddered, sensing the rumblings of the nightly mutation prepare to take him over. It did not require a full moon. He was not Lon Chaney, fretfully watching the clouds part, knowing the night of the dreaded lunar transformation was upon him. Knowing that in a few short moments the monstrous, murderous werewolf would devour his personality and begin a night of carnage.

Jimmy's change happened regardless of what phase the moon was in. It occurred each evening like clockwork. Usually around 9:00 o'clock. Hungry or not. It began with a murmur and ended in a roar. Hair did not cover his body, but his mouth turned into the want of a hungry wolf in winter. Fangs did not grow from his gums, but he stalked the house like a predator growling and foraging for food.

His mouth widened to half the size of Chicago. It was a Godzilla mouth, ready to devour all the sushi in Tokyo. It was a groundswell of hunger. Unstoppable as an avalanche. Must feed. Granola and milk. The sweet milk at the bottom of the bowl. Peanut butter and toast. Followed by milk. Ice cream by the pint. Chocolate Fudge Brownie or Dulche de Leche: the creamy Haagen-Dazs variety. Popcorn and cider. Peanuts. Cashews. Bananas and cream. He ate fast. As though the hyenas were coming to take his catch from him. He fed himself until something subsided. Until the furious storm passed. A restlessness so deep it could not be perceived. He ate to quiet that groundless fall. He ate to keep quiet. To muffle himself. To feel nothing. To be lazy and placid. He ate to eliminate anger. To kill all tension. All desires. And he ate to fill himself, to know a fullness that did not allow for emptiness. That coated the lining of his mouth and stomach with the lotion of presence. As though he were truly there with another, carrying his mother's love in an imagined womb for the comfort of his missing soul.

God forbid if there was nothing to eat in the house that could satisfy Jimmy's cravings. He was every bit as bad as a pregnant woman. Any delay in feeding caused him to snarl and grow fangs. His face and body covered with coarse hair and he pounced on the nearest prey. Being without was insanity. Waiting was intolerable. Was rage.

Jimmy hated any waiting. Waiting in line at the grocery store. Waiting for the traffic to begin moving. He thought of buying a tank and rolling over the cars that blocked his way. But these were minor offenses. Satisfying the demand to eat was tenfold more urgent and the rage that swelled, and at times overflowed, could only be compared to the thunder and lightning of an infant deprived of mother's milk in its moment of need. Told it wasn't time. Told it was wrong to want now. Wait until it is time. The sound and the fury.

The werewolf prowled the premises of the kitchen every night around 9:00 PM. He preferred to move in the shadows away from the sight of others. Quietly and secretively. He stole his food. And it was not the gleeful Dagwood Bumstead who ate the ice cream and cake. There was no gleam in Jimmy's eye. The wolf was grim as he ate. Grim as Gerald sitting alone in his chair. Grim as a starving pup who eats to survive. Jimmy saw himself as weak and pathetic. His flesh swelled with self-contempt. The mirror sent him to the stockades.

Jimmy racked his brain trying to think of how he might make an escape. How he might rid himself of this stain. The late '60s provided a score of possible exits that promised everything from the moon to the stars. In fact, free love, the get-your-shit-together growth movement and spiritual enlightenment were all part of the Baby Boomers' Declaration of Independence, their pursuit of happiness. Each beckoned to the seeker desperate to leave himself behind. Each promised its own version of liberation and renewal. Especially the West Coast variety. A new world had been discovered: an Eden of sensual flowering. Jimmy migrated westward like so many others. And on the eve of that great exodus, he fell apart. He cracked like a window hit by a rock. His identity was thin as single-pane glass. What he knew as Jimmy covered only the surface of his frame from his face down to the ribcage. Rarely did he feel his legs and feet, or the strength of his back and spine. Breathing was shallow and irregular. So that when something within broke, it shattered and a flash flood of anxiety roared through the channels of his body.

California promised to return him to his native land. Sex promised to renew the energy of delight. Therapy promised to make him whole. Meditation promised to end suffering. Jimmy scurried from one to another like a mouse in a cage. A rainbow of offerings greeted his hungry eyes. A smorgasbord of choices was arranged on the table. Sex was as plentiful as candy.

Jimmy fell in love a hundred times a day. He had sex with teenagers and women old enough to be his mother. Made love morning, noon, and night. Copulated in closets and showers, on the lawn and in the car, in the bathroom of a 747 with a stranger and on the kitchen table with his best friend's wife.

Therapies were every bit as abundant. They appeared like orange blossoms in April. He screamed a primal scream alongside his pal John Lennon. Dialogued with empty chairs. Traced his pathology back through generations of pain. Pinned his thinking errors on the donkey. When the werewolf survived these extermination efforts, he traded in the empty chair for a zafu and sat for a week staring at a Zen wall in the hills outside Santa Cruz. From 4:00 in the morning until 9:00 at night, he sat and tried to empty his mind. The 5:00 AM rooster call sent him into peals of laughter, but by midweek he went running from the meditation hall wailing like Adam fleeing the garden.

The next stop was Boulder, where he sat in meditation until blisters covered his butt. A gymnasium full of werewolfs and orphans sat in that hot stuffy cavern waiting for the Tibetan genius to arrive and bless them with the secret teachings. More often than not, he showed up drunk on saki, sixty to ninety minutes late, stumbled across the stage to the guru's chair on his one good leg where he sat for the next ten minutes smirking at the seekers obediently seated on the floor beneath him. When he finally spoke, it was with provocation: "Pissed off, huh? Very Christian, this pissed off." With a shit-eatin' grin, he drop-kicked every single ego and good intention half-way to Kansas City.

Jimmy liked the part where he mocked the Christians. Four years of catechism classes with Pastor Sauer taught him that Christianity and the mirror were on the same side. He left Boulder in despair, convinced his spiritual strivings were fraudulent attempts to escape life.

Back in Portland Jimmy threw himself into psychotherapy. Into BioEnergetics, Neo Reichian body work, Rolfing, Tai Chi, into virtually anything that promised a new life. He saw only his flaws and blemishes. Only the defects in himself. A long-standing childhood fear returned. He worried that his hunger was the result of a tapeworm growing in his stomach. A disgusting creature that had grown as large as twenty yards long and might one day, if he opened his mouth to speak, show its repulsive head and reveal his true ugliness. Likewise, the dreams of overflowing toilets and public nakedness tried to tell him that shame was the ruler of his inner world. Shame was the hit man for the mirror and every time he got hold of something real and good in himself, shame knocked him down again. He tried living the life of Don Juan. He tried living the life of Timothy Leary. When these failed, he tried to live the life of his brother. Surely if he could be like Frank, all would be well. He invented lives and scorned all attempts at authentic living. He tried living, and not living, every life but his own.

∾

Exhausted and defeated, Jimmy slumps to his knees. His forehead touches the ground where finally, some fifty plus years into his life, the realization appears from out of nowhere: he wants to nurse. He wants to nurse at the breast of mother. A mother big enough to hold him. Big enough to survive the fury of his hunger. He wants to hold back nothing. He wants to give everything, take everything; eat to his contentment from her nipple, from her flesh and her eyes. Pressed against her body, chest to her tummy, mouth surrounding the breast, fingers mapping her face, legs wrapped around her ribs, making rope of their bodies. Until he is done. Until he finds satisfaction. And feeling peaceful at last, swimming in the pool of being, released from the tensions of desire, he is free to play with her. And free to bask in the glowing presence uniting one to the other.

Jimmy lifts his head from the floor. The truth is now obvious. With one breath, he is humiliated by the honesty of his desire. With another, he is calmed. The epiphany will ease but not extinguish the urgency of his hunger. It will soothe but not remove the frenzy of his soul. What was known but could not be thought is now both. What could not be found with the short stick of awareness is now illuminated. The quakes that upended his equilibrium took place at such depths as to be imperceptible. They made a mockery of willpower and sent him blindly to the refrigerator like the subject of a hypnosis experiment who raises his arm on command. He paced the halls of his home like an Arctic fox in winter. But there was no understanding the tectonic activity of that beleaguered self. No way to comprehend the force of a living trauma that returns unbidden. Until now. Jimmy rose to his feet sobered and ashamed. Knowing the thrusts and screams of infancy had not ended. Would not end. An unfamiliar warmth met him as he stood. A warmth that spoke words of pity. Pity that was not demeaning. That could stand in his place and look into the eyes of shame and not blink.

But there was yet another feature to the epiphany. Something nearly overlooked in the background and not really in the background. A presence in the cracks, beneath the fold. In-between. Intermittent as light from a distant star. Flickering. So subtle, and, once perceived, so distinct. A radiance without a source. It appeared and vanished.

Jimmy thought he was making it up. He thought he was nearing a seizure. But it persisted and was unforgettable. It spawned a new yearning. A yearning for contact. Contact with that radiance. Hunger for the real. He felt the presence of spirit calling. A spirit embodied in all his life experience. That used every twisted circumstance to make itself known. Bypassing none. Not the naively blissful Dagwood eating his evening snack. Not Gerald, forlorn and inconsolable, sitting in his chair. Not even his own dismal attempts at living.

This yearning would lead him back to Daisy. To the mother who could not let him touch her body. Who fed him self-loathing from a bottle. The same Daisy who charmed the world, whose smile could warm a winter's night. Whose kindness touched the lives of many.

There would be many remarkable experiences along the way in meditation. Joy would flow from mountain lakes into the dry bed of Jimmy's heart. Much would occur that revealed the presence of invisible realms. But realizing the epiphany would require something different. Outside the ashram. Outside everything he thought he could bear.

It would mean returning to Daisy. To his mother. Not as a wanting child. But as himself at her side. Holding her hand while Daisy slowly crumbled. While the present and then the past evaporated into ether, taking every scrap of dignity that was hers, so that the only bits of Georgia Daisy left were held by Jimmy in his battered heart. And when the time came when she looked at him without a trace of recognition, when smiles ceased to blossom across her dear face with his approach, it was he who held her life story out of the reach of mud and decay. It was he who held her hand in the last hours and heard her last grateful breath.

And in doing so he was dumbfounded to find the light of her being undiminished. To find the epiphany shining in the tattered scraps of Georgia Daisy. To realize that all the while what he took to be the Queen of Persona was that and more. To realize the ubiquitous spiritual quest accepted and used the very Daisy he fought and rejected to embody and actualize what could be.

Jimmy wept and he laughed. His cherished ideas rotted on the limb. Fifty-nine years of pushing her away and a few lousy hours of letting her be. And in his awakening, he felt something bigger than he and Daisy lifting. Something heavy and soaked in sweat. What remained was desire. But not the desire to nurse. What remained was the desire to know this radiance. To know its glistening presence. To feel the fullness of plentiful being. And not just in the beautiful and succulent. But in the lowest. In the unacceptable: the ugly and the false. Within the slightest morsel.

# CHAPTER 9
# Forgetting: A History

෧

Three AM. Dead of night. No light. No world. No body. Infinite silence. Deep sleep and dream images. Consorting. Nothing and something. No mind. Particles of becoming make love with deep space. Creation moans. Nothing in something and something in nothing. Being before sound and shape. Non-being before an after. Three AM, clouds forming low on the water. Spirits roam. Eternal peace No self No place Unbroken quiet, unbounded love

A bolt of lightning. Another. Something like thunder. Shaken. No sound. The crack of lightning. No place. A long way to return. Am I tumbling? Where am I? What? That sound. Lightning strikes like a spear. What, a body, which way? Something tugging, urgent, come. Crash, hitting the atmosphere. Slammed into consciousness. Shit. The phone. Oh no. Where? What time? Fuck, 3:00 AM. What are words? Speaking through miles of clouds.

"Hello?" A voice opening like a door with old hinges.

"Hi Jimmy, whatcha doin'?" Georgia's voice was chipper. She could have been a 12-year-old eager to go on a picnic.

"Sleeping."

"Sleeping?" Instantly Georgia is annoyed, sensing she may have done something wrong. "Well, why are you sleeping at this time of day?"

"Mom, It's 3:00 o'clock in the morning." Don't get mad.

A silent gasp comes from the receiver. She's done it again. No. Don't give in. Georgia reflexes to denial.

"No, it isn't 3:00 in the morning. Really? It can't be." She rustles with her phone straining for the clock. Prove it wrong. All wrong. "Well, I can't seem to find the darn clock. Are you sure?"

"I'm sure, Mom. You all right?"

"Oh sure, I'm fine." There is a crack in her voice.

"How about if I call you in the morning?"

"When are you going to come see me?" Georgia tries to camouflage the demand and the panic. Her voice morphs into the shrill growl of a cat, cornered, her back arched.

"I don't know, Mom, soon, I'll try to get over Thursday morning before work."

"Thursday!" She is stunned. Thursday is never. She feels slapped and reacts by collapsing into angry despair. "You mean I have, I have to stay in this God-forsaken place by myself until... When did you say you were coming? Oh God. Do you have any idea what it's like to be here alone all the time? God, I wish I'd never left home."

"Mom, take it easy."

"Take it easy? I thought you were going to help me. When can I come over?" By now her fury is burning the wires.

"I'm sorry, Mom, I'm trying to help."

"You haven't lifted a finger since I got to this awful place. You don't give a hoot. Oh Georgia, what have you done?"

Don't be defensive. "Haven't lifted a finger?" Stop.

"That's right. Not a damn thing. Just dropped me off at this place and left. Why are you asleep now? Why aren't you working at least?"

"I'm sorry you're not happy, Mom. I'll try to get over tonight. We'll have some dinner. Okay?"

"When?" Daisy perks up.

"Soon. About 3 or 4."

"Oh sure, sweetie. That sounds lovely. Okay! I won't keep you now. See you then. Bye-bye, Doll."

∾

Gerald stood by the back door waiting for Georgia to ready herself for their golf date. He was amused by the predictable last-minute delay. It wasn't the bathroom that held Georgia up, though she did require an empty bladder before leaving the house. She had to avoid using the Honey Buckets, which always left her feeling messy. It wasn't the extensive checklist required by the mirror, the hair just right, makeup, lipstick, brush teeth and use water pick, final check on clothing and overall appearance. She had allowed ample time for these preparations. At least an hour before an outing, Georgia closed the door of the bathroom and began her ritual of readying. Gerald could hear her singing her favorite songs from his spot in front of CNN out on the screened-in porch. The silence of her tardiness meant she was searching the house for one thing or another.

So it came as no surprise when from the family room, he heard her call, "Honey, have you seen my glasses?"

Gerald laughed to himself and shook his head. "Which ones?" He was playing with her.

"Honey, you know, my sunglasses."

"I haven't seen them."

A delighted shriek came from the living room, "Gottcha! Where have you been hiding?" Georgia walked through the kitchen and saw Gerald smiling by the door. She let out one of her self-effacing bursts of laughter and exclaimed, "Georgia girl, where is your head? I could swear I put those glasses on my bed stand this morning. You're laughing at me, aren't you?"

And he was. Gerald looked at Daisy with affection and amusement. He got a kick out of her absent-minded ways. Laughter was soon to leave their home but in these final years of their fifty-eight together, enough room existed to enjoy the goodness of their lives and find humor in the eccentricities of their personalities. They shared a good laugh over the normal signs of aging. All their friends reported the same gaps in memory, and they thought nothing of the lost glasses, the missing grocery lists, the strange disappearances of mobile phones and car keys. Even when Georgia's grey wool slacks vanished and showed up one day in the utility closet, the two old companions managed to joke about it and go on without a trace of concern.

Gerald and Georgia were seasoned at remembering only those memories that brought good feelings to mind. They were skilled practitioners of forgetfulness and lived without self-reflection, which allowed each to maintain a state of equilibrium within. When they passed through the security gates of the Hilton Head Plantation each day, the couple was convinced they had banished the past and prevented any trespasses on their future. Only the occasional nightmarish dream or the rare demonic memory interrupted the tranquility of the life they'd made in Hilton Head. Georgia sang to herself and Gerald watched the news and neither paid much attention to the growing pattern of forgetfulness infiltrating Georgia's life.

Once Gerald was diagnosed with a rare bile duct cancer, all attention went to his needs. Humor evaporated quickly. Gerald sank into a frowning despondency. Georgia was confined to the house to care for him, and anxiety began to eat away at the structures of her memory as efficiently as the cancer ate up his healthy cells. While she couldn't stop the landslide of forgetting, what she had for dinner, where she placed her rings, what day of the week it was, she was also deluged with remembering. The memories came unbidden. Forced to think of and attend to what she did not want to know; namely that the great fear of her life was closing in on her: the dread of becoming her mother in senility and viciousness.

It was 1971 and Georgia's father was dying of prostate cancer. The cells had moved to his bones and he was losing weight rapidly. She commuted from New York to Pittsburgh to care for her parents who were now living in a small apartment. She spent one full week with them and then returned home to be with Gerald. Frank was serving in Vietnam, and Jimmy was in his junior year of college. Daisy never complained about her situation though it went on for months and without a drop of assistance from her brother. She tired but never once considered a different approach. Her father grew sullen and resigned while her mother grew frightened and nasty. She criticized Georgia relentlessly. Georgia watched helplessly as her mother became more and more irrational toward her.

"Where have you been?" This was the typical greeting Georgia received from her mother toward the end. "Why aren't you around here when we need you?"

"Mother, I live in New York. I come as often as I can. Can't you understand that?"

"What I understand is you're not here when you're needed. When your father is wasting away to nothing. I'm by myself. Do you understand that? Where do you live? Why are you so far away? You should be with your family. Why do you live with that man? He doesn't talk, he doesn't smile, he's terrible."

"Mother, he's my husband. Don't talk like that."

"Don't tell me how to talk. I'll talk, I'll talk. Why don't you live here with your parents? Are you too good now? Is that it, you're too good for us?"

"Mother, stop."

"Don't tell me to stop. Stop. I'll stop, I'll stop. He won't stop, he just stares out that window. He won't stop, how can I stop? Stop? Ha."

"Come on, let's go for a walk, get some fresh air."

"Oh no, oh no you don't. You're not taking me away. Oh no. You and your tricks. Smart little college girl. You won't fool me. Oh no. You won't take me away." Victoria was screaming now. Her eyes bulged with paranoid contempt.

William Sinclaire spoke up but his voice was weak and he simply uttered her name. Her head jerked his way, but her attention quickly snapped back to her daughter, who was pleading now.

"Mom, all I said was, 'let's get some fresh air.'"

But it was no use. Georgia's mother was going quickly. It was worse with each visit. Her mother's belligerence took Georgia from her father's side all too often, and she felt a hurtful resentment that she could expect no comfort or appreciation in return for her efforts. She worried about the future and what would happen to her mother after her father passed.

"You'll have to put her in a home, Daisy. There's no other choice. Dr. Eckhardt said so, didn't he? You can't take care of her. She's too sick. Besides, you've worn yourself ragged flying back and forth to Pittsburgh and for no appreciation to boot. She'll be taken care of."

"Honey, she'll never understand. She'll hate me. I don't know if I can take that." Georgia couldn't tolerate anyone being angry with her, much less her mother whom she loved and feared most of all. She knew Gerald was right, but she was worn out and couldn't fathom how in the world she might manage that kind of fight with her mother.

"It's the best thing. You'll get by."

But Daisy shuddered inside. And she was right. It was several months before her father succumbed to the cancer. Many more trips to his bedside. Bill showed up once. He sat and stuffed his mouth with greasy french fries the entire visit. Daisy warned him that he was eating himself into an early grave, but he smirked and went right on. Two years later his heart blew up on the train to Boston. He was a strange man. In the midst of their father's decline, he seldom visited and never offered to spell Daisy. On an off-week at home, Daisy received a call from her brother to talk about the situation with their parents. At the end of the conversation, she asked where Bill was calling from and learned, to her astonishment, that he had moved to the neighboring small town six months previously without so much as a phone call to let her know. She was furious with him. She wondered what had gone so wrong between them? She didn't dare remember and the distance he kept wouldn't let her forget.

On the occasion of this visit, Victoria was silent and flitted around the house like a nervous cat. Her eyes watched for any signs of danger. Bill left and she asked who the stranger was and why was he there. Daisy was the only one she spoke to any longer. She had turned from her husband when the pain became too great.

Daisy died a thousand deaths watching both her parents perish. Gerald was of little comfort as his energies went to shoring up the emotional dam separating his waking mind from memories of Ruth. Victoria's outbursts oscillated with long periods of smoldering and vacant withdrawal. The periods of silence were nearly as awful as the rage that spewed from her mother's mouth. Daisy trembled wondering when the next eruption would occur and what would set it off. How would she ever forget this misery?

When her father passed, Daisy made all the preparations to move her mother to Connecticut. Of course she tried to keep it from her but Victoria was suspicious and kept asking, "Where are we? Where are you taking me?"

Daisy tried to put her off. "We're taking you where we can take care of you, Mother. We'll be close."

Victoria huddled in the back seat staring at the foreign landscape. But for the rancor and flashes of fear, she was a shell of a person, hollowed out by the ravaging disease in her brain. When they arrived at the Stamford Care Center, she stiffened and began to cry. She took her place silently and without incident, which saved Daisy from the embarrassment she expected, but the anxiety only worsened when her mother looked at her as if she were a strange intruder. For several visits she said nothing. Daisy sat with her nearly every day.

At night she complained to Gerald, "She won't talk to me. She just stares at the wall. She'll barely look at me, Honey. It's awful."

"Daisy, you don't have to go so often. Your mother's too far gone, she won't notice. You have to take care of yourself. You've been through so much."

"I can't, Honey. I just can't. The thought of leaving her there alone is...well I just can't do it. I couldn't live with myself." And she didn't. She went nearly every day and sat with her stone-faced mother.

Victoria looked at Daisy when she said hello as she walked into her room. She said nothing but turned her empty gaze to the wall. Georgia sat with her for hours. At first she tried to engage her in conversation about the boys but soon gave up as her mother gave no indication of having heard a word. Until one day two weeks after her arrival, as Daisy was nodding off in her chair she heard a low hoarse voice, crackling with the heat of contempt, "How could you put me here?"

Georgia started awake. "What?"

"How could you put me in this place?"

"Mother, I'm sorry. I really am but I couldn't take care of you the way you need. Please understand. This is a good place, really, give it a chance, I'll visit every day if you want."

"I never want to see you again."

"Mother, don't."

"You're not my daughter."

And with that Victoria rolled over on her side and closed her eyes. She never spoke again. She refused food and died of pneumonia two weeks from that moment when she branded her only daughter with everlasting guilt.

Daisy buried her mother in Pittsburgh next to her father. When she left Pennsylvania for the last time, she thought of the large stone house and the memory of her parents happily tending the roses. She remembered the aroma of her father's tobacco wafting through the large comfortable rooms and the smell of her mother's pot roast beckoning from the kitchen. All the disturbing memories she placed in a coffin of their own. It overflowed like a suitcase bulging at the seams. For the rest of her days she kept that locker closed. Only the little man with red hair caused her to wonder if she'd overlooked something. The little man and the vision of her mother's back shouting hateful curses from her broken ribs. Curses that echo across time and generations of living and unborn sons and daughters.

∽

Georgia set her mind to forgetting what was unforgettable. The anguish of her mother's demise and the terror of repeating with her own children what was so dreadfully painful haunted her from behind the curtain of denial. She forgot her mother's burning eyes. She forgot herself and who she could have been. And, like Gerald, she forgot entirely the specter of death and heartbreaking loss. So complete was the evacuation of unpleasant memories from her waking life that when Gerald was diagnosed with a terminal disease, she had to go about her business, forgetting as quickly as perception forged an impression.

It began with the ordinary things of daily life: the lists, the car keys, a hat and scarf. Her purse was a favorite. Twenty minutes or more could be lost to the search for the missing purse. She was adept at losing. Soon she was losing everything. Everything but him. Around the house she floated: a moth trapped inside for the winter. Hours passed in pursuit of the missing and oblivious to the threat of what she might find. Days shrunk down to moments, solitary moments, lost in the whirlwind that scattered beginnings and endings, and splintered the continuity of events like old teeth.

Daisy walked about in a sand storm. The details of the hour slipped from her mind and disappeared before they could be remembered. She pulled stories from the closet and found them moth-eaten. It became harder and harder to forget that something terrible was happening. She admonished herself to pay better attention. But still she left the water running in the bathroom to answer the phone and, to her dismay, found the room flooded on her return. She covered it all with that gorgeous smile. Her last line of defense. But in her failures to forget, she remembered the terrifying face of her mother cursing her and rolling over on her side to kill herself in Daisy's presence. And even more terrifying were the flashes of experience that intruded on her fragile mind. Flashes of lightning that illuminated the landscape of her dark night and revealed Daisy standing before a mirror and seeing for the first time that she was vanishing. It was to become a Holocaust of memories: the dismemberment of a life. A Trail of Tears stretching from Hilton Head to Portland. Beginning with the present that went up in smoke like paper lit by a match. Ending in the slaughter of the entire narrative of her history. Gone with the wind. Never happened.

~

Jim hung up the receiver and stared at the black ceiling. His spirit was flattened. He felt nothing but a dull heaviness perched on his chest. Emily touched him there above his heart and said softly, "Sorry, Honey." Her sympathy helped but the weight was immovable.

The night calls were coming more often. Two times a week at least. Always the same jolly greeting, the incredulous gasp when she discovered the time and the retreating shame of her goodbye. Georgia's anger was a new development and so out of character, Jim was stunned. His mother was deteriorating every day. Her world rocked on its axis and turned night into day and day into night. It exposed the neat narrative of her life as an assemblage of bits and pieces of memory and fantasy glued together like a child's model airplane.

Jim was the first to notice the erosion. He found it odd the way Georgia went about the house losing things during his father's illness. He found it alarming when she flooded the bathroom. When he moved her into the retirement home a year after Gerald's death, he noticed she was still losing her keys at every turn but by then she was also losing recall. She asked him a hundred times where they were going with all the boxes. When they arrived at her apartment, Georgia was so overwhelmed, she went to bed and Jim stayed up all night unpacking the kitchen. Six months later alarm turned to devastation when he visited and found mail stacked up ten inches high on nearly every surface in the apartment including months and months of unpaid bills.

He was appalled to find Kleenex littering the carpet. Georgia had a habit of sneezing after meals. She went through a lot of tissue in her lifetime. Most likely it was a substitute behavior for the tears she never allowed. In any event, when Jim entered her bedroom, he found half a box of used tissues crumpled up beneath her bed. What was more disturbing was that his fastidious mother was oblivious to the collective mess growing up around her like rampant weeds in an untended garden. And when Jim got to the bathroom and found cut-up towels serving as toilet paper, his heart broke. She was hiding her desperation so well, Frank would not believe the seriousness reported by his brother. He resisted the idea of her dementia and nearly fought Jim at the suggestion she be moved to the West Coast to live near one of them.

"I just don't think she'll be happy moving out west, Jim. She's not a West Coast person and she's never handled changes. It seems to me she's just better off in Hilton Head where her friends are."

"Happy went out the window a while ago, Frank. I've been looking into this and I'm pretty sure she has Alzheimer's."

"Jesus. She doesn't sound all that bad when I talk to her."

"It's an act, Frank, she's faking it. She can still hide how bad it is. For Christ's sake she was using cut up dish towels to wipe her butt!"

Silence. What was happening here? Jim couldn't figure it out. What was Frank fighting? Was it just the usual adversarial position of the litigator? Was it the typical aversion to painful situations?

He managed to stay away from his dad until it was too late and then nearly vomited when Jim suggested the three of them visit the funeral home together to be with Gerald's body before cremation. He balked like a frightened horse and only after Georgia agreed to go did he accompany them, biting at the reins the entire visit. "I don't want that to be my last memory of Dad" was his alibi, but the truth seemed to be he couldn't handle a drop of emotion. Maybe, as the oldest, he felt a responsibility to take care of his mother and knowing he never would allow his life to be changed by her needs recoiled from the guilt by rationalizing staying put as being in her best interests. On occasions he said he didn't want Jim to be burdened but it seemed to Jim that Cain and Abel were fighting again over something more fundamental. Something to do with Eve that would remain a mystery shrouded in debate.

"Well, I think Mom's just going to get worse and we better make the move now while she's still able. Emily and I have talked and we're willing to move her to Portland and take care of her."

"Jim, do you have any idea how that will up-end your life? She'll be all over you to take care of her."

"I know. I know. But I just can't see leaving her there alone. It'll be a nightmare trying to manage this from three thousand miles. Believe me."

It was already a nightmare as Georgia had become so fearful she couldn't be alone and the facility had helped the boys arrange for twenty-four-hour care. She was reduced to the state of a frightened child, except when she picked up the phone to talk and then the faithful persona of Daisy kicked in and she sounded for a few moments like a million bucks. It was only when the conversation lasted longer than those few minutes that it became evident she didn't recall a word of what was said or notice when she repeated herself for the fourth time.

"Why don't we get a diagnosis? I'll come out and take her to a neurologist and see what they come up with. Maybe that will help us decide what's best."

Frank couldn't argue with gathering evidence so Jim arranged a referral from Georgia's internist and flew East for the appointment. He felt like an undercover agent ratting on someone he'd grown to like. Why was he so compelled to take care of his mother? A profound sense of duty had taken over his relation to her. But he couldn't say why. His heart felt dry. In fact, most of the time he felt annoyed with Georgia, a cause for more guilt and reason to suspect his own motivation. Was he competing with Frank for favored son status? Was he trying to make amends for being such a bad son all those years? Hitchhiking through North Africa after college without so much as a postcard or phone call home. Moving three thousand miles away to the Pacific Northwest was bad enough, but it was the blame-your-parents-for-everything era and Jim expressed his by having little to do with Gerald and Georgia.

There was plenty to feel guilty about, including the present-day oscillation in his feelings toward his mother. As Georgia's world rocked this way and that between lucidity and bewilderment, normalcy and chaos, his own climate teetered between sympathy and judgment. Fondness to contempt. His own confusion built. Why was he sacrificing so much of himself? Why was his service so joyless?

By the day of the visit to the neurologist's office, these questions were pounding on Jim's brain. He woke from a fitful sleep on Georgia's couch. It must have been 100 degrees inside. He could hardly walk through the heat blasting from the registers. He did manage to shower and get dressed, but when he walked into Georgia's room Jim found her still lying in bed and looking terrible. All the air had leaked out of her body. She was limp and depressed.

"Hi Mom."

"Hi Sweetie."

"You all right?"

"Oh sure. Just tired, that's all. Jimmy, I can't go to that doctor today. I just don't feel up to it, Sweetie. I don't know why but mornings are just awful. Can't get going. But I just can't go today. I'm sorry, Honey."

Jim was clutching inside and the annoyance factor jumped a notch or two, but he stayed calm. "That's okay, Mom; we don't have to be there for a few hours. Let's get some breakfast in you and see how you feel." He would soon learn never to schedule her for a morning appointment. Not even a beautiful Carolina morning helped lift her spirits. The mysterious morning blues would last until day and night switched places.

"Oh, I'm not hungry. I just don't feel like doing anything. Who is this doctor anyway? Why are you taking me there?" Her suspicions were up.

"Dr. Teller recommended him to help you with this morning energy problem." The hundredth explanation did no more than the first, but he answered her each time she repeated the question.

"I could sure use help with that. I don't know what's wrong with me. Never in my life have I felt this way. I always get up and get going. Oh God, I don't know." She was slipping deeper. "I just can't go today, Jimmy. Why don't you cancel the appointment and we'll go tomorrow. Okay Sweetie?"

Jim knew the whole plan was collapsing and so he took her by the hand, like he had with his two-year-old son years back, and redirected her into a different world. He told her funny stories about the boys' latest tricks. He told her funny stories about the dog. They reminisced about old days in college. The old memories were tattered but still standing. She began to laugh and before his eyes the organization of her brain shifted, and a coherence in the Daisy personality emerged like magic. Soon she was talking on and on about Sophie, the last of her great talking partners.

"Bonjour, Georgia. Bonjour. It is a beautiful morning, n'est-ce pas? Oui, Oui, beautiful. How are you this beautiful morning my dear." Daisy laughed at her friend's exuberant way of expressing herself. She loved the dramatic European flair. Before long Daisy had perked up like a dry plant after a watering. Jim seized the moment.

"Let's get some pancakes, Mom. I'm starving." Never one to deny her son food, Daisy was all agreement now.

"Yum, sounds good, Jimmy." And a perky 11-year-old climbed out of bed and got changed.

And they were on their way. The morning confirmed Jim's assessment and as he drove Georgia to the doctor, the clamor of contradictory feelings quieted and he felt certain he was doing the right thing. Georgia sat in the passenger seat like a cat going to the vet.

"Where are we going?"

"We're going to see a doctor, Mom."

"Why are we going to see a doctor? I'm fine. Is it Dr. Teller? I just saw him last week."

"No, it's a new doctor that Dr. Teller recommended to help with the morning problem."

"Oh, I don't have a morning problem, Jimmy. What do you mean?"

It went like that until they reached the medical office. Over and over again, Georgia asked the same questions. She didn't like what was happening even though she couldn't remember what was happening. By the time her name was called and she walked into the examination room, her mood was tense and gloomy. She looked like a girl in trouble, as though she expected her father to open the door and scold her. But it was a stranger who opened the door and walked in with a smile on his face.

"Hello, my name is Dr. Sauberhaven. You must be Mrs. Brennan. How are you doing, Mrs. Brennan?" He was East Indian, handsome and warm. When he gave Georgia his hand to shake Jim was flabbergasted to see the downcast little girl transform before his eyes into the graceful and glowing Georgia Daisy.

"Good morning, doctor. Oh I'm fine, thank you, and how are you? Why, this is my son, Jimmy."

Georgia gave Dr. Sauberhaven her hand and smiled up at him like sunrise on Easter Sunday. Jim saw the good doctor fall under her spell. He watched dumbfounded as Daisy charmed the Harvard-educated neurologist into the diagnosis of mild memory issues. It was a masterful performance. Mesmerizing. When Jim recounted the meeting with Emily later that day, he could only compare it to Ethel Merman's command of the audience in *Hello Dolly*.

Ethel Merman had nothing on Daisy. Neither did Carol Channing or Ginger Rogers. Daisy saw the curtain go up and it was show business all the way. There's no business like show business. Jim had heard her sing that one over dirty dishes. It was all a dress rehearsal for this moment.

"Very good, Mrs. Brennan. I'm going to give you three words to remember and in a few minutes I'll ask you to repeat them for me. Okay?"

"Certainly."

"The words are sugar, house, and bear. All right?"

"All right."

"Mrs. Brennan, can you tell me what year it is we're in?"

Georgia laughed like this was some foolish kid's game. "Well of course I can. It's, well let's see, 2004, I believe."

"Very good. And who is currently the President of the United States?"

"That would be George Bush."

"Excellent."

Georgia passed with flying colors. Jim felt foolish and flummoxed. Frank would love this. How could it be? They rode back to her apartment in silence, and Jim reprimanded himself for not being more prepared. He thought it would be a piece of cake. If he could identify her dementia, how could a trained neurologist miss it? He hadn't counted on an Academy Award-winning performance for Best Actress going to his mother for the portrayal of a sweet old lady foiling the efforts of her neurotic son to lock her up. He could hear Frank smirking now.

He would have to write the doctor a detailed letter explaining Georgia's personality and describing her everyday reality in detail. In the meantime, he put up with Georgia's incessant questions, the constant anxiety about her missing keys. He roasted again that night in the overheated apartment and left for home the next afternoon. His mother walked him to the parking lot and said goodbye. They hugged and she held back tears. Jim pulled away and saw Georgia in the rear view mirror watching her son disappear. She looked like a five-year-old dropped off at boarding school. He watched as the Daisy in the mirror grew smaller and smaller. He watched and saw her throw her shoulders back, turn, and walk back to her room composing herself. Making right. She is a child lost in the woods. Daylight is fading and she has only her smile to find the way. He left in chains.

Back home Jim wrote a two-page assessment of Georgia's personality changes and deterioration in cognitive functioning. Dr. Sauberhaven interviewed Georgia again two weeks later and without the support of Jim close at hand, her true condition became clear. Dr. Sauberhaven phoned Jim the next day and shared his observations as well as the new diagnosis of Alzheimer's disease. He recommended she be moved to a memory care facility near the home of one of her sons as soon as possible.

Jim passed on the news to Frank, who submitted to the authority of the neurologist with surprisingly little opposition. And so it was done. Georgia would move to Portland to be looked after by Jim and Emily. Frank worried about Jim and Emily and the burden they were assuming.

Jim worried about his mental state. Something more than the constant ambivalence was creeping into his psyche. What was it? He felt as though he were being taken over. Possessed. It was subtle but tangible. The invasion of a foreign spirit. Heavy, as though a second body had entered his. This strange new presence was impossible to talk about. He tried to speak with Emily but could not articulate this new and disturbing experience. And so it moved in alongside the collection of festering emotions already weighing him down as he went about doing what he believed was necessary to insure his mother's well-being. But his service was joyless. He was reminded of the feelings when Gerald told him to mow the lawn. The same stubborn resistance. The silent no. Was he a boy or a man? Living his life or watching it? Why was he always wanting things to be different from what they were? For and against? Bouncing between sympathy and judgment. He was tiring and she hadn't reached Portland. And now this new development, this occupation of his soul, this trespassing of a foreign entity. What next?

The move took place on election day 2004. Georgia couldn't find her social security card or voter's registration and was denied the right to vote in the last election she would live to see. By this time she could not answer, if asked, who the President of the United States was. Their votes would have certainly canceled each other since she was an ardent life-long Republican and Jim was a McGovern Democrat.

That evening they watched the returns in the Savannah Airport Sheraton. Watched as the country divided into red and blue. As those busy forgetting the ugly past faced off against those unable to forget the nation's evil history like lines of infantrymen in a bloody Civil War battle. Meanwhile George Bush and his friends lined their pockets with the people's gold and claimed the rights to another four years in the White House. Jim watched the results of yet another Republican victory with contempt and nausea. He watched his own red and blue states bicker and snarl at each other as his mother asked him what they were doing here. "Where are we going, Jimmy?"

"We're going to Portland, Mom. You get to live near Austin and Charlie."

"Oh sure, Sweetie. Of course. That's wonderful."

It wasn't wonderful that morning. She balked as soon as the sun came up. Claimed she couldn't possibly make the move. It was all too much. She thanked Jim for his efforts, apologized for the inconvenience, and went back to bed forlorn as a dog who has to suffer through another day inside. Jim did his best to distract Georgia from what he could only imagine was an avalanche of feelings so overwhelming that what little of her remained was easily buried in the landslide.

They made it to breakfast and the tide turned. Sophie came to say good-bye with red eyes. Georgia didn't seem to understand and wanted to say funny things in French. They drove to the airport in the shuttle van as the sun rose over Georgia. Georgia Daisy sat in the passenger seat smiling at nothing and Jim felt as awful as he could remember. It was the journey of a thousand questions. Without the Xanax it would have been ten thousand. And since there were only two, "What are we doing?" and "Where are we going?", Jim was grinding his teeth by the time they flew over Tennessee. He was ordering Scotch by the time they reached Missouri and thinking about the boy in his mother's closet covered with ketchup when they passed the Tetons.

He asked himself a question or two as well. What the hell was he doing? Was it true, as Jeff Anderson's mother had said, that he was just a Momma's boy wanting to be near his Mommy? Was he hiding from the hate that he couldn't bear to admit to himself? Maybe he just wanted to look like the most wonderful person on earth and have others admire his selfless love and sacrifice while all the time secretly loathing every minute of it. Surely it was all vanity.

Frank was right. Jim was nuts to think he could pull this off. Georgia would surely drive him crazy and they would end up hating each other. He would need an exorcism to free himself from this newest intrusion. And still, amidst the storm of confusion and gusting emotions, he knew bringing Georgia to Portland was the humane thing to do. Emily and the boys had agreed with Jim and backed him up. They were hopeful that some time remained to enjoy together before the illness made it impossible. Jim was ready to manage the gaps in memory and the barrage of questions. He was ready to manage the visits and meetings with nursing staffs. He was ready to manage her finances and pay the bills.

He wasn't prepared for his mother to reek of urine. He wasn't prepared to buy her adult diapers at Costco. He wasn't prepared to walk into her bathroom and find dry excrement on the floor while she went on her way oblivious to the mess she had left behind. Nor was he prepared to hear his kind mother cursing, scratching and fighting with all her might against the nurses attempting to assist her to the toilet. He was not prepared for the terrible sadness that engulfed his world. That made it easier for whatever it was that possessed him to take a deeper and deeper hold on his spirit.

And yet, Georgia did not become her mother. She did not shoot flaming arrows at those closest to her trying to help. Yes, there were the angry night calls to Jim in the early days. And there were the screaming fits when her aides tried to get her to the toilet. But these passed and though the disease ate away the present to nothing, and in good time exterminated the past as well, from the ashes of her life Daisy rose up with her everlasting smile and each and every attendant fell in love with Miss Daisy from Savannah. She smiled and called them Darlin'. She smiled and called them Doll. Daisy was beloved to them. Angelic. Depression, which was the last remnant of memory, the last sense of a self to remember, faded along with yesterday and tomorrow.

And Daisy began to glow a strange and lovely glow. She was as beautiful as ever. Without trying. It was a puzzle to Jim. How could she be so gone and so radiant? She could no longer remember the lyrics to her favorite songs but on occasion she could be heard humming the tune to "Diamonds Are a Girl's Best Friend" or "Deck the Halls" even though the halls were lined not with boughs of holly but with women like herself wandering about the edges of things looking for their lost lives. Still it was humorous when in the dog days of summer, Daisy lit into a measure of "Joy to the World." Her life was an old jig-saw puzzle scattered on a card table with too many missing pieces to make sense of.

None of this stopped Daisy from talking. In fact she talked incessantly for a time. She didn't have a partner like Millie or Sophie and she didn't need one. Talking went on pretty much like breathing. She seemed quite pleased with what she had to say and carried on as if she were at a cocktail party conversing with a neighbor. The words came out like salad. All chopped up and tossed with various vegetable ideas and story lines. It could be quite amusing to listen to her Canterbury Tales. She spoke with real earnestness about her mother and father taking a shower in her room. The pink flamingo on her bureau top that kept her roommate awake puzzled her. Of course she spoke at great length about the unfortunate ladies walking about the facility. She felt sorry for them. Why did they look so sad? But much of her conversation was in a language of her own. The deck of cards was well shuffled and the sentences dealt were an artful mix of verbs and nouns, adverbs and prepositions. It all made perfect sense to Daisy and she went on without hesitation describing a world without end. Amen.

Her discourse reached its expository peak in the rehab center after surgery to repair a broken hip. The break came as no surprise to Jim. That it happened just two weeks after the difficult move to a more competent memory facility did. Jim was still reeling from the move and the rapid decline that led to the decision. Georgia had fallen before and was fortunate she hadn't suffered a concussion or worse. Her legs were weak and her field of awareness so far-sighted that any change in her environment brought the possibility of tripping into play. Curbs were the worst. Leaving a baseball game at Frank's, she walked off a sidewalk not recognizing the drop to the street, stumbled, and fell. Six hours later she left Marin General with a nasty bump on her forehead.

There were many phone calls to Jim and Emily from her new home at the Hampton. Jim came to flinch whenever the phone rang. His stomach did a triple somersault from the high dive.

"Hello, Mr. Brennan?"

"Yes?"

"Mr. Brennan, this is Nurse Richardson from the Hampton." It sounded like the grim reaper calling from a funeral home. "Your mother has taken a fall." Pause. An eternity later, "She's all right now. We found her on the floor in the group room after dinner. Nothing broken or anything, but we are required by law to inform family members."

Jim thought the law should require they begin the phone call with the reassurance part. And some were sensitive enough to do so. But not on the night of the big crash. It was the last night of her life to walk to dinner. To walk to the bathroom and brush her teeth. There, standing before the mirror and an image she no longer recognized as herself, Daisy turned and fell. Her hip shattered.

When Jim reached the emergency room at Providence Hospital, she was still in some pain. Writhing under the skimpy sheets and hospital gown, groaning and asking for help. She grabbed Jim's hand and held on for dear life. They were familiar with the Providence ER. Only three weeks after Georgia's arrival in Portland on the morning of Thanksgiving, they spent a lovely four hours waiting to have her heart checked out. She'd had a stent put in the year before and woke that morning with more chest pain. The hospital released her in time to make the turkey dinner, and she was all smiles and apologies while Jim was tired and cranky. The care was good but the sitting around four hours for no apparent reason was upsetting. Even if there were the usual ER sound effects and drama to entertain.

On another occasion she ended up in the ER with serious flu symptoms. By the time Jim arrived, she was in a room shivering uncontrollably and, half asleep, crying for help under her breath. The resident came in and, very mechanically, informed Jim that because of the shivering they suspected a serious blood infection. Jim listened and when the doctor left asked the nurse if she would bring several blankets for his mother. The shivering stopped. But the doctor appeared insulted and stayed away for another two hours.

This night was different. Georgia's pain was brought under control, and the ER doc arranged for a surgeon to talk with Jim and planned the surgery for later that night. It was a long night. Frank was phoned and agreed to come up the next day. Jim was glad of that but spent that night and the following days wrestling with the worst of the many mental states he had to encounter: the wish to have it over. The wish that made him shrink into self-loathing. How could anyone wish for his mother's death?

Jim found himself looking for death in every corner of day and night. He hid the part of himself that yearned for the final call. The announcement that the end had come. He felt pulled to endings, pulled to a melancholy that wrapped his spirit in a particular warmth. The mirror found him guilty of criminal intent and sentenced him to life in prison without parole. Being locked up behind bars didn't stop the dreadful thoughts from coming. With every call they started up again. Was this the time? It was as though death were the sacred moment. The moment of utmost presence.

But this was not the time. Georgia came through surgery in good shape. Though she would never walk again, she was fitted to a wheelchair and got around quite well. In fact, when she returned to the Hampton after six weeks of rehab, she became quite a celebrity motoring about the long hallways with her nimble little chair. She took to the inside lane, always the conservative one, as though she were blind and keeping a hand on the wall gave her the security of knowing her location.

What stood out was her determined expression. She looked like a woman with a mission. What could it be? Endlessly retracing her tracks up and down the corridors of this purgatory, this death row lined with despairing women standing and sitting, wringing their hands and some arguing with invisible visitors, all of them, poor beautiful souls, deserted by their lives and memory and staring into a fog that would never lift.

Her boys found a suitable rehab center near Jim and Emily's home, and Georgia settled in for six weeks with other wounded and aging warriors of her generation. The anesthesia wore off and Georgia Daisy woke up talking. This was not a dialogue between two old friends. This was a solo shot. A monologue that would have made Spalding Gray stand up and bow. Her greatest performance. The stage was her semi-private room. A curtain divided the room and strangers came and went. On the wall was a television monitor that played a non-stop nature video twelve hours a day. Pastoral scenes with New Age sound tracks designed to put the most agitated soul into a stupor. Georgia's monologue matched the non-stop movie frame for frame. Hers resembled an old-fashioned South Pacific malaria-induced delirium. At first it scared the hell out of Jim. He was certain she'd been further damaged by the surgery and would never come out of this wild place.

After a few days he began to marvel at the dexterity of her language. By day five, he was laughing and appreciating her every take. There were the one-liners that would have brought tears to Henny Youngman's eyes. Like the Sunday afternoon Jim went to visit, and Georgia looked out the window, got a coy glint in her eye, and said, "Hey you, who what you could peek at my panty hose?" The play of word salad reached its pinnacle on that stage. William Burroughs would have been consumed with envy. His naked lunch spoiled. E. E. Cummings would have taken notes. A moving collage poured from her mouth. Headwaters of a river. From the moment he walked into the room until the moment he left, Georgia carried on. She seemed to be teaching, lecturing her students on the proper uses of grammar, raising her hand to point and emphasize the last remark.

Dozens of visitors arrived. Jim was unable to perceive her guests, but she greeted them warmly and conversed as if it were another day on the patio at the country club. A few received harsh words. Admonished for one thing or another. But mostly she just chatted and chuckled in a newsy sort of way. Raising her eyebrows here and there to dramatize what looked to Jim like some rather juicy gossip. More panty hose stories, no doubt. It was impossible to discern the actual story line because by then the delirium was so strong, word salad had transformed into a confetti of syllables. A ticker-tape snowstorm of broken nouns and verbs falling on Manhattan. Where she'd picked up the post-modern flair for meaningless symbols he did not know. This Georgia was a graffiti artist. Ella Fitzgerald climbing and descending scales like a cat with only sounds and soul to convey her meanings. Jim sat and marveled. This was his mother going on, speaking with spirits, speaking in tongues, speaking like a lunatic. She spoke as though she had the ear of other worlds, other gods. For moments he forgot whom he was with. He forgot his annoyance and sat with her without fighting. Without rejecting his mother.

Georgia went on for days. She might have been reciting the twelve books of *Paradise Lost*. When the delirium wore off, she looked at Jim in disbelief.

"Jimmy! What are you doing here?" Throughout her week-long oration, she had never addressed him directly. They seemed to be in different auditoriums. And now she was startled to find him in her world at all. The moments of lucidity returned and though terribly tired, she smiled and said, "So good to see you, Darling."

"Good to see you, Mom."

"Let's go went, left-over sand in the fridge then, shall we?"

"Sure, Mom, we'll do that."

"Oh good, Doll. Gool. You take that wrapper and put it up..."

"Mom, it's Emily's birthday tomorrow. I have a card for you to sign."

Georgia smiled. The clear moments were few, but she was back from her voyage to other universes and looked at her son with much love. "Sure Doll. You take that barbeque and eat it now." Jim handed his mother the birthday card, somehow believing her handwriting had survived the carnage of capabilities lost in these days of decline. Georgia was the quintessential English teacher. Correcting the grammar of her caretakers and complaining about educated people who spoke poorly were favorite pastimes. Her handwriting was impeccable and a measure of an allegiance to the etiquette and rules of language.

But on that day her signature was no more possible than walking. Daisy took the pink birthday card in her dry hand, smiled her smile, and in the other she held the pen like a stick or a straw. The two, pen and hand, floated above the page making several attempted landings. Each time the pen veered off and climbed like a balsa wood glider to a safe height before descending once more to the field without a runway. When she did land and attempt her signature, Jim thought of all the newsy cards and letters ending in "Love, Mom." He saw the elegant spacing, the perfect slant of penmanship; but when he looked at the card, what he saw was letters broken into tiny scratches. They lay on the paper like dead inch worms, dried out and curled up. Daisy smiled and handed Jim the pen. She was satisfied with her work. Jim thanked her and put the card away, wondering if he'd been cruel to ask her to sign her name. Telling himself he should have known better. He looked at the tiny scratches and felt his heart crumble like dry twigs. There was no Mom in those markings. Her smile did not reach her fingers.

Daisy's smile was the last of her possessions. All the miniature cups and saucers, the porcelain figurines, the mink stole; all the beautiful objects that she collected and enjoyed so much over the years were gone now. All the lovely reminders that she had left her past behind vanished along with the past itself. What remained was her smile and the last enduring memory of a lifetime: her son.

When she returned to the Alzheimer's home after the six-week absence, she roamed the halls on her new wheelchair. She wore tracks in the carpet like the wheels of a covered wagon crossing the muddy trails leading west. It appeared that she was going somewhere important. Looking for a doorway out. And as she met people along the way, she called out "Jimmy, Jimmy? Jimmy, come here." Her voice carried like the song of a loon over a lake at midnight. It was a haunting, mournful call to the one string left holding her up. She listened for a response and heard nothing but a voiceless echo swallowed by a ruthless void. When she discovered it was not Jim approaching, she put her feet in gear and shuffled off into another dream, another cloud without end.

ை

It was on a Sunday visit, while observing his mother's determined pursuit from a distance, that Jim finally understood the nature of the possession holding him prisoner. He had become the experiencer of Georgia's life. The one who suffered her losses. The one who suffered her humiliations. Who kept alive an I otherwise ravaged by the decay of her neurons. He had considered for some time the impact his mother would have felt had her self remained intact through the fall. Georgia would have been completely mortified. Degraded beyond her capacity to endure.

Jim knew this. He watched as her dignity was destroyed. As her self slowly died like an old shrub, branch by branch. And what happened inside his own psyche went beyond recognition, beyond empathy. Beyond what could be easily assessed as good or bad, healthy or sick. It happened quite unconsciously and naturally that he took on her soulfulness. He did not volunteer for the part. As gradually as darkness turns to light, he became the mind of her being. Preserving in the only way possible what was more than a memory of Daisy, more than a translation of her experience, as an actor might give life to a character. What was no less than the temporary embodiment of her spirit at first baffled and then frightened and finally amazed the son of this lovely, lonely lady who brought his flesh and spirit into the world.

She was readying to leave this world for another and Jim was pleased to give her a way station until it was time. Pleased and quite taken with the elasticity of his own being. Being, that proved so able to hold his mother's existence as well as his own in the same space. And in so doing revealed the porousness of all this terrain taken to be a self. This density, this marbled slab of what must be a me. This papier-mache shell. There seemed to be room for most anything. For countless shapes and selves. They seemed to come and go like ghosts or images projected on a screen. In fact, rather than a self, Jim began to experience an infinite Self, unfolding and forming with a fluidity that was both terrifying and beautiful, unwanted and longed for.

Georgia Daisy lay in bed at her new and final home. She slept on her side with her knees pulled up. Even dozing she looked like someone behaving well. Jim watched his mother sleep and listened to her breath enter and leave. It was three months since she'd moved to the skilled nursing facility. By that time, most of Daisy and Georgia had departed. A few remnants of persona stuck around like old faithful pets. The reflexive smile. The familiar greetings. Mostly she was silent. The grand conversation over. Jim knew that if she opened her eyes now and saw him sitting there, she would stare at him passively as though she were observing a fence post or a giraffe or a dream that had not ended with waking. Actually, the expression on her face was blank, as though no one were observing. As though nothing was observed.

Jim was no longer a son. He no longer visited his mother. The home was near his office and he visited every day but for shorter and shorter periods. Now that she was gone, he missed Daisy. He wanted to hear her say his name, call him "Darlin'." And yet, something in him wanted to turn away. He wanted to walk away and not return. He never wanted to feed her another spoonful of food. Or hear her housemates squawking like prehistoric reptiles. Or push her down another God-forsaken hallway. He was no longer able to cry. No longer able to joke with the staff. They came to him and asked,

"You all right, Jimmy?"

"I don't know. I guess so."

It was his way to make friends with the nurses and aides. They bantered and told jokes and he grew to like most of the people who cared for Daisy. They loved her. Everyone loved her.

"How is Mom doing do you think? She seems to sleep a lot."

"Oh she doing fine, Jimmy. I just love Miss Daisy. She the sweetest lady ever your mother. We just love her."

"She doesn't know who I am."

"You don't think so, Jimmy? I bet she does."

"She just looks at me like a stranger."

"Oh come on now, Jimmy. A mother always know her boy. Miss Daisy, she knows. Look at her, how happy she is."

Jim hadn't looked for a long time. It was too hard to look and remember. But it was true. Not that she was happy but something else. Something Jim had overlooked. Something eclipsed by the absence of the person who first loved him. Who first said his name. But there it was. How could he have missed it? He was every bit as blind as Oedipus. Conditioned to see faces and forms, letters and not the page. Georgia wasn't there but a radiance was. A glow. The body of Georgia Daisy sat slumped in the wheel chair, eighty-two years of motion winding down to the slightest of life-sustaining movement. The personality of Georgia Daisy was now dissolved and along with all the great mysteries of the world departed to the subtle realms of being. And yet, Jim's eyes were met by a light so luminous he forgot himself and his grief, a light that seemed to have no cause. That was not her smile. A light now free to burn undiminished by the filters of knowing and not knowing. Jim stood there speechless.

"You all right, Jimmy?"

"Yes. I'm good. Thanks, Betsy."

In an instant he realized his error. His big mistake. And when he did, a thousand pictures of Georgia and Daisy flooded his mind. Each image went through a transformation inspired by a recognition of the glow that was now so obvious. The glow that had always been there but clouded and obscured by the good little girl, by the gracious Southern Lady, and by the mother caring for her son. Jim was dizzy and sat down on a sofa in the hallway. His mother sat beside him. Her eyes closed. Revealed at last. Known. Glowing.

# CHAPTER 10
# The Necklace

❧

*I can tell you now, having said many things which are false, lies are not stories and stories contain much that is not true. These are not sins but the strivings of the blind groping for something real much like a diver lost in a cave struggling to find his way out. I can tell you what I know; the opposite of one truth is another...and another. And another. Each is strung like glass beads and glistening jewels on silk, winding and unwinding around the neck and shoulders of a silence so grand that universe upon universe desires to come and listen. And bathe.*

*Because I am no longer, I can tell you this: everything dies. Dies and is born to die again. And again. Eaten by silence and returned as song. Songs of love and sorrow. Becoming this and becoming that: all of it fleeting. The story that never ends. Fleeting reflections of that jeweled necklace, of all that is invisible, all that is brilliant. Strands of pearls draped over and around the body of a world you cannot see or touch, a world without edges that is the womb of your being. Everything, everything, my dear, is from and of that radiance and has nowhere to go but here, where the silence is deepest and most near, where stories melt and beauty lives.*

❧

The wind came for Daisy. It took forty-eight hours for her breath to empty, leaving her spirit free to slip effortlessly into the heart of nothing. Into the freshness of nothing but weightless being.

Jim felt the wind on his neck when the phone rang that Sunday. A chill went up his spine. All the nights spent imagining her end did not prepare him for the actual force of the gusting energies of death. Two strong legs were not enough to keep him from staggering backwards when the nurse informed him that she was unable to rouse Georgia after breakfast and that the ambulance had just left to take her, unconscious, to the hospital. They had been concerned for weeks as mysterious red blisters grew in number all over Georgia's body. But the nurse couldn't say, without a clear diagnosis, if her current condition was related to the strange spots taking over her skin.

None of this mattered to Jim. He wasn't listening to the nurse after her first words. The wind howled in his ears. It entered Jim's mind through holes left by the anguish of the past two years and he was overcome by vertigo. Suddenly the annoyance that was his constant companion vanished. The wish for his mother's demise fled. An anxious dread twisted in his belly like a wet towel being squeezed dry. The world without a mother loomed over him and overwhelmed what little capacity there was to think. Whether he said good-bye to the nurse or hung up the phone was impossible to say. Something like sleep engulfed his consciousness like a dream that can't be escaped. Not until Emily entered the kitchen and saw him staring at the trees outside the window was Jim able to find himself in the whirlwind.

"Honey, what's wrong?" She knew that look was reserved for Georgia.

"Mom's in the hospital. Unconscious. I've got a bad feeling."

They packed the boys in the car and headed out immediately. Georgia waited for them to arrive at the Good Samaritan Hospital across the river in Northwest Portland. When they got there, they found her one floor above the birthing center where their youngest was born. The irony of this juxtaposition was not lost on Emily, who was aware of the subtleties and symbols of life's crazy twists and turns like no one Jim had known.

They met at a plant sale on a Friday morning more than a decade earlier. Neither had been scheduled to work that morning, but each had found it necessary to change shifts for reasons other than those the fates had in mind. Jim sat at the cashier's table when Emily walked through the portable garden, through the throngs of customers and into his field of vision, unexpected as a hummingbird suddenly appearing from nowhere. Time and space parted as she walked toward him. She glowed like the first sunrise.

Jim's heart did a triple somersault with a half twist and landed with an effortless splash in his future. He dropped the quarters and dimes in his hand onto the table and beamed at her without embarrassment for what must have been long enough for all the molecules of their bodies to line up and say yes.

When Jim looked closer at Emily, mingling with customers, offering suggestions about perennials and flowering baskets, he noticed a caring attention to the detail of the moment that pleased him. What he noticed next cast a spell over everything. The plants disappeared. The people searching for the perfect addition to their gardens: gone. Only Emily inhabited the space that was now wide as the Columbia River.

Hovering over each of her bronze shoulders was an orb of bustling energy, impossible to describe because nothing was there except for invisible motion spinning like a thousand electrons around a point in another realm. Jim tried to dismiss the perceptions as a strange psychic construction but his attempts failed. The impression of the two strange vortexes never left his memory. Whether Emily sensed the presence of her two companions, he could not tell.

Two years later the first of the two whirling forces was born: Austin Martin. Twenty-three months later the second entered his incarnation: Charles George. Named, in part, after his grandmother who now lay one story above the place of his birth nine years earlier.

Emily was a gift from the moon. Jim fell and fell for her warmth. Their bodies touched and bloomed desert flowers that would last the rest of their days and weather storms of thunder and lightning. They spoke in tongues together and rolled over spring grass by the Metolius. They bled together and sang a song that woke the red earth from a millennium of slumber.

Jim handed the babies to Emily and watched them take her breast into their open mouths. He watched them become her body and then their own and he smiled a smile he had never known before. And he handed the boys death. Beginning with Gerald, who was diagnosed weeks before Charlie's full head of black hair appeared to the world for the first time. Austin had already felt the wind blow across his face as he and his mother gave so much to bring him to the world of flesh they both nearly expired from the effort. But once here, loved beyond measure, he thrived and walked on the earth with delight, accompanied by the knowledge of endings.

ᗆᗩ

The doors to the hospital opened automatically. Not since leaving Good Sam with Charlie in their arms had they crossed that threshold of birth and death. As they did so that day, both Jim and Emily paused and felt a trembling pass between them. They looked at the sad eyes of their children and ached for the young hearts about to lose another grandparent. Not knowing what condition Georgia was in, Emily and Jim left the boys in the waiting lounge and went to find Georgia's room by themselves. Her room was bright with afternoon sunlight. Georgia lay in bed breathing heavily, her eyes closed. She stirred slightly when they entered and called to her by the name she knew best.

"Hi Mom." Tension was absent from Jim's voice at that moment, but a great fear choked off the love and sadness welling up in his chest. "You look beautiful, Mom." Emily took Georgia's hand and they both saw a glimmer of a smile pass over her face.

"We're here, Mom. The boys are here too. Don't worry. We'll be right here with you." Jim did his best to sound calm.

Georgia did not move. She took in breath after breath as though she were laboring to lift one heavy stone after another. Jim and Emily stood next to her and watched the determined effort of her body. They listened to the sound of air being swallowed by hungry lungs. And they marveled at the force driving each breath, driving life onward.

"The doctor can see you now, Mr. Brennan."

Jim stepped through deep puddles of anxiety making his way to the hallway where a kind-looking middle-aged woman stood taking notes.

"Hello, I'm Dr. Wilson."

"I'm Jim Brennan, Georgia's son, and this is my wife, Emily."

"Pleasure to meet you. Why don't we go sit in the lobby and talk."

Dr. Wilson's presence was immediately reassuring to both Jim and Emily. Besides the warmth of her greeting, she was calm and unpretentious. She gave the impression of unlimited availability and respect. They sat down in the lobby outside the intensive care unit. Austin and Charlie were watching something funny on the TV in the corner of the room, out of hearing range.

"Well, I'm sorry to tell you that your mother is quite ill with a bad infection. We're not entirely certain what is causing the infection, but there are two possibilities and either of them is very serious." Dr. Wilson slowly explained each scenario and what the treatment procedure entailed. "I'm afraid that if we find the infection has eaten into the colon, there isn't really anything we can do. And if it hasn't, we can operate but it's a terribly difficult surgery for a person in her condition to recover from."

"How difficult? What would it be like for her?" The fear in Jim's gut was growing.

"At least two or three weeks in the hospital. She would be very uncomfortable for much of that time."

"And the results?"

"The prognosis is mixed at best. Your mother is not strong. There are lots of complicating factors, as you know."

Grief began to overcome the attention Jim wanted to give to Dr. Wilson's explanation. It began to spill from his heart with a force that matched his mother's last gasps. He struggled to control himself when he said to the good doctor, "Well, what do you think is best for her, Dr. Wilson? What is best for her?"

"You should know that you do have the option of making her comfortable and letting this take its course." Silence stepped up like a fifth family member. They heard the boys laughing at the TV show.

"It's that bad? You think it's bad enough to let her go?" Now Jim was straining for oxygen.

"I do. Your mother is weak to begin with. I think the chances are strong that we'd go in and find there was nothing to do, that the infection had gone too far and killed a stretch of colon. And really, if it hadn't, I'm not sure she would survive the ordeal of surgery and recovery."

"So you think letting her be is an option?" Jim was aware of a vise tightening around his throat. Something moved in his spleen. Something nocturnal and sinister creeping through the bush.

"I do, Mr. Brennan. I know it's a terribly difficult decision but I believe it is a reasonable and moral one."

"You do?" Jim was trembling by now. Looking to Dr. Wilson for comfort and guidance. He began to sob and Dr. Wilson touched his arm.

Emily took over and Jim was relieved. The emotion swamped his defenses but it was the sinister presence that made him shake. It was an infection in his soul, ageless bacteria gone berserk, green and draining into his blood.

Emily asked the good doctor, "How long would she live?"

"I'd say a couple of days. Three at the most but probably no more than two. We can keep her comfortable and out of pain without any problem. Palliative care is quite good at helping families and patients get through. She'll be taken care of. I promise."

"What would you do if it were your mother?" Emily didn't mind putting her on the spot.

"Oh dear, well I think I'd be just like you and not know what to do, but in the end I'd figure it was time to let her go."

Jim and Emily loved Dr. Wilson. They wanted to take her home and make her dinner. "We'd better think about this for a while and call Frank. My brother is in San Francisco."

"Of course. I'll be around. You take all the time you need and in the meantime we'll make sure your mother is comfortable. And really, whatever you decide is fine."

"You really think it's all right to let her go?" Jim looked deep into Dr. Wilson's eyes and found only acceptance looking back.

"I really do."

∽

Frank answered the phone. Jim was surprised to find him home on a Sunday afternoon in mid-summer. Typically, Frank and his family were out enjoying the pleasures of Marin. But this was July, and Frank was in the third month of chemotherapy. He spent many days sitting in the sun on the back patio. Steroids helped prevent the vomiting that consumed him the first month of treatment, but they also enabled his denial to claim the upper hand over the advancement of the disease.

On this particular day, denial was a far more arduous achievement because Frank found it increasingly difficult to breathe. No one asked if he was experiencing an uncanny synchronicity with Georgia. His oncologist certainly didn't when she wrote off his symptoms as anxiety. When Frank was admitted to Marin General with pneumonia a week after his mother's death, Jim decided to phone the world-renowned expert and give her hell. By the time Frank reached Georgia's death bed, he could barely walk, the fatigue was so great.

However, on the afternoon Jim called with the information from Dr. Wilson, Frank lay in the sun dozing and worrying about the secrets knocking at his front door.

"Hello."

"Frank, it's Jim."

"Jim, how are you?"

"I'm all right, but Mom isn't. You'd better get Sally on the speaker phone."

"Hold on a minute, Jim, hold on."

Jim wondered if it was the same phone they'd all used on the Sunday afternoon in April when they'd called with news of the cancer. He pictured them sitting in the chairs around the table outside.

"Jim, can you hear?"

"Hi Jim." It was Sally joining in, bright as a search light. "How's Grandma?"

Sally knew all about death. She'd been initiated early to life's cruelties when she woke up one night in her eleventh year surrounded by flames and fled the inferno with her baby sister in her arms and her parents trapped in the smoke and fire. For the rest of her life she walked, talked, and thought in fast forward. Stuck in one gear. Jim loved her just the same and anguished for her when Frank went on about the latest PTSD fraud he'd exposed on the witness stand. He wished Sally could find some ease in her life, but Frank's illness only exacerbated the intensity at her core.

"Hi Sally, I'm glad you're both home. Yeah, well, Grandma is in bad shape. Emily and I just spoke with the doctor, who, by the way is wonderful; she gave us so much time and explained what she could so that we could understand it. She's a blessing. Anyway, the deal is that Mom has some sort of infection in her intestine. She's not conscious at the moment but she seems comfortable. The infection has either killed off part of the colon or severely compromised it."

"When did this happen?" Frank sounds grim and contracted.

"She's had these strange red spots on her body for a few weeks they haven't been able to get rid of. No one seems to know if they're related, but the nurse was unable to wake her this morning. She thought Mom was dehydrated and when they couldn't get enough fluids in, sent her to the ER. They discovered the infection and admitted her."

Silence.

"What can they do?" Each of them felt the cloud of death descend. They watched it swallow Daisy and rob the world of her smile.

"Well, here's the tough part." Jim tried his best to stifle the emotion rising in his throat. "Dr. Wilson says they could go in and determine what the condition is, if the colon is salvageable or if a portion has all ready been destroyed. She suspects it's the latter. If it hasn't, they could operate but it's a very arduous surgery and recovery is doubtful. The other option is to let her be. Let her go." As he said the words to his brother, the last line of suppression broke and sobs washed up over the sea wall. Emily put her hand on his leg. The boys looked their way and stopped laughing.

"Oh Jim, poor Grandma." Sally had no one but the Brennan family. She kept what distance she could by calling Georgia "Grandma." Although she never considered calling her Mom, knowing in her heart she couldn't call her anything so intimate, Sally loved Georgia as much as anyone. "What do you think, Jim, is it time to let her go? She's suffered so much."

"I don't know. It may be. The odd thing is she doesn't look all that bad lying there in bed. You know how Mom is. When we went in, we expected her to look awful but she actually looked beautiful. It's hard to think of just not doing anything when she looks so good." Fear sat like a stone in his stomach.

"I just don't think we have a choice, Jim. I mean she's not herself anyway and to put her through that, she'd never survive it, she's too weak."

"I know." Yes, he knew, but something in Frank's voice threw him off. He made it sound too easy, like he was almost eager to have her gone. The hair on Jim's neck bristled and he felt the age-old battle between him and his brother heating up.

"What did the doctor say, Jim?" Sally intervened and brought the two big-horned rams back from the pending square-off.

"What did she say? She said it's all right to do nothing. Like Frank said, she's too weak and the procedure is grueling." He tried to mute his disdain.

"Jim, it's the best thing. She's had enough; if she had a chance at some semblance of living it would be one thing but she's not capable of having a life so why put her through this too?"

"I know, I know. It's just hard." Jim couldn't stop the tears and Frank seemed surprised his brother was having such a tough time of it. Their perennial battle over reason versus emotion took center stage again. Jim knew he'd better end the call before his feelings became a downpour.

"You'd better come soon, Frank."

"How long do they think she has, Jim?" He knew Sally couldn't bear seeing Georgia in her last hours but he didn't blame her.

"They figure two days, possibly more, but not likely."

"I'll try to get up there tomorrow."

"What do you mean you'll 'try'?"

"I'll be there. You just can't imagine how much is going on but I'll be there tomorrow as soon as I can get a flight out."

"Okay, good."

"You take care, Jim, and I really think it's the right thing. Poor Grandma, my heart breaks for her but we can't put her through any more at this point after all she's been through."

"Sally's right, Jim, she's better off..."

"Right, I gotta go." Jim handed the phone to Emily and left the lobby. That conversation would replay in his head again and again for years to come. He wondered what motivations his brother was hiding. He was suspicious of his brother. But those questions didn't stick around for long.

He walked down the bright hallway to his mother's room. As the door opened, he heard the long draw of breath. Her lungs pumped stubbornly. She hadn't changed position since they were last in. Her head leaned to one side and her mouth hung open just slightly. Georgia was working hard, and the effort required to feed enough oxygen to her body was incongruous with the sunken figure lying in bed. Her face looked serious. The famous smile was missing. She could not throw her shoulders back and go on.

Jim stood by her side and wiped burning tears from his eyes. He couldn't wipe away the nauseating anxiety. He felt sea-sick. Her hand was warm and relaxed in his. It made him cry harder. So soft. So defenseless. Jim found himself weeping and trying to say something to his mother through the convulsions of grief. Georgia did not move. "I'm sorry, Mom, I'm sorry." The apologies gushed out of his mouth as fast as the flood of teardrops stained his face. "I'm so sorry." And as he spoke Jim realized he was apologizing to a host of listeners but mostly because of the menacing presence he'd sensed earlier. Because here he was, at last, face to face with the killer. His murderous self finally revealed. For it was now his to take his mother's life. His to remove the oxygen tube from her nostrils. His to remove the IV from her vein. His to say no to the surgeon. His to watch, alone, as the life force emptied from her flesh.

The little boy who plotted her end recoiled in horror. The man who wanted to strangle her hung his head in shame. He hid his face as he walked down a corridor of accusers: "Murderer! Mother killer! Wicked, wicked man." He wanted to escape. He wanted to disappear. His legs were heavy and numb and reminded him of childhood dreams when he couldn't run. Predators drew near and he was immobilized. Trapped.

The warmth of Georgia's hand in his brought him back to the room. The room above the birthing suite where he caught Charlie slipping from Emily's womb into his own fatherly hands and the crisp flush of that first breath. Jim wondered who would catch him. And he fell through this floor and the next. This world and the next. A free fall into a night without mercy. Without a God or saviour. And he landed where he began, at his mother's side, prepared to assume the final duty, the final joyless service of ending her life.

∾

*The anguish of a mother over the suffering of her children is unsurpassed. Even greater is the anguish of the dead for their loved ones still struggling on Earth. However, there is a difference. The ordinary daily pains and disappointments no longer concern the dead. These are a trifle to us, and we know hardship to be as unavoidable as snow in winter. Even death means nothing to us who know the ease with which the spirit moves from one sphere to another. No, it is none of the usual earthly setbacks that cause the dead to despair. What causes us such heartache is to helplessly witness the folly of our children and survivors.*

*It is the ignorance of the human mind we so recently shared that makes us moan and lament. The needlessness of such torment is now as obvious to us as the sun is to you. We see the luminous light of spirit permeating every last inch of space, permeating every molecule of matter. We know the bliss that is being itself residing in the breast of every creature. Can you see how it grieves us to watch those we love sitting on such an exquisite treasure bemoaning their sad fate and blind to the riches so close at hand? It grieves us to hear the fallacies of the mind elaborated into stories that scar the face of creation. It is the saddest of ironies that the dead know only possibilities while the living know only limitations. Limitations bound at the spine like books. Bound by the very stories that insure the slavery of the spirit. Bound to toil and sweat in attempts to free the self that only tighten the knot.*

*It is not vanity that rules. Vanity is merely the prop that holds up the storefront of personality. It is perversion that drives the activity of the hive. Perversion. Misguided souls lost in a boggy woodland tapping tree after tree for golden syrup and coming up with nothing but handfuls of termites and grubs.*

*I have seen the stories come undone. Seen them crack open like mudflats baked under the desert heat. Gerald's was the first to crumble. Iron gates the height of a king's couldn't keep death out of his castle. Couldn't keep age and an infantry of loss from infiltrating his illusion of security. One week before his death he wondered aloud to the hospice nurse, "When am I going to beat this thing?" His story was replete with omissions and erasures. He dreamed of a world without pain and woke up screaming, every muscle in his body cramped and contorted.*

*We wrote the introduction to the stories our children would tell. It revolved around work. Gerald vowed to eliminate work from our lives. He forced me to stop cooking. He didn't want to lift a finger ever again. We went out for every meal. I was permitted to slice bananas and floss my teeth. Black people came to our home and cleaned the toilets. More black people cleaned the pool and cared for the yard.*

*Our story was to make us free from hardship. We slowly wasted away in our success. You see, to us work was the villain. The dirty thug that enforced the dictatorship of poverty. And Gerald was convinced that it was poverty that took his mother from him. Sweat reminded him of that grand theft, of the hour they closed the casket on his heart.*

*Our first-born, Frank, became addicted to work. He tried to paint over his father's depression with unlimited success. Work was his brush. He was unstoppable. He resembled an ant, working day and night and lifting weights far beyond his own. He dined with the wealthy and used his will like a crowbar to make a place for himself alongside the rich and powerful. When his story broke, the crack was louder than a giant Sequoia toppling in the forest. And like the great tree he fought every inch of the fall to right himself, to deny the impact. But fall he did.*

*I tried singing to him in a dream. I pleaded with him from the other side to surrender. To no avail. And when he hit the hard ground the earth shook, many limbs shattered, and the lies and secrets of his life tumbled out like marbles from a jar.*

*My own story was simple. It was the poem of every mother, though background to the larger myths of the men in my life. Mine was a quest for love. Like many of my sisters of the day, I told myself love could be had by giving everything, and asking nothing. Pleasing and acting pleased. Love waited at the foot of the rainbow. Love that would wash away the stain hidden beneath my smile.*

*You simply can't imagine the relief death brings. The effortlessness of being. What foolishness the living engage in. You are missing the bounty of delight waiting to be found right here within the music of your very own breath. The dead mourn for you. Heaven does not wait at the end of a bus line.*

*James was our youngest. His story was altogether different. For some time he seemed intent on not having a story. Gerald wrote that James was lazy, allergic to work. But he was wrong. Something else was at play. Perhaps James heard his grandmother whispering from the blue. He seemed to see the gaps in our stories. More than that, he saw shafts of light streaming from those gaps. On more than one occasion, he entered an opening and tasted the nectar therein. Now that I have joined the splendor, I can see that he lived on a fault line between those worlds. In his earliest days, he lay on his back like an Indian sage on a pile of leaves. We were unsettled by the way in which he looked at us. Our motion seemed awkward and misplaced.*

*Soon he was forced to make a story. What came of it was a story without a story. He seemed to float above the ordinary world we knew, more like a bird zigzagging with the wind. When older, sensing the roar of approaching waterfalls, he adopted the prevailing custom of his generation and made the making of himself into the story. Loss, or threat of loss, haunted every turn of the page.*

*What else could he do? Ours was not a home warmed by the telling and retelling of the histories of love. The only surviving stories were the hieroglyphics etched on our faces, the constant mournful frown of his father and the frozen smile of his mother. Because he could not touch my body, he touched my shame. Have you remembered this? He found his flesh littered with holes. From the holes poured vitality and meaning, pleasure and a feeling for what is real. Into the holes he stuffed whatever he could when self-forgetting failed. He fell apart and glued himself together. And yet, there was something that never perished. Something other than the broken logic of his life. Something related to beauty and the friend of wind and song, something blessed and nameless.*

༄

Jim is walking down Santa Monica Boulevard toward a mobile ashram built on the parking lot of a seaside hotel. It is a Saturday morning in 1980 shortly after Christmas. As he draws closer, he feels the nervousness of hope and dread arm-wrestling in his stomach. He has flown to Los Angeles to attend a weekend meditation intensive given by the guru sweeping the country, Swami Muktananda. Great expectations are swimming in his heart as he walks the five blocks to the meditation hall.

Jim is no stranger to meditation or spiritual pursuits. He has sat in sweaty gymnasiums with Tibetan Lamas, listened to roosters chant while he stared at Zen walls fourteen hours a day for seven days and even attempted to find nirvana doing the tantric tango with Cheryl Topas straddling his pelvis. What he found were aching knees and an abundance of fragmented thoughts in his head. After a week of trying to get comfortable on a zafu, he did find a great clarity of mind. Driving back to San Francisco the world was scintillating. Color and a presence of life unlike anything he'd known made him glad he'd endured the week-long sit.

Certainly imitating Shakti and Shiva with Cheryl had made an impression, and he vowed to be more active in that practice. But the world soon faded. Cheryl decided to meditate in the full lotus. And Jim turned against the practice of meditation and spirituality, convinced he was hiding from life and the psychological problems influencing his retreat. He threw himself into therapy and bicycling. Lust required no such discipline. It clung to him like a virus.

But as Jim grew into more of a person, as he came to resemble a real character in a 20th-century novel, he became more despondent and restless. Once again he felt the pull of what he took to be a terrible yearning, a hunger for something real. He tried to analyze it in order to extinguish its force. He tried to sublimate it into art. He bought a how-to book (*Drawing on the Right Side of the Brain*), a sketchpad, and some charcoal pencils, and began to draw the portraits of famous people. Drawing worked. It was an active meditation. In the three hours that passed, sketching the face of one celebrity or another, he forgot himself and seemed to enter a stream of experience unrestricted by time and memory. To his astonishment, the likeness of Pope John and Jacques Cousteau emerged from the white pages. Nabokov was his favorite subject. There was something complex in his eyes that defied understanding, a sly mischievous expression that he felt could be either playful or sinister. A face he couldn't easily read were he sitting across the table at a poker game.

One night Jim was enjoying the famous photo of Einstein, the sad, thoughtful eyes looking for company, the grand white mane, the deep, dark creases in his skin. He enjoyed the play of black and white, the blurring of light and dark, the meaningful shadows meandering across that unforgettable face. As he sat with his Einstein, a friend entered the room and dropped a magazine in his lap with a smiling Swami Muktananda on the cover. Jim stopped drawing and turned his attention to the chuckling image in his hands.

This man was playful. He seemed to be laughing for no reason. The orange wool hat on his head made him appear casual, as though he didn't take himself too seriously. Jim dipped into the testimonials and was taken with the remarkable spiritual experiences reportedly happening in the presence of this Baba, as they called him. Some spoke of tremendous openings into joy. Stories of expansiveness and unbounded love were common. Forays into a freedom so vast the world and its sufferings just fell away. These lined up with accounts of blissful states and, like the other tales of spiritual breakthrough, such expansive openings were attributed to the touch of Muktananda and a thing called *shaktipat*.

According to the article Baba was not an ordinary guru. He was a Siddha, a perfected being capable of awakening the kundalini lying dormant at the base of the spine. The awakened kundalini released tremendous energy and connected individuals with their source, the unbounded Self. Muktananda walked the rows of seekers during the intensive and touched them on the head and the rest was a magical, sometimes explosive, birthing of spirit. A second coming into being. Spiritual fireworks.

Jim put the magazine down. He looked at Einstein and he looked at Muktananda. They were as different as zebra and rhino, but as his gaze moved from one to the other he began to see just one being looking back. Soon he found that the being in the pictures was identical to the one doing the looking. Without a thought, Jim drifted into a spaciousness far removed from charcoal and paper. His body grew ten thousand meters in every direction. Grew into the Eagle Nebulae, where he roamed weightless and free. It was a hundred times better than the flying dreams he loved so much. After what felt like an hour, Jim slowly opened his eyes. The room looked at him like a dog not sure if its master is right. He put down his pencils and drawing pad and stood up cautiously. From there he went directly to make plans for the trip to Santa Monica.

Outside the huge white tent Jim can hear the voices of a thousand men and women singing the holy mantra *Om Namah Shivaya*. The singing is deeply personal and mysterious. Wave after wave of the beautiful chant breaks over him at the entrance to the darkened hall. Gods on one side and goddesses on the other chanting with a passion that is spellbinding. Call and response, back and forth, give and take: the rhythm is intoxicating. A love song between the sun and the moon. A love supreme washing smooth the edges of Jim's heart. Before he enters the hall, before he smells the wonderful aroma of burning incense, before he takes his seat among the throngs of bodies singing the name of God, his body begins to sway with the rise and fall of the sacred syllables. His mind is captured and stilled by the resonant tones. A smile spreads within, sublime and full.

Celebrities file in and take their places near the front of the hall where an empty chair sits under a large photo of a nearly naked man with a huge round belly. The chair is slightly elevated and a table with flowers stands beside it. Jim assumes that Swami Muktananda will take that seat. The swami is not in the hall and Jim is again taken over by the chanting. The seashore has never sounded so lovely.

Soon the lights are raised and the program begins with introductions, more chanting and another talk, by a young American swami. He is funny, articulate, and a fountain of remarkable stories about meditation and interactions with Muktananda. Jim can sense his own expectations, and those of his neighbors, growing with every account of a fantastic spiritual experience.

The atmosphere in the room is buzzing. As the bald, white man in orange robes goes on delighting the crowd with promise, Muktananda enters the hall quite inconspicuously. Jim is reminded of the steaming gym in Boulder with the Tibetan genius and notes the punctuality of Muktananda's arrival and the confident, uninebriated step with which he walks to his chair. Once there he bows to the picture above his seat and sits down in a half-lotus. He appears entirely comfortable and unassuming. The trademark orange wool cap is on his head and the playful smile of the magazine cover on his face. The Siddha guru smiles and waves to the guests nearest his spot in the hall. He is warm and friendly and often breaks into a hearty laugh. Soon the first speaker concludes his talk and all attention shifts to the man in orange. His voice is soft but strong. Speaking in Hindi, he begins by saying, "With great love and respect, I welcome you all, with all my heart." His words are translated by a beautiful young Indian woman, who stands at a microphone before the audience. She shines like a star sapphire mounted in gold. With every word she seems to fall deeper and deeper into a love that is intoxicating. Muktananda, the bliss of freedom, moves as easily as his name suggests between themes and moods that are one moment serious and the next full of merriment.

The talk lasts for thirty minutes and then the hall darkens for meditation. This is the big moment. Time for the touch and the awakening of the kundalini. Shaktipat. Jim is uncomfortable sitting on the floor but his anticipation is so great he barely notices. He can still hear the pulse of the mantra within the grand silence that falls upon them all. He tries to meditate but really he is watching the figure of this short-robed man walk between the lines, stopping to give the touch to every aspiring meditator in the room.

As Jim senses his approach, his body tingles. What will happen? Will it be auspicious? Suddenly Muktananda stands before him. He presses two fingers in Jim's eyes and mutters something under his breath. Jim is taken by surprise. It all happens so fast. He had expected the touch on the crown of his head. Never mind, he says to himself, and awaits the big moment. Within the hall he hears the moans and exclamations of ecstatic worshippers. Within himself he feels nothing but discomfort and a sore knee. His circulation is poor, and soon feet and ankles are numb. He lifts his knees up and tries his best to open to the Inner Self. What did Muktananda say? "God dwells within You as You." Closing his eyes he waits for the gates of heaven to open and does his best to ignore the pain in his body and the voice of ridicule beginning its own mantra of negation.

Shortly after noon Jim and a thousand other pilgrims leave the great white tent and move to the lunch line for the meal included in the cost of the retreat. Jim eats alone and in despair. Nothing earth-shattering has happened and he has begun to admonish himself for his foolish fantasies. After lunch he walks the streets of Santa Monica mocking his naiveté and criticizing the poor judgment that led him down another dead-end path. His father was right; when was he going to accept reality? When was he going to face life as it is and stop asking it to be more?

He considers taking a cab to the airport and heading home early but something in the Midwest pragmatism of his psyche convinces him to stay on. Not that he believes anything different will happen. But he had enjoyed the chanting. At the designated hour, he walks back into the hall as despondent as he'd ever felt. This time he takes a chair near the back to at least spare himself the ordeal of aching knees. The despair grows heavier and heavier, swamping Jim like a rogue wave. He is defenseless. The program begins with more talks and chanting. Jim doesn't hear a word. He is flying through storm clouds without radar. Turbulence tosses him this way and that. There are no instruments to guide him. He is certain to fly into a mountain and die. Why hadn't he just left?

Twenty minutes into the program, his mind spinning out of control, he is caught off guard by a spontaneous prayer reaching out from the hurricane of thought. There is no time to wonder whose voice it is calling from that forsaken place because in the instant he utters the words, "Please help me," a flash occurs and the enclosed shell of being Jim has known as his self blows open and expands at what seems like the speed of light into a boundless space. Not only does his spirit soar like a bird freed from its cage but it is now infused with a joy beyond recognition. A joy beyond words. Beyond cause. He seems to have died and left his body light years behind and become a field of radiance.

What remains of Jim Brennan has nothing to do with depression and restlessness and everything to do with a crazy love, a love without an object. A love that is everything. A bit of Jim watches in marvel and awe but this is a sliver of what is primarily the bliss of consciousness unfolding and delighting in its unfolding. And it was not to be short-lived. Love everlasting had Jim in her arms and was not letting go.

The afternoon meditation with Muktananda is even stronger. Jim disappears into the joy of pure, unborn being and doesn't return until the lights go on and he hears Muktananda's sweet voice beckoning him and the others back to this world. But it is no longer the world he'd left. This world is suffused with a new, blissful vibration residing in his chest. A vibration so tender and delicious Jim listens for it like a new mother listening for the breath of her baby. He wakes in the middle of the night to make sure it is still there. It is a candle in the dark. A shadow turned into a jewel. Scintillating. Breathtaking. In fact, when meditating, he notices himself taken over by a stillness so profound that he barely needs to inhale. His lungs rest as he takes in the life of another source. Another source all together.

Walking back to his dorm room, Jim does not feel the earth beneath his feet. He does not hear the surf pounding on the shoreline. Only the music of that dear vibration sings for him. The magic of shaktipat plays again and again in his mind. Enormous thankfulness swells in his heart and the desire to give something in return takes over his thoughts. During the darshan, he saw people approach Muktananda and give him a gift of one addiction or another. A sacrifice at the foot of the guru. Some gave cigarettes, some gave alcohol. They came and bowed and exchanged pettiness for the sublime gift of grace.

Jim decides he will surrender the virus of lust. He stops into a Plaid Pantry and buys the silliest porn magazine he can find. This particular issue has the photo of a shapely girl flashing her ass at the photographer. Perfect.

At the evening program that night Jim enters the darshan line with the prize sacrifice wrapped in a paper bag. The line moves slowly and Jim approaches the short brown man with the bemused but loving smile with glee and trepidation. He is trembling by the time he kneels and lays the bag at the feet of Muktananda. Nityananda, the naked one above the chair, the bliss of eternity, stares down at him with the stern look Jim mistakes for the mirror.

He stands and walks off exhilarated by the adventure of surrender. Twenty paces away someone taps him on the shoulder. It is one of the Swamis. He says to Jim, "Baba wants to talk to you." A bolt of energy strikes him below the ribs. The next moment Jim stands before a chuckling Muktananda waving the magazine and the naked bottom in his hand for everyone to see. The swamis fall over themselves reeling in laughter. Jim's heart is pounding like a steel drum. Baba looks Jim in the eyes and pointing to the ass so flagrantly exposed says to him in a voice embroidered with amusement and tenderness, "Do they shit out of this?"

Jim nods.

"Then why do you have to look at it?" Baba laughs and laughs and motions Jim to go on his way. But Jim can tell he isn't laughing at him as he throws the cheap magazine into the growing pile of self-medicating, self-enhancing drugs the faithful have brought him. He and the rest of the witnesses to Jim's sacrifice are poking fun at the folly of the human being. At the endless string of distractions cooked up by the mind. At the desperate, futile grasping for happiness.

Jim walks away stunned at the silence of the mirror. A force far greater, a force of kindness, has made his executioner speechless. Impotent. Allowing Jim to walk into the sea of devotees laughing out loud, overflowing with energy as though every cell in his body were a whirling dervish spinning and spinning, faster than the fastest electron, into a field of unbridled love.

Home was never the same. Jim longed to be in India living in Muktananda's ashram. He longed to begin his days with chanting as he'd done that morning in Santa Monica. His yearnings were frustrated but he built himself a meditation room off the garage and sat religiously every morning at 5:30 AM for over five years. Just as religiously, he checked to see if the awakened vibration was still there.

Fearful that it would abandon him, he kept a close eye out for the blissful visitor whenever he woke in the night or lost track of it during the day. After some time, he learned to trust in the presence and found himself able to go into meditation just about anywhere: waiting in the grocery store parking lot, at work with his patients, under a hot shower at day's end. In the meditation room he had visions of Krishna and gilded celestial bodies. He dissolved into luminous fields of love and bliss. The ripple of what the sacred texts refer to as Shakti flowed over and through his being. He felt as if he were the headwaters of the Ganges.

The problem came when he ended meditation and opened the door to the world. There he walked into a resentment he found troubling and perplexing. A resentment he later recognized as identical to the feelings he held for his mother. An inner resistance to the world. Against life. What was he against?

In fact, though the bliss of shaktipat had not gone away, neither had the forces of the world. The mirror found its tongue and, though somewhat weakened, set about to reestablish its authority.

Jim suffered and railed against his world because he could not reconcile the wondrous expressions of consciousness with the ceaseless assaults of life. The whole dynamic ferris wheel of fortune and loss endlessly circling. Circling, always circling, capturing the soul and taking it to great heights and great lows. Spinning through the thrill of flight, the fear of falling, the urge to jump, the transcendent view, the descent to the ordinary. Pain and pleasure proved as enduring as the rising and setting of the sun. As everlasting as surf pounding on the beach: the multitude of waves coming into being, rising in power, crashing on the shore, and vanishing in the sand.

He couldn't stop the moods that behaved like waves. Thoughts and desires that apparently had lives of their own. The mirror reminded him of the foolishness of his strivings. The bliss of consciousness reminded him of a real Self. He oscillated between joy and shame. Between forgetting and remembering. How was it possible to forget so easily what was so unforgettable? So indelibly tattooed to his soul? And what caused him to remember? Was it a memory at all? Or was it contact? Contact with that nameless radiance at the heart of every instant. Contact with that which restores what needs no restoring. That which returns what has never been lost.

∾

By the time Frank arrived in Portland to say good-bye to his mother, nearly thirty years had passed since Jim first met Muktananda and received shaktipat. Baba died two years after of heart failure and the organization he founded suffered political in-fighting over his successors. Jim went his own way, struggling to reconcile his disparate experiences and working to bring psychological knowledge and spiritual awareness closer together. Increasingly he came to acknowledge that the way to acceptance and peace led through his mother. Try as he might, the tension remained. The impatience, the damn impatience, even in dying, made him feel small and loathsome.

Frank looked well enough. It was a family trait to look good no matter what. He hadn't lost much weight and his face had good color. But when he walked it showed. He couldn't hide the fatigue. He couldn't hide the weight on his shoulders causing his body to stoop forward. Perhaps for the first time as an adult, he bent to something beyond his control.

The chemo was working, but at a cost. Frank was weakening. No one suspected he was walking around with pneumonia. One week later and he would be in the hospital struggling to breathe. This day, though, he was in the Good Samaritan Hospital struggling to see his mother. The man who faced down the toughest judges in the country, the Charles Atlas of San Francisco litigators (never a grain of sand kicked in his face), could not, in sickness or in health, struggle to bring himself to face his parents on their death bed.

Frank walked into Georgia's room looking like he needed a bed of his own. His gait was slow and labored. When he saw his mother lying there on her side with her mouth open and working hard to draw each breath he grimaced and cursed, "Jesus." His eyes begged to look away. They half-closed as if he were squinting into the sun. He walked to her bedside but he could not bring himself to touch her body. He folded his arms. It was the last time he would get that close.

"Hi Mom." Even his words struggled for air. To go beyond himself. In a short four months he would take her place on that bed. Jim wondered if Frank was seeing himself in the grasp of the beyond. "Has she been like this the whole time?"

"Pretty much. Her breathing is more labored now but still fairly strong. I'm surprised."

"It's hard to see her like this." Frank shook his head and looked at the wall.

"Yeah, it is. At least she's not in pain."

"What are the doctors saying?"

"Not much. Just keep her comfortable. Maybe another day. Who knows?"

"Christ." He looked at Jim and shook his head again. His eyes were pleading to be excused. He sat down on a chair like a soldier in the last days of a war certain to end in defeat.

"How are things, Frank?"

The old mule of silence stood between them again. At the first sight of it, Jim grasped for something to engage his brother. Death was far more tolerable an opponent than the awkward tension that could build between them.

"Fine, fine. The usual struggles and frustrations." Frank's voice was tight and brittle. He looked like a beaten boxer in his corner, hoping the bell won't ring for another round. Jim found he could barely look at his brother. They sat there in Room 360, the final stop on Georgia's itinerary, on opposite sides of the bed their mother lay in.

Had she always been the one between them? Was it a simple competition for her favor? In a matter of hours she would be gone and they would be face to face. What then? What would be left? Privately the brothers feared being alone together with their differences. But it was the growing similarities that truly bothered them when they looked across the abyss of Georgia's body into each other's eyes.

By morning they would wake up to a world without their mother for the first time. Frank would wake up knowing he was no longer invincible. Knowing his lungs were filling with unshed tears. Knowing pain and failure were stalking him relentlessly.

Jim knew failure and pain. He saw the helpless, desperate shadow pass over his brother's face and wanted nothing more than to help Frank with his suffering. And yet, there was that gap. That space between them where their mother lay taking breath after useless breath. A gap Jim longed to close but could not. He told himself it was his fault. And so he sat there alone with longing on one side and shame on the other.

Frank looks at the floor and he looks at Jim. He tries not to look at Georgia. When he does, his face breaks into pieces. Jim recognizes the anguish and annoyance.

"Are you hungry?"

"I'm starving. Is there someplace nearby we can eat?" Frank is visibly relieved by his brother's rescue.

"Sure, NW 23rd is a block away. Let's get you something to eat. You look like you need some food."

Jim recognized Frank would be absent for the long night of silent waiting, and he couldn't help wonder why he ended up alone with so much in his life. His work. The care of his mother. In a matter of months, he would be completely alone; the last of his family. How would he manage that? He shuddered and turned his back on those thoughts.

Annoyance sat there waiting but soon gave way to feeling sorry for his brother. Not only for the cancer taking him down inch by inch. That was terrible, but what was worse, what was heart-breaking, was the emotional weakness and fear that made any vulnerability whatsoever dangerous, a threat to Frank's identity that compelled him to clamp down on his heart and hold back. Hold love in check. Love. Love is the culprit. Gerald knew it. Frank knows it. Love is the mother of pain. And pain is always the villain of the story: the memory of loss, of the forgotten waiting in ambush.

"I don't know. It's really tough seeing her like that. Just hard to believe." Something was trying to penetrate his stone fortress. Something he no longer had the strength to hold off. Frank shook his head once more and walked at a turtle's pace to the elevator. Jim wanted to sympathize but found himself thinking it wouldn't be so surprising if Frank had watched her fall face first into her soup. Or if he'd cleaned up the mess in her bathroom. He tried to stifle the resentment and warm to his brother but Frank's condition pained Jim greatly and anger seemed far preferable to seeing him fight a futile battle. Better than feeling the tensions holding him together like rubber bands.

⁓

If only Frank could have been there to hear the music therapist sent up that afternoon by Palliative Care. She would have soothed his frantic soul. Emily arrived in time. She came after lunch with a bouquet of flowers from home. Always the sensitive one, Emily walked into Room 360 with a vase of fresh white daisies. In the middle of the arrangement was one brilliant red rose. It glowed like a ruby from the crown of a Maharaja. Jim and Emily bought the rose years before when their beloved Lab died. His name was Magic. And he was.

They found this particular rose in the same way they found each other. In the midst of a hundred rose bushes it called to them. The huge cherry red blossoms, the rich deep perfume. Love at first sight. And when they checked the tag to identify the name what they found made them smile all the more. It was a German name which Emily translated as "the magic of love."

Emily placed the bouquet on the night stand by Georgia's bed. "Hello Mom." She took her hand and rubbed it gently. Jim was so happy to have her with him. He looked at the bouquet and felt something change in the atmosphere of the room. Emily had that effect on him and the world she touched. She seemed able to attune herself to the music of the spheres, to the deep rhythm of her babies, and to the longings of her husband.

Jim was appreciating the pleasure of looking at his wife and the thoughtfulness of her soul when the musician entered the room. She walked in on a cloud. Quiet as the moon.

༄

*She was an angel. Her wings were translucent as the platinum blue of the sea at dusk. Her hair was long and chocolate-brown. She held a golden harp in her arms and sat down without a word. I wondered if I was at the gates of heaven until my angel folded whatever breath was left to me into her heart and with her fingertips encouraged those golden strings to sing like a choir of birds bathed by the pink glow of dawn. I felt her hands glide across those strings like the dancers in Swan Lake. And then she came and offered her hand to my heart, her song to my spirit, and we danced a beautiful waltz upon the dream of this world. A beautiful waltz that flowed like stardust across the universe.*

༄

Emily and Jim sat by Georgia's bedside and let the music take them. The flowers sang along and turned to butterflies flying in the splendor of being. Death disrobed and revealed its true colors, revealed its twin-ship with life and the energies of eternal becoming. Emily and Jim closed their eyes and opened to the sound enveloping the room. The sound dissolving the thin lines of self outlining their thoughts. They melted into one being. Into the life without closings.

༄

*Life is a dream. Death is also a dream. That music lifted our hearts from dreaming and sent them soaring. It turned my coarse breath into pelican wings gliding inches above the ocean waves.*

෴

The harpist played on, but for Jim and Emily there was no musician or instrument, nor even music, only that sweet wordless lullaby, the transformer of sorrows, carrying them into the silence of the ocean's depth. Into the deep space of cosmic breath. There, in the nucleus of creation, within the large and the small, that radiant link, friend to wind and song, comforted them.

෴

*Seeing my family at peace, I could begin the final preparations for my departure. With one breath and then another, my soul went about unpacking a lifetime of gatherings. Dying is nothing but subtraction and the soul needs no instruction in arithmetic. It feels no remorse laying aside the fondest of keepsakes. Like the sage in a Himalayan cave my soul went about its business uttering those sacred words...Neti Neti...not this, not this...and with a farewell kiss I said goodbye to my family and to everything I thought myself to be: the obedient daughter, fun-loving Daisy, the selfless Mother, all the articles of clothing accumulated over time like patina on a sculpture, until all that remained was a ripple, not even a breeze, a celestial gown from the cloth of moonlight*

෴

Evening comes slowly in July. The midsummer nights stretch far into the turn of the earth before the last of daylight paints an enchantingly deep blue makeover on the face of darkness while quietly slipping into the land of tomorrow. By the time the first star began to sparkle, Jim sat alone in Room 360 with Georgia. Frank had retreated to his hotel exhausted and disturbed. Emily was home with the boys helping them to bed and sharing stories about their grandmother. She had stayed for as long as was possible. Together they encouraged Georgia to let go, assured her that all was well and it was her time to be at peace. Emily said goodbye to the woman who had been a mother to her. She tearfully kissed her cheek for what was sure to be the last time. Jim hugged her and they both cried in each other's arms a long soft cry.

Quiet descended on the room as Jim took a chair to his mother's bedside. He stroked her hand and said softly, "I'm here, Mom. I'm here."

Georgia had not moved for two days. The only sign of life was a simple sound. The rhythmical sound of one breath followed by another. That one chord, repeated and repeated like the drone of an Indian tambura, resonated deeply within Jim and became, in those forty-eight hours, so familiar that he barely noticed when the pace began to change. When the urgency of each claim to life softened.

When he did sense the engine of Georgia's body begin to slow, he saw her face relaxing as well. Jim could sense in those moments the great exertion of survival ever so gradually winding down like the blades of a fan unplugged. Georgia had finished her business and was gliding home. Her body accepted the news without a struggle. And as it did so, Jim realized with some embarrassment that while he thought he'd been encouraging Georgia to let go and while he thought he'd been accepting and reassuring when he told her the family would be fine and she was free to go, now, in the presence of her peaceful descent, he knew that he'd been pushing. Pushing against her way of dying like he'd pushed against her way of living.

For a moment he felt terrible. Shame reared over him like a grizzly bear on its hind legs. But the sound of his mother's dear lungs rising and falling woke him from the lifelong nightmare of shame, and Jim watched with astonishment as the grizzly went down on all fours and disappeared into the brush.

Georgia's breathing was no longer the labored story of going on. A different song arrived on the wind, a song of surrender. Jim lay his head on her hand and sobbed. For this moment the fight was over. The fan would take time to run down. The ferris wheel of pleasure and pain would not stop on a dime. Perhaps it would take the rest of his life. Perhaps Jim would be on his own death bed before he could truly reach out a hand of friendship to himself and life. But in that moment it all stopped.

Jim raised his head and through eyes clouded with tears and a voice choked with yearning he'd kept prisoner all these years, he said to his dying mother, "I'm sorry, Mom. I'm sorry. I love you, Mom."

And he cried for himself and for his brother and for all the ancestors waiting to accompany Georgia Daisy on her way. And especially for Frank, he said again, "I love you, Mom. Frank loves you. We all love you." This was not the joyless service of the preceding months and years. This was the service of thankfulness.

His heart swelled and went out to Georgia's and she accepted him with the formidable compassion of the dead. Their spirits met and soared into the moonlit sky. They flew directly to Frank. There they hovered over his fitful sleep and touched his forehead while promising to be with him always. Georgia kissed her first-born and whispered something in his ear. He stirred in his bed and rolled on his stomach, muttering something only Georgia understood. She said goodbye, and mother and son returned to her room at the hospital where they settled in for the night.

∽

Jim sat by Georgia's side and told her stories he'd kept from her all these years. He told her about the ring, the dog who ate the ring, and Mary Jo Bellinger. He told her about the midnight races to make curfew through the winding roads of New Canaan in the old Mercury bought from the husband of Agi, the talker. She never knew about the day he and Jeff Anderson were arrested in the great Pyramid for breaking into a secured burial tomb. Nor did she know about hitch-hiking through the desert of Libya on his way to Egypt. This after spending three weeks on a beach in Morocco smoking hashish and body surfing with five hundred hippies from all parts of the world. He told her his adventures and brushes with danger while his mother listened like a boulder that has heard everything there is to hear for a million years or more. He laughed and shook his head thinking back on the highlights of his youth.

Gerald and Georgia disapproved of every step he took toward life. But in the last full day of his mother's life, he remembered his rebellious determination with pride. And somehow as the clock approached midnight, he felt Georgia on his side and on the side of passions she had long denied herself.

He apologized for laughing at her the day she came home with frosted hair. He apologized for the self-centered years when he couldn't even remember to send a Mother's Day card. With an ache in his heart, he thanked her for all she had given and sacrificed. For her unfailing love.

Once again his heart beat loudly for his mother. He looked at her face and knew he would miss seeing her lovely green eyes. He would miss her smile and the light she brought to the world.

As Emily had remarked the first afternoon in the hospital, Georgia was still beautiful. Beautiful to the end. And in the space of that thought Jim was taken by an inspiration. A wish to celebrate and adorn his mother properly. Remembering the flowers Emily brought earlier in the day he turned and took one from the vase. He cut the stem and placed the daisy in Georgia's hair behind her ear. Lovely. Wasn't she lovely?

Just then a gust of wind upended the quiet. It sounded like a choir of hummingbirds, like a river of silver in flight. Jim had never before heard such singing. His body melted away to nothing. His personality turned to vapor. Something moved and yet nothing moved. Something and nothing lay like lovers where surf meets sand. And the consciousness Jim thought was his folded seamlessly as the most fluid of dreams into one being after another. Some of them formless, some recognizable, some familiar. All seemed to inhabit the same space. The identical molecule of existence. And yet none had any more substance than a cloud. Dissolving and forming. An endless parade of coming and going. Old, old faces. Native American women whose lined faces looked like canyons seen through the eyes of an eagle. Georgia's mother, finally at peace and draped in the compassion of the dead, put her hand over her daughter's heart. Ruth, who smiled and made galaxies glow. Ancient Tibetans knelt on rocks, forming the rivers of the world with their tears. Gerald, minus the woe, having discovered laughter on the moon. A kaleidoscope of souls emanating from and returning to nothing as the wheel of birth and death turned and turned. The only constant being joy. A great joy that arose from the sound of the hummingbirds' wings beating faster and faster until there was only one sound, one syllable, singing the unbounded song of joy.

Angels brought Jim back to his body and the chair beside his mother's bed. They were invisible to him but he could feel their gentleness. He came back to himself with ease. Georgia's breathing greeted him with its distinctive hello. Jim saw the daisy in his mother's hair and smiled. He stood and went to the vase and one by one brought the white daisies to his mother and fitted each to her soft gray mane. Georgia looked like a noble queen. She wore the crown of creation. The collection of Van Gogh's celestial stars formed a halo around her quiet face.

Jim reached for the red rose. He removed one velvet petal after another. With tenderness he placed them around his mother's neck and shoulders until they formed a necklace equal in beauty to the crown on her head. They reminded him of Indra's gems radiating out into the universe and beyond.

Georgia wore them with grace. She would be happy to leave this world dressed for the occasion. He imagined her taking the Lord of Death by the arm and walking like a lady into the mist. When he looked down at his mother, it was easy to see her smiling and admiring the necklace and crown. In those moments past midnight, before the sunrise of her last day on earth, Jim accepted the smile and life of Georgia Daisy with all his heart. The struggle of for and against subsided, and he sat with his mother for another thirty minutes admiring the beauty of the moment and allowing the peace between them to permeate the body of memory. And before he lay down on the cot at her feet he smiled and said with love and respect, "Good night, Mom. You're doing great, Mom. You're doing great. Whenever you're ready. You let me know. I love you."

# CHAPTER 11
# The Last Breath

❧

I'm sure I was asleep before my head touched the pillow. And yet I dimly remember listening for Mom's breath one last time and making a mental note of its rhythm and volume. The end was near and I wanted to make sure that I would be awake when the bell sounded. No doubt it was also comforting to hear and feel the presence of her life surrounding me. I suppose it is likely that I drifted into a deep sleep remembering being a baby in a crib when her breath was my breath and her life the only life. However, the only conscious thought in my mind as I lay down that night was the pleasing image of the daisies in her hair and the blood-red rose petals on her chest. The hope to be awake for her passing was less of a thought and more the prayer of my body as I pulled a sheet and blanket over my shoulder.

I was thankful for a few hours of nothing and took the elevator straight to the bottom floor of oblivion. Deep sleep is the most soothing form of forgetfulness, isn't it? Such a benevolent eraser. Gone was the hospital, Mom, and most of all me. What a relief. A few hours away from the helter skelter and commotion of this confusion called my self was a Godsend.

Yes, the last few hours with Mom were precious. At last I found a way to put aside annoyance and accept her. That allowed a big love to settle into the hollow carved out by decades of conflict with my self. But as I lay down in the dark silence of that hour, I had little confidence that the bristling grievances occupying my mind for nearly sixty years would remain quiet for long.

I was right and I was wrong. At the first disturbance of that blessed state beyond the senses, I suffered the common, but still unnerving, experience of being unable to locate myself. Unable to recognize existence. Groping for a switch in the dark: a me to pull myself up from nowhere. It was like waking up inside a Zen koan without a guide. No bearings whatsoever. No footing.

Gradually faces emerged from the dark and the fragile coalition of me scrambled like a bunch of exhausted young soldiers struggling to wake up and cohere into an acceptable unit for their sergeant. Confusion and disorder. Love bumping into hate. Tripping over fear. Remembering clawing its way up from the bottom of a rock face. Memories of quicksand and collapsing bridges. Wrestling with zero. Wanting to breathe. Wanting to be. Where? Why am I here? Do I want to be here? Yes, yes. No. I don't know. Yes.

In the end it was her breath that brought me back. That brought form to a dark mindless room. The breath of our mother running slowly into still water. I opened my eyes and crows landed with a shriek. I closed my eyes but the world did not disappear. Forgetting was impossible. Remembering floundered.

Her breath was so weak it barely reached my ears. But it was strong enough to wake the love in my bones which lifted this body of resistance with one massive effort the way I'd seen those Russian Olympic heavyweights lift a sagging barbell and throw it to the floor. My spirit shook like a water-soaked dog and the crows angrily dispersed to the four corners of the world. I sat up and tried to steady the whirlpool in my head.

Once again, it was Mom's breath that brought my attention to a focus. Softer than a whisper. Light as a feather falling from a nest. I cannot recall a more tender touch. A more gentle request. It brushed fear from my heart and inertia from my brain, and I moved toward her bedside unencumbered. In the four steps it took to reach her, my body became weightless. My eyes glanced out the window at the first colors of sunrise appearing on the horizon. The long arms of sunlight moved like watercolors up the curtain of early morning and left a golden pink farewell on the horizon for Daisy. Songbirds perched outside her window and serenaded their departing friend with her favorite songs.

And when I reached her side, I was dazzled to find her turned toward the window with her clouded green eyes open and looking directly into mine as though seeing her son one last time was her soul's final request of this life. She looked through me as though there were no difference between the sunrise spreading in the East, the grown body of her youngest child, and the last few breaths floating from her lips like falling cottonwood blossoms. We held hands and let the pauses between each precious rise and fall of her lungs, slight as they were, hold our hearts together. Mom took three more shallow breaths. She gave her final wind to the world as a kiss, a puff. Like a little girl who takes a dandelion in her hands and gently blows the delicate seedlings into the air scattering them on a passing breeze. And she was done. The final note.

Another remarkable incarnation untangled from its earthly knot. Freed from the bonds of the known. And the silence, oh Frank, the silence that stood over her body, that filled her body, that quieted in one motion, like the baton of a great conductor, the orchestration of a trillion cells. That silence, itself the story that has no end, that cannot be told, that goes on with the telling into infinity. I wish you had been there to behold our mother enter that silence. I wish that silence would find and name you. Perhaps it would help you, if with your own eyes and senses, you could perceive death as something other than the destruction of everything you hold dear. Perhaps you could learn to accept it as an intermission, a pause in the extraordinary, revolving story of your spirit. Maybe then you wouldn't be so afraid. Maybe then you could say goodbye to Sally and the boys and leave them with the blessing of your thankfulness. They need your love. As do I.

Dear Frank, I love you. There, I said it. For the first time in my adult life and maybe ever. I love you and I fear for you. Please don't think I'm pious or beyond fear. Believe me, I'm terrified. For years the thought of my death has made me shiver and shrink. In my psyche, Hell is eternal annihilation. Worse than being buried alive. I remember that television show we watched once as kids, the one about the convicts who tried to escape by digging a tunnel from their cell block just wide enough for their bodies to crawl through. Do you remember? And as they were making their escape the authorities, having discovered the plan, sealed off the entrance and exit of the tunnels and the prisoners were trapped and left to die like worms. This is the dread I have felt despite the teachings of the ages to the contrary. I can't shake it. Even though the experiences of meditation and the readings of sacred texts have shown other possibilities to be true, I tremble in terror. How do we know?

Sometimes you and I seem like those prisoners, Frank. Desperate to escape confinement. Desperate to get somewhere. Fighting against the penitentiary guards. What are we fighting? Are we fighting for something or are we nothing unless we're fighting? It seems like shadow boxing to me. Do you really love the battle so much?

Frank, you are dying. I'm so, so sorry. So sorry. But Frank, it's true. Listen to me. What do you love? Success and wealth? The Olympic Club? No, you love your boys. Your family. Sally. Use your dying. Let it help you. It is breaking down everything and it can't be stopped. Let it break down the vault enclosing your heart. You've worked yourself to the bone to give them everything. Now give them this. Give them your heart. And let them give it back. Please. Be more than a memory to them, Frank. Live on in their souls.

You and I were born on opposite sides of the great divide. When the earthquake of '68 hit, the world split in two. We watched as a gaping hole opened where solid land once lay. We watched as the hole widened and our separation grew. You fought the conventional war, and I went underground and joined the guerilla forces of the counterculture. We clashed. Our swords crashed against each other like lightning bolts dueling over the Rockies. Why?

We both grew up under the scorching heat of mushroom clouds exploding in the sky. We've known since that day we had only seconds to live. We fought against that terror. But our emotions turned brittle as crackers, paper cuts on the skin of our hearts. Of course we ran from our emotions. You were faster. You are still running. Outrunning pain. Outrunning Dad. Outrunning cancer.

Of course. We are white men and we don't surrender. We glorify the battle. We are white men. Educated, middle-class men. Sons of privilege. Offspring of heroes and triumph. We remember our father going to work in a suit and tie. We remember our mother making breakfast in an apron. We remember ourselves on dusty ball fields, dreaming in church pews. Lusting in science class, drinking under age, cheating on geometry tests. We remember lying to our parents, falling in love, having wet dreams, running away from home. Running from our mother's smile. We remember Vietnam, atomic bombs, assassinations. We remember lynchings and murders. Feeling small and weak, wanting to be James Bond. Kissing girls in the dark. Drinking way too much, liking drugs way too much, wanting sex way too much. But lately, feeling little and weak is what we remember most: little and cold alone at night, trying to forget. Little and frightened of everything in the room. Our covers pulled over our heads.

And like those little boys trapped in the memory bank, we cry for no reason. We cry and cover our faces. Because we are ashamed. Because we are sixty years or more and still boys with emotions we thought extinct. Still running. And fighting. Aren't we?

What are we fighting, Frank? Is it Dad? Are you still trying to outdo him? Are we fighting the giant squid of poverty? Or does it always come down to death? To loss. To Ruth leaving our father helplessly alone with unbearable pain. Is that the fight? Are we fighting against a world that is always taking back what we love? Or have we come to do battle with love itself? With Mom. With neediness. Is that the real enemy? Need and longing? Is it weakness we're shooting at? Softness we detest? And crave. No wonder our wanting is so huge. Our yearning makes us tremble. We are not different, Frank, even though we set out in opposite directions like we did as kids playing hide-and-seek in the dark. I seek you. And I believe you also seek me.

It will always please me and seem perfectly right that Mom died as the sun rose on a new day. As the sky blushed like a Georgia peach and birds sang Hallelujah to all who would listen. It will always astound me and be of some comfort when I think of the mystery of the moment of her death. The trembling pulse of life and the absolute stillness of the body, abiding together in the breath that does not return and the space that does not end.

I went and fetched the doc. He did his duty and pronounced her dead at 4:15 AM. He was kind and expressed his sympathies. When he left the room, I sat down by Mom's bed and looked at her slowly. I looked at her unwrinkled skin. At her silent mouth. I looked at her resting eyelids. At her tender young ears. At the portrait without a pose. Without a smile. She lay there on the bed of her life. Motionless as water in a cup.

I could feel the memories of her time floating toward daylight until every last drop evaporated and the cup stood empty. I could imagine her viewing the parade from her place in the luminous morning of her spirit's renewal. Holding the ribbon of her days in her fingertips like a child opening her birthday gifts. I thought I could see the green pool of her eyes grow large as a lake and take in every molecule of what did and did not occur in her lifetime from the reserved seat of acceptance and marvel. I thought I could hear her sigh and exclaim to herself, "Oh my, Georgia! Oh my!" Soon I closed my eyes and joined her in the peace which passeth all understanding. We met there. In the ever new. In effortless being. Until the unwrinkled sky turned blue and full of the light of her soul.

I stood up and stretched. Bent down and kissed our mom on the forehead. A kiss for all of us who loved her. I walked to the door of Room 360 and paused. When I turned to look at her for the last time, my heart broke and for a second I couldn't breathe. How could I leave? She might have been taking a nap. A sob the size of a sneaker wave heaved in my chest and nearly knocked me down. The body that made us and delivered us to life on earth lay there before me like a fallen tree.

The mother who loved us and smiled upon our days was gone. I felt incapable of opening the door or closing it. Petrified. Petrified to leave and enter a motherless world. A world I'd never known. She was delivering me to that world as well. Alone. Alone in the company of the one. Without a thought I went back to her bed and held her hand once more. The rain of tears was heavy but quick. I know it's stupid but I wanted so much for her to squeeze my hand and say "It's all right, Sweetie." Instead I said "Goodbye, Mom. I love you. Farewell." With that I threw my shoulders back, the way I'd seen her do a thousand times, took the deepest breath I could, and walked out the door and through the corridors of the hospital and out into the hum of morning.

And that's the story, as I recall it, Frank. Please forgive my ramblings and preaching. I'm hoping a piece of you wants to know this. We are all that's left. Let's be good to each other.

Call me soon.

With love, your brother,

Jim

# EPILOGUE
# Walking

༄

J im left the hospital and walked out into a delightful morning, already fully in bloom. He turned his back on the house of birth and death, on the home of happiness and grief, and began walking. The air was pleasingly cool and light, free of any humidity whatsoever. It was 5:15 AM, and few people were awake and fewer still out and about other than those arriving at Good Sam for a change in shift. Emily and the boys would still be sleeping, having endured the curmudgeonly chorus of crows, who greeted every daybreak as if it were a nasty intruder. Frank would still be sleeping, he hoped, and getting the rest he dearly needed.

The morning belonged to Jim and the birds and random squirrels racing up the rough-edged bark of redwoods and giant Doug Firs. Some played a game of tag, running through the branches at breakneck speeds. Others preferred to travel across the highway of power lines stretching every which way above the city landscape.

It was a quintessential summer morning in Portland. Not as fine as a Carolina morning, perhaps, but in its own way incomparably wonderful. The air was crisp. Not the soothingly lazy air of the South. Crisp and scintillating, brimming with inspiration. The sky had a bit more blue to it. A western version of blue that made the soul long for the mountains and a closer read. It was the kind of morning that made life out to be utterly beautiful. Seductively manageable. As if nothing bad could possibly happen in a world so glorious as this. Jim walked slowly down the old cracked sidewalks, half expecting the world to say, "I'm so sorry. How are you?" But the circus of the living paid no attention to his sorrow and went on with the play of creation and survival, as oblivious as a three-year-old with blocks.

Jim had no one to take care of and nowhere to be. For the first time in his life he met the day a motherless child. When he looked into the sky, he saw the clear and cloudless invitation of the wild blue yonder. He heard birds beckon and saw trees gesturing for him to join them. A desire to wander entered his heart. Just then his eyes returned to the brilliant blue cradling the fresh infancy of yet another morning on the planet Earth. He sensed something else looming in the beyond. He saw and felt the presence of Georgia, already fully absorbed into the vast parabola of sky extending from the Great Northwest, over her birthplace in the Great Lakes, to her heart's abode in the islands and wetlands of South Carolina.

This was not the first time Jim had witnessed the recently departed soul of a loved one arching across the sky. Nor was the experience dependent on him holding to a spiritual state of mind. When his beloved mentor died unexpectedly a few years back, following a kidney transplant, the radiance of his dear self found Jim in the same way. Likewise, when Gerald passed, the entire night sky glowed, luminous as pearls, from the light of a blue moon reflected off the marshlands of South Carolina, glowed and pulsed with the spirit of his father as Jim's plane slowly descended into Savannah.

Because of those moments, and because Georgia's essence, shimmering and unbounded, touched him without reaching, he knew her to be in all places at all times. He imagined her hovering over what would be Milwaukee and Cleveland watching the great ice fields carve out the basins that would become the Great Lakes and the flat land of the Midwest that would be the place of her becoming. Ridiculous as it was, he imagined his mother, of all people, swimming with alligators and turtles in the lagoons and inward water-ways of the deep South, bidding farewell to this teeming sanctuary of life with a love that has no measure. In the same surprised breath he realized, and welcomed, the company of Georgia into his heart. Georgia's presence was palpable and easily recognizable. What could be more familiar? It did not require memory or imagining. It did not require reaching or asking. Her spirit was now synonymous to his own being.

In recognizing this grand commonality, Jim relaxed the possessive hold and claim he made to his differences. He relaxed the fight to maintain and distinguish himself. Standing still on the street corner, a bit taken aback by the magnitude of this new feeling, he said yes to his mother and to the freedom that immediately opened its arms to him. And with his inner world now warm and expansive, he accepted the invitation of the birds and trees and followed them into the song of that remarkable morning.

Walking slowly and without a destination, Jim passed gardens and old Portland homes. Climbing roses and twisted Japanese maples. On one corner lot he noticed a large pile of fresh wood chips waiting to be spread over the garden paths. It was hemlock and from more than thirty feet he could smell the sweet, fermented aroma of decomposing wood. A plume of steam rose from the center of the pile reminding him of cremation pyres he'd seen in India.

As he drew nearer, he could feel heat radiating from the mass. The smell was intoxicating. A morning raga played on the breeze curling through the neighborhood. The melodies were enchanting and led him further and further from the hospital.

Soon Jim turned toward the West Hills and the thick forests of Portland. Sunshine warmed the muscles of his back and as it did so cast a long shadow ahead of his footsteps. He watched the shadow grow long and flat. Under his breath he chuckled and felt a tender affection for the elasticity of his person. For this crocodile self and submarine ego: periscope up, looking for safe waters. He held his arms up just so and voila, he was a Saguaro cactus reaching for the stars in the Arizona desert and so pleased was this cactus, with its existence, that he stopped and danced a jig right there on the sidewalk. The dancing Saguaro.

And just as suddenly his shadow rose from the featureless, flat road like evolutionary man and assumed the form of a totem pole towering above the world's insistence on singularity. He saw an infinite array of sculpted figures come into relief. A chain of characters cut from the same log of being circling the globe of this speck of self. The numbers grew fast as Jack's beanstalk and quickly were out of sight, lost in the crystal imagination of a perfect sky.

The many faces brought Jim to a halt and he stood there swaying and dizzy from the encounter with the whole rag-tag gang of pirates, the hurricane of impulses, the mudslide of mistakes, this crazy cubist psyche packed to the gills. This totem self, this stack of impersonalities scrambling for a moment in the sun, arranging and rearranging, matching and mismatching: one series of portraits after another, one erratic dream after another. When he finally settled, he turned and looked back at the sun slowly climbing its faithful bridge. It's all right. It's all right, he assured himself. A smile returned to his face. It seemed like years since he'd been here and able to smile and laugh.

By now he was near the forest. Dizzy with grief and joy, not knowing what was coming next, he continued walking toward the magnificent trees waiting for him in the sunlight. And as he gazed ahead into the dazzling display of light and shadow, he felt the readiness of spirit to reveal its beauty. How can the simplest meetings throb with such delight? And not just the grand stars of nature like the Sequoias but the slightest of happenings, the haikus of existence brushed by this radiance, this presence, a pine cone tumbling to the forest floor, a dapple of light on Irish moss, a spider web suspended between trees gently rocking in the wind. Along with the readiness of spirit, he noticed the readiness of this thing called soul. This hungry colt. This eagerness to be infused with meaning and joy. This erotic longing for the kind of love-making that dissolves inner and outer. That makes water colors flow where solid shapes once perched.

Jim was now in the heart of the forest. His heart grew heavy again thinking of his poor brother. He shook with sobs remembering Georgia on her death bed. Maybe he should run back to her. Was it right to be seeking his own fulfillment just moments after her death? For an instant the old temptations charged like medieval warriors slinging arrows and stones his way. For a second the mirror flashed and the demons of shame jumped from the trees like a band of monkeys. But on this day, they were fleeting apparitions. Here and gone. Jim paid them no regard. Instead he gazed into the forest, which was aglow with the play of light glancing from tree to tree.

Few things were as pleasing to Jim as the old woods of Oregon. He sat down on a stump and listened for the quiet within the music of the place, the quiet surrounding the chatter of birds and the musings of a light breeze. As he took in the silence with nothing better to do than sing, his eye moved into the far reaches of the forest and he noticed something different about his way of seeing. His vision was more active. More probing. The image that was once flat as a photograph was now three dimensional. What was glazed over was distinct. He looked into the near and the far. Into the depth of field and the close at hand. Well into the center of things. He saw the particulars as well as the space uniting them. A tender space. A tender space with a mother's touch that seemed to give birth to every instant and particle of existence and then take it all back, all of it, inhaling every prodigal son and daughter into her womb, where the shapes fall apart and turn to dust.

And as his eyes moved about the woodland, free of the usual restrictions, free to delve into the depths of every breath of creation, seeing became the bird of paradise. Perception flew through the shadowed canyons effortlessly, until perception alone filled the space and the masquerade of this and that evaporated. Until the strain of self and other vanished. Leaving the air so clear. So light. Allowing the exquisite ballet of energies and the erotic embrace of color and sunlight free to play on and play on into eternity, to the everlasting delight of the presence at the heart of every bit of it.

And where Jim had been, where sorrow too great to hold had lain down, where hope and dread had married and borne children, where all this had lived and vied for position, a great peace settled in. A peace that was inclusive. A space that was not separate: close but not local. Dispassionate but not removed. Where Georgia resided, though dead. Which Frank inhabited, though alive. Where the passions and emotion of his life could live and roam like cattle on a thousand-acre ranch. Where a motherless child could find that the love he longed for was near. Nearer than he ever dreamed possible. Closer than his own breath.

Gradually the world returned and Jim with it. Slowly the figure of I emerged. And when his mind remembered its place, he thought of the little boy running home through a summer night in Ohio and the sensation of losing his body to the dark and running into the arms of being. He smiled and wondered if death was like that. If the soul moved faster and faster and faster until it went beyond the limits of movement into the great pool of light waiting in the heart.

Maybe it was like taking off in a jet airplane and climbing forever through gray cloud formations until at last the moment came when the aircraft burst through the final layer and into the transcendent blue light of the beyond. Everything is melting away, at last. Melting. Slowly. It will be years before it is clear. Years before the promise of yoga is fulfilled. Years of chanting the Vedic affirmation, *Om Namah Shivaya.* Before the ice has fully melted and water flows again. Before the disguises of the self peel away. Before the freedom of spirit is renewed. Jim will have to stand and follow his footsteps back to the city, back to the urban amusement park. Back to the noise: the black exhaust, the horns and frantic pursuit. Back to the nightmare of Frank's dying. Back to the terror and dread of his own mortality and to the stuff of his mind careening about his head like kids in bumper cars. To what his friend Zorba called full catastrophe living, replete with the joys and sorrows of the marketplace.

Back to the story that has no end. The incomprehensible, bewildering tale of the ages. The story that dwarfs all stories. That should be making him feel small. Standing next to the 200-foot trees. Standing in the shadow of death. He thought he should be feeling small, insignificant really, looking out to the massive volcanic mountains, themselves dwarfed by the sky and the 13-billion-year-old cosmos rollicking through its lifetime.

So small, like a feeble campfire spark that leaps into the air straining for a future. Straining to become a blaze on its own, only to die quickly in the cool grasp of night. But strangely he was not. He felt boundless as laughter. Big as the sky. And he started down the path leading to his life in a world in constant flux. A life constantly flickering between agitation and strife and the sublime ease of pure being. Constantly turning out stories to remember and forget. Appearing and disappearing.

Feeling Georgia near to his heart, he hummed a favorite tune as one foot landed and the other lifted. He began to sing that song to the woods and sunlight. Most of all he sang for his mother. He sang wholeheartedly, without a trace of shame, the way he'd heard her so many times before. This time it was "Here comes the Sun," the sutra of eternal return, that came to his mind walking down the path to the city below. It was George Harrison singing along with Jim the lullaby of reassurance, the song of fresh beginnings.

And it was all right. All right to be kind like her. To give without trying to get. Free to touch lightly this fragile body of life. Free to care. Yes free to care. To care about the least of things. To offer warmth in the cold lonely winter. And free at last to love. A big love. Love like a mother's. And while loving, with every breath, free to tell the story that has no beginning. The story that has no end.

And feeling the music lifting his spirit and the newly released soul of his mother, he began to run. He ran slowly at first. Slowly down the path that led back to town. Slowly. Still singing. Slowly and then faster. Faster and faster, aided by the slope of the land, until he outran singing, outran his breath and body, outran morning and night, waking and sleeping. Until he outran running itself and the sure life of the spirit, moving and not moving, carried on, yes, carried on into the glow that smiles upon birth and death alike. That smiles upon and within the heart of all of this and all of that. The entire stir-fry of existence: the coming and going, remembering and forgetting, loving and hating, the beauties and the beasts, Daisys and Warrens, the whole rootin', shootin' galaxy of the unimaginable, stories within stories and people within people, all of it wrapped in a trillion tiny pieces of silver and cast to the wind landing where it may, if at all. Radiant. All of it, radiant.